THE PHANTOM DEATH
AND OTHER STORIES

THE PHANTOM DEATH AND OTHER STORIES

W. CLARK RUSSELL

WILDSIDE PRESS

THE PHANTOM DEATH AND OTHER STORIES

For more information, contact:
www.wildsidepress.com

CONTENTS

THE PHANTOM DEATH

On the 24th of April, 1840, having finished the business that had carried me into the Brazils, I arrived at Rio de Janeiro, where I found a vessel lying nearly loaded, and sailing for the port of Bristol in four or five days. In those times, passenger traffic between Great Britain and the eastern coast of South America was almost entirely carried on in small ships, averaging from 200 to 500 tons. The funnel of the ocean mail steamer, with her gilded saloons and side wheels, which, to the great admiration of all beholders, slapped twelve knots an hour out of the composite fabric, had not yet hove into sight above the horizon of commerce, and folks were very well satisfied if they were no longer than three months in reaching the Brazilian coast out of the River Thames.

The little ship in which I took passage was a barque called the *Lord of the Isles*; her burden was something under four hundred tons. She was a round-bowed wagon of a vanished type, with a square, sawed-off stern, painted ports, heavy over-hanging channels, and as loftily rigged, I was going to say, as a line-of-battle ship, owing to her immense beam, which gave her the stability of a church. I applied to the agent and hired a cabin, and found myself, to my secret satisfaction, the only passenger in the ship. Yes, I was rejoiced to be the sole passenger; my passage out had been rendered memorably miserable by the society of as ill-conditioned, bad-tempered, sulky a lot of wretches as ever turned in of a night into bunks, and cursed the captain in their gizzards in a calm for not being able to whistle a wind up over the sea-line.

The name of the skipper of the *Lord of the Isles* was Joyce. He was unlike the average run of the men in that trade. Instead of being beef-faced and bow-legged, humid of eye and gay with grog-blossoms, he was tall, pale, spare; he spoke low and in a melancholy key; he never swore; he drank wine and water, and there was little or nothing in his language to suggest the sailor. His berth was right aft on the starboard side; mine was right aft also, next his. Three cabins on either hand ran forward from these two after-berths. Two of them were occupied by the first and second mates. Between was a roomy "state-cabin," as the term then was: a plain interior furnished with an oblong table and fixed chairs, lighted by day by a large skylight, by night by a couple of brass lamps.

We sailed away on a Monday morning, as well as I recollect, out of the spacious and splendid scene of the harbour of Rio, and under full breasts of canvas, swelling to the height of a main-skysail big enough to serve as a mizzen topgallant-sail for a thousand-ton ship of today, and with taut bowlines and yearning jibs, and a heel of hull that washed a two-foot wide streak of greenish copper through the wool-white swirl of froth that broke from the bows, the *Lord of the Isles* headed on a straight course for the deep solitudes of the Atlantic.

All went well with us for several days. Our ship's company consisted of twelve men, including a boatswain and carpenter. The forecastle hands appeared very hearty, likely fellows, despite their pier-head raiment of Scotch cap and broken small clothes, and open flannel shirt, and greasy sheath-knife belted to the hip. They worked with a will, they sang out cheerily at the ropes, they went in and out of the galley at mealtime without faces of loathing, and but one complaint came aft before our wonderful, mysterious troubles began: the ship's bread crawled, they said, and, being found truly very bad, good white flour was served out in lieu.

We had been eight days at sea, and in that time had made fairly good way: it drew down a quiet, soft, black night with the young moon gone soon after sunset, a trembling flash of stars over the mastheads, a murky dimness of heat and of stagnation all round about the sea-line, and a frequent glance of sea-fire over the side when a dip of the barque's round bends drove the water from her in a swelling cloud of ebony. I walked the quarter-deck with the captain, and our talk was of England and of the Brazils, and of his experiences as a mariner of thirty years' standing.

"What of the weather?" said I, as we came to a pause at the binnacle, whose bright disc of illuminated card touched into phantom outlines the hairy features of the Jack who grasped the wheel.

"There's a spell of quiet before us, I fear," he answered, in his melancholy, monotonous voice. "No doubt a day will come, Mr. West, when the unhappy sea-captain upon whose forehead the shipowner would be glad to brand the words, 'Prompt Despatch' will be rendered by steam independent of that most capricious of all things—wind. The wind bloweth as it listeth—which is very well whilst it keeps all on blowing; for with our machinery of trusses, and parrels, and braces, we can snatch a sort of propulsion out of anything short of hurricane antagonism within six points of what we want to look up for. But of a dead night and of a dead day, with the wind up and down, and your ship showing her stern to the thirty-two points in a single watch, what's to be done with an owner's request of look sharp? Will you come below and have some grog?"

The second mate, a man named Bonner, was in charge of the deck. I followed the captain into the cabin, where he smoked a cigar; he drank a little wine and water, I drained a tumbler of cold brandy grog, then stepped above for an hour of fresh air, and afterwards to bed, six bells, eleven o'clock, striking as I turned in.

I slept soundly, awoke at seven o'clock, and shortly afterwards went on deck. The watch were at work washing down. The crystal brine flashed over the white plank to the swing of the bucket in the boatswain's powerful grasp, and the air was filled with the busy noise of scrubbing-brushes, and of the murmurs of some livestock under the long boat. The morning was a wide radiant scene of tropic sky and sea—afar, right astern on the light blue verge, trembled the mother-o'-pearl canvas of a ship; a small breeze was blowing off the beam; from under the round bows of the slightly-leaning barque came a pleasant, brooklike sound of running waters—a soft shaling as of a foam over stones, sweet to the ear in that heat as the music of a fountain. Mr. Bonner, the second mate, was again in charge of the deck. When I passed through the companion hatch I saw him standing abreast of the skylight at the rail: the expression of his face was grave and full of concern, and he seemed to watch the movements of the men with an inattentive eye.

I bade him good morning; he made no reply for a little, but looked at me fixedly, and then said, "I'm afraid Captain Joyce is a dead man."

"What is wrong with him?" I exclaimed eagerly, and much

startled.

"I don't know, sir. I wish there was a medical man on board. Perhaps you'd be able to tell what he's suffering from if you saw him."

I at once went below, and found the lad who waited upon us in the cabin preparing the table for breakfast. I asked him if the captain was alone. He answered that Mr. Stroud, the chief mate, was with him. On this, I went to the door of Captain Joyce's cabin and lightly knocked. The mate looked out, and, seeing who I was, told me in a soft voice to enter.

Captain Joyce lay in his bunk dressed in a flannel shirt and a pair of white drill trousers. All his throat and a considerable portion of his chest were exposed, and his feet were naked. I looked at him, scarcely crediting my sight: I did not know him as the man I had parted with a few hours before. He was swelled from head to foot as though drowned: the swelling contorted his countenance out of all resemblance to his familiar face; the flesh of him that was visible was a pale blue, as if rubbed with a powder of the stuff called "blue" which the laundresses use in getting up their linen. His eyes were open, but the pupils were rolled out of sight, and the "whites," as they are called, were covered with red blotches.

I had no knowledge of medicine, and could not imagine what had come to the poor man. He was unconscious, and evidently fast sinking. I said to Mr. Stroud, "What is this?"

The mate answered, "I'm afraid he's poisoned himself accidentally. It looks to me like poison. Don't it seem so to you, sir? See how his fingers and toes are curled."

I ran my eye over the cabin and exclaimed, "Have you searched for any bottles containing poison?"

"I did so when he sent for me at four o'clock, and complained of feeling sick and ill. He was then changing color, and his face was losing its proper looks. I asked him if he thought he had taken anything by mistake. He answered no, unless he had done so in his sleep. He awoke feeling very bad, and that was all he could tell me."

I touched the poor fellow's hand, and found it cold. His breathing was swift and thin. At moments a convulsion, like a wrenching shudder, passed through him.

"Is it," I asked, "some form of country sickness, do you

think—some kind of illness that was lying latent in him when we sailed?"

"I never heard of any sort of sickness," he answered, "that made a man look like that—not cholera even. And what but poison would do its work so quickly? Depend upon it he's either been poisoned, or poisoned himself unawares."

"Poisoned!" I exclaimed. "Who's the man in this ship that's going to do such a thing?"

"It's no natural illness," he answered, looking at the livid, bloated face of the dying man; and he repeated with gloomy emphasis, "He's either been poisoned, or he's poisoned himself unawares."

I stood beside Mr. Stroud for about a quarter of an hour, watching the captain and speculating upon the cause of his mortal sickness; we talked in low voices, often pausing and starting, for the convulsions of the sufferer made us think that he had his mind and wished to sit up and speak; but the ghastly, horrid, vacant look of his face continued fixed by the stubborn burial of the pupils of his eyes; his lips moved only when his frame was convulsed. I put my finger upon his pulse and found the beat threadlike, terribly rapid, intermittent, and faint. Then, feeling sick and scared, I went on deck for some air.

The second mate asked me how the captain was and what I thought. I answered that he might be dead even now as I spoke; that I could not conceive the nature of the malady that was killing him, that had apparently fastened upon him in his sleep, and was threatening to kill him within the compass of four or five hours, but that Mr. Stroud believed he had been poisoned, or had poisoned himself accidentally.

"Poisoned!" echoed the second mate, and he sent a look in the direction of the ship's galley. "What's he eaten that we haven't partaken of? A regular case of poisoning, does the chief officer think it? Oh no—oh no—who's to do it? The captain's too well liked to allow of such a guess as that. If the food's been fouled by the cook in error, how's it that the others of us who ate at the cabin table aren't likewise seized?"

There was no more to be said about it then, but in less than half an hour's time the mate came up and told us the captain was gone.

"He never recovered his senses, never spoke except to talk in delirium," he said.

"You think he was poisoned, sir?" said the second mate.

"Not wilfully," answered Mr. Stroud, looking at me. "I never said that; nor is it a thing one wants to think of," he added, sending his gaze around the wide scene of flashing ocean.

He then abruptly quitted us and walked to the galley, where for some while he remained out of sight. When he returned he told the second mate with whom I had stood talking that he had spoken to the cook, and thoroughly overhauled the dressing utensils, and was satisfied that the galley had nothing to do with the murderous mischief which had befallen the skipper.

"But why be so cock-certain, Mr. Stroud," said I, "that the captain's dead of poisoning?"

"I am cock-certain," he answered shortly, and with some little passion. "Name me the illness that's going to kill a man in three or four hours, and make such a corpse of him as lies in the captain's cabin."

He called to the second mate, and they paced the deck together deep in talk. The men had come up from breakfast, and the boatswain had set them to the various jobs of the morning; but the news of the captain's death had gone forward; it was shocking by reason of its suddenness. Then, again, the death of the master of a ship lies cold and heavy upon the spirits of a company at sea; 'tis the head gone, the thinking part. The mate may make as good a captain, but he's not the man the crew signed articles under. The seamen of the *Lord of the Isles* wore grave faces as they went about their work; they spoke softly, and the boatswain delivered his orders in subdued notes. After a bit the second mate walked forward and addressed the boatswain and some of the men, but what he said I did not catch.

I breakfasted and returned on deck; it was then ten o'clock. I found the main-topsail to the mast and a number of seamen standing in the gangway, whilst the two mates hung together on the quarter-deck, talking as though waiting. In a few minutes four seamen brought the body of the captain up through the companion hatch, and carried it to the gangway. The corpse was stitched up in a hammock and rested upon a plank, over which the English ensign was thrown. I thought this funeral very hurried, and dreaded to think that the poor man might be breathing and alive at the instant of his launch, for after all we had but the mate's assurance that the captain was dead; and what did Mr. Stroud know of death—that is, as it would be indicated by the body of a man who had died from some swift, subtle, nameless distemper, as Captain Joyce seemingly had?

When the funeral was over, the topsail swung, and the men returned to their work, I put the matter to the mate, who answered that the corpse had turned black, and that there could be no more question of his being dead than of his now being overboard.

The breeze freshened that morning. At noon it was blowing strong, with a dark, hard sky of compacted cloud, under which curls and shreds of yellow scud fled like a scattering of smoke, and the mates were unable to get an observation. Mr. Stroud seemed engrossed by the sudden responsibilities which had come upon him, and talked little. That afternoon he shifted into the captain's berth, being now, indeed, in command of the barque. It was convenient to him to live in that cabin, for the necessary nautical appliances for navigating the ship were there along with the facilities for their use. Mr. Bonner told me that he and the mate had thoroughly examined the cabin, overhauled the captain's boxes, lockers, shelves and the like for anything of a poisonous nature, but had met with nothing whatever. It was indeed an amazing mystery, he said, and he was no longer of opinion with Mr. Stroud that poison, accidentally or otherwise taken, had destroyed the captain. Indeed, he now leaned to my view, that Captain Joyce had fallen a victim to some disease which had lain latent in him since leaving Rio, something deadly quick and horribly transforming, well known, maybe, to physicians of the Brazils, if, indeed, it were peculiar to that country.

Well, three days passed, and nothing of any moment happened. The wind drew ahead and braced our yards fore and aft for us, and the tub of a barque went to leeward like an empty cask, shouldering the head seas into snowstorms off her heavy round bow, and furrowing a short scope of oil-smooth wake almost at right angles with her sternpost. Though Mr. Stroud had charge of the ship, he continued from this time to keep watch and watch with Mr. Bonner as in the captain's life, not choosing, I daresay, to entrust the charge of the deck to the boatswain. On the evening of this third day that I have come to, I was sitting in the cabin under the lamp writing down some memories of the past week in a diary, when the door of the captain's berth was opened, and my name was faintly called. I saw Mr. Stroud, and instantly went to him. His hands were clasped upon his brow, and he swayed violently as though in pain, with greater vehemence than the heave of the deck warranted; his eyes were starting, and, by the clear light of the brace of cabin lamps I easily saw that his complexion was unusually dusky, and darkening even, so it seemed to me, as I looked.

I cried out, "What is the matter, Mr. Stroud?"

"Oh, my God!" he exclaimed, "I am in terrible pain—I am horribly ill—I am dying."

I grasped him by the arm and conducted him to his bunk, into which he got, groaning and holding his head, with an occasional strange short plunge of his feet such as a swimmer makes when resting in the water on his back. I asked him if he was only just now seized. He answered that he was in a deep sleep, from which he was awakened by a burning sensation throughout his body. He lay quiet awhile, supposing it was a sudden heat of the blood; but the fire increased, and with it came torturing pains in the head, and attacks of convulsions; and even whilst he told me this the convulsive fits grew upon him, and he broke off to groan deeply as though in exquisite pain and distress of mind; then he'd set his teeth, and then presently scream out, "Oh, my God! I have been poisoned—I am dying!"

I was thunderstruck and terrified to the last degree. What was this dreadful thing—this phantom death that had come into the ship? Was it a contagious plague? But what distemper is there that, catching men in their sleep, swells and discolours them even as the gaze rests upon them, and dismisses their souls to God in the space of three or four hours?

I ran on deck, but waited until Mr. Bonner had finished bawling out some orders to the men before addressing him.

The moon was young, but bright, and she sheared scythelike through the pouring shadows, and the light of her made a marvellous brilliant whiteness of the foam as it burst in masses from the plunge of the barque's bows. When I gave the news to Mr. Bonner, he stared at me for some moments wildly and in silence, and then rushed below. I followed him as quick as he went, for I had often used the sea, and the giddiest dance of a deck-plank was all one with the solid earth to my accustomed feet. We entered the mate's berth, and Mr. Bonner lighted the bracket lamp and stood looking at his shipmate, and by the aid of the flame he had kindled, and the bright light flowing in through the open door I beheld a tragic and wonderful change in Mr. Stroud, though scarce ten minutes had passed since I was with him. His face was bloated, the features distorted, his eyes rolled continuously, and frequent heavy twitching shudders convulsed his body. But the most frightful part was the dusky hue of his skin, that was of a darker blue than I had observed in the captain.

He still had his senses, and repeated to the second mate what he had related to me. But he presently grew incoherent, then fell delirious, in about an hour's time was speechless and lay racked with convulsions; of a horrid blue, the features shockingly convulsed, and the whites of his eyes alone showing as in the captain's case.

He had called me at about nine o'clock, and he was a dead man at two in the morning, or four bells in the middle watch. Both the second mate and I were constantly in and out with the poor fellow; but we could do no good, only marvel, and murmur our astonishment and speculations. We put the captain's steward, a young fellow, to watch him—this was an hour before his death—and at four bells the lad came out with a white face, and said to me, who sat at the table, depressed and awed and overwhelmed by this second ghastly and indeterminable visitation, that the chief mate was dead, had ceased to breathe, and was quickly turning black.

Mr. Bonner came into the cabin with the boatswain, and they went into the dead man's berth and stayed there about a quarter of an hour. When they came out the boatswain looked at me hard. I recollect that that man's name was Matthews. I asked some questions, but they had nothing to tell, except that the body had turned black.

"What manner of disease can it be that kills in this fashion?" said I. "If it's the plague, we may be all dead men in a week."

"It's no plague," said the boatswain, in a voice that trembled with its own volume of sound.

"What is it?" I cried.

"Poison!" he shouted, and he dropped his clenched fist with the weight of a cannon-ball upon the table.

I looked at the second mate, who exclaimed, "The boatswain swears to the signs. He's seen the like of that corpse in three English seamen who were poisoned up at Chusan."

"Do you want to make out that both men have committed suicide?" I exclaimed.

"I want to make out that both men have been poisoned!" shouted the boatswain, in his voice of thunder.

There was a significance in the insolence of the fellow that confounded and alarmed me, and the meaning was deepened by the second mate allowing his companion to address me in this roaring, affronting way without reproof. I had hoped that the man had been drinking, and that the second mate was too stupid with horror to heed his behaviour to me, and without giving either of them another word, I walked to my cabin and lay down.

I have no space here to describe the wild and terrifying fancies which ran in my head. For some while I heard the boatswain and the second mate conversing, but the cabin bulkhead was stout, the straining and washing noises all about the helm heavy and continuous, and I caught not a syllable of what they said. At what hour I fell asleep I cannot tell; when I awoke my cabin was full of sunshine that streamed in through the stern window. I dressed, and took hold of the handle of the door, and found myself a prisoner. Not doubting I was locked up in error, I shook the door, and beat upon it, and called out loudly to be released. After a few minutes the door opened, and the second mate stood in the threshold. He exclaimed:

"Mr. West, it's the wish of the men that you should be locked up. I'm no party to the job—but they're resolved. I'll tell you plainly what they think: they believe you've had a hand in the death of the captain and the chief mate—the bo'sun's put that into their heads; I'm the only navigator left, and they're afraid you'll try your hand on me if you have your liberty. You'll be regularly fed and properly seen to; but it's the crew's will that you stop here."

With that, and without giving me time to utter a word, he closed and secured the door. I leaned against the bulkhead and sought to rally my wits, but I own that for a long while I was as one whose mind comes slowly to him after he has been knocked down insensible. I never for an instant supposed that the crew really believed me guilty of poisoning the captain and chief mate: I concluded that the men had mutinied, and arranged with Mr. Bonner to run away with the ship, and that I should remain locked up in my cabin until they had decided what to do with me.

By-and-by the door was opened, and the young steward put a tray containing some breakfast upon the cabin deck. He was but a mule of a boy, and I guessed that nothing but what might still further imperil me could come of my questioning him, so in silence I watched him put down the tray and depart. The meal thus sent to me was plentiful, and I drew some small heart out of the attention. Whilst I ate and drank, I heard sounds in the adjoining berth, and presently gathered that they were preparing the body of the chief mate for its last toss over the side. After a bit they went on deck with the corpse, and then all was still in the cabin. I knew by the light of the sun that the vessel was still heading on her course for England. It was a bright morning, with a wild windy sparkle in as much of the weather as I could see through the cabin window. The plunge of the ship's stern brought the water in a roar of milky froth all about the counter close under me, and the frequent jar of rudder and jump of wheel assured me that the barque was travelling fast through the seas.

What, in God's name, did the men mean by keeping me a prisoner? Did they think me a madman? Or that I, whose life together with theirs depended upon the safe navigation of the barque, would destroy those who alone could promise me security? And what had slain the two men? If poison, who had administered it? One man might have died by his own hand, but not both. And since both had perished from the same cause, self-murder was not to be thought of. What was it, then, that had killed them, visiting them in their sleep, and discolouring, bloating, convulsing, and destroying them in a few hours? Was it some deadly malady subtly lurking in the atmosphere of the after part of the vessel? If so, then I might be the next to be taken. Or was there some devilish murderer lying secretly hidden? Or was one of the crew the doer of these things? I seemed to smell disease and death, and yearned for the freedom of the deck, and for the sweetness of the wide, strong rush of the wind.

The day passed. The second mate never visited me. The lad arrived with my meals, and when he came with my supper I asked him some questions, but obtained no more news than that the second mate had taken up his quarters in the adjoining berth as acting captain, and that the boatswain was keeping watch and watch with him.

I got but little rest that night. It blew hard, and the pitching of the vessel was unusually heavy. Then, again, I was profoundly agitated and in deep distress of mind; for, supposing the men in earnest, it was not only horrible to be thought capable of murder, there was the prospect of my being charged and of having to clear my character. Or, supposing the men's suspicion or accusation a villainous pretext, how would they serve me? Would they send me adrift, or set me ashore to perish on some barren coast, or destroy me out of hand? You will remember that I am writing of an age when seafaring was not as it now is. The pirate and the slaver were still afloat doing a brisk business. There often went a desperate spirit in ships' forecastles, and the maritime records of the time abound with tragic narratives of revolt, seizure, cruelty of a ferocious sort.

Another day and another night went by, and I was still locked up in my cabin, and, saving the punctual arrival of the lad with my meals, no man visited me.

Some time about eight o'clock on the morning of the third day of my confinement, I was looking through the cabin window at the space of grey and foaming sea and sallow flying sky which came and went in the square of the aperture with the lift and fall of the barque's stern, when my cabin door was struck upon, and in a minute afterwards opened, and the boatswain appeared.

"Mr. West," said he, after looking at me for a moment in silence with a face whose expression was made up of concern and fear and embarrassment, "I've come on my own part, and on the part of the men, sir, to ask your pardon for our treatment of you. We was mistook. And our fears made us too willing to believe that you had a hand in it. We dunno what it is now, but as Jesus is my God, Mr. West, the second mate he lies dead of the same thing in the next cabin!"

I went past him too stupefied to speak, and in a blind way sat down at the cabin table and leaned my head against my hand. Presently I looked up, and on lifting my eyes I caught sight of two or three sailors staring down with white faces through the skylight.

"You tell me that the second mate's dead?" said I.

"Yes, sir, dead of poison, too, so help me God!" cried the boatswain.

"Who remains to navigate the ship?" I said.

"That's it, sir!" he exclaimed. "Unless you can do it?"

"Not I. There's no man amongst you more ignorant. May I look at the body?"

He opened the door of the cabin in which the others had died, and there, in the bunk from which the bodies of Captain Joyce and Mr. Stroud had been removed, lay now the blackened corpse of the second mate. It was an awful sight and a passage of time horrible with the mystery which charged it. I felt no rage at the manner in which I had been used by that dead man there and the hurricane-lunged seaman alongside of me and the fellows forward; I could think of nothing but the mystery of the three men's deaths, the lamentable plight we were all in through our wanting a navigator, with the chance, moreover, that it was the plague, and not poison mysteriously given, that had killed the captain and mates, so that all the rest of us, as I have said, might be dead men in another week.

I returned to the cabin, and the boatswain joined me, and we stood beside the table conversing, anxiously watched by several men who had stationed themselves at the skylight.

"What we've got to do," said I, "is to keep a bright lookout for ships, and borrow someone to steer us home from the first vessel that would lend us a navigator. We're bound to fall in with something soon. Meanwhile, you're a smart seaman yourself, Matthews, as well qualified as any one of them who have died to sail the ship, and there's surely some intelligent sailor amongst the crew who would relieve you in taking charge of the deck. I'll do all I can."

"The question is, where's the vessel now?" said the boatswain.

"Fetch me the log-book," said I, "and see if you can find the chart they've been using to prick the courses off on. We should be able to find out where the ship was at noon yesterday. I can't enter that cabin. The sight of the poor fellow makes me sick."

He went to the berth and passed through the door, and might have left me about five minutes, evidently hunting for the chart, when he suddenly rushed out, roaring in his thunderous voice, "I've discovered it! I've discovered it!" and fled like a madman up the companion steps. I was startled almost to the very stopping of my heart by this sudden furious wild behaviour in him: then wondering what he meant by shouting "he had discovered it!" I walked to the cabin door, and the very first thing my eye lighted upon was a small snake, leisurely coiling its way from the head to the feet of the corpse. Its middle was about the thickness of a rifle-barrel, and it then tapered to something like whipcord to its tail. It was about two feet long, snow white, and speckled with black and red spots.

This, then, was the phantom death! Yonder venomous reptile it was, then, that, creeping out of some secret hiding-place, and visiting the unhappy men one after another, had stung them in their sleep, in the darkness of the cabin, and vanished before they had struck a light and realized indeed that something desperate had come to them!

Whilst I stood looking at the snake, whose horror seemed to gain fresh accentuation from the very beauty of its snow-white speckled skin and diamond bright eyes, the boatswain, armed with a long handspike, and followed by a number of the crew, came headlong to the cabin. He thrust the end of the handspike under the belly of the creature, and hove it into the middle of the berth.

"Stand clear!" he roared, and with a blow or two smashed the reptile's head into a pulp. "Open that cabin window," said he. One of the men did so, and the boatswain with his boot scraped the mess of smashed snake on to the handspike and shook it overboard.

"I told you they were poisoned," he cried, breathing deep; "and, oh my God, Mr. West—and I humbly ask your pardon again for having suspected ye—do you know, sir, whilst I was a-talking to you just now I was actually thinking of taking up my quarters in this here cabin this very night."

BROKERS' BAY

Brokers' Bay is situated on the West Coast of England. You may search the map for it in vain, and the reason why I call it by any other name than that it bears will, when you have read this story, be as clear as the mud in the water that brims to the base of Brokers' cliffs. Brokers' Bay is a fine, curving sweep of land. For how many centuries the sea has been sneakingly ebbing from it who can imagine? The time has been when the galleon and the carack strained at their hempen ground tackle at anchors six fathoms deep where the white windmill now stands within musket-shot of the Crown and Anchor, and where the church spire darts the gleam of its weathercock above the green thickness of a huddle of dwarf trees near the little vicarage.

About fifty years ago a company of enterprising souls took it into their heads to reclaim some of the land which the subtly and ceaselessly ebbing sea, rising and falling with moonlike regularity, yet receding ever, though noticeably only in spans of half-centuries, was leaving behind it. They armed themselves with the necessary legal powers, they subscribed all the capital they considered needful, and by processes of embanking, draining, manuring, and the like, they succeeded in raising wheat and grass, vegetables and flowers, where, since and long before the days of the painted Briton, shuddering in the November blast, or perspiring away his small clothes under the July sun, nothing had flourished but the dab and the crab.

Vet the speculation on the whole was a failure. It was a patriotic achievement in its way, and those concerned in it deserved well of the nation; for if it be a fine thing to bleed for one's country, how much finer must it be to add to its dimentions to enlarge its latitude and longitude, and extend the home-sovereignty of the monarch? Yet, though a pretty considerable village stood hard by the reclaimed land, houses did not increase. The builder, whose Christian name is Jerry, came down to Brokers' Bay, and took a look around, and went home again, and did nothing. He was not to be decoyed, he said. Brokers' Bay was not the right sort of place to start a town in, he thought. There was too much mud, Mr. Jerry considered. He calculated that when the water was out there was a full mile and three quarters of slime. Oh yes, whilst the slime was still slimy it reflected the sky just the same as if it had been water, and it took a noble blood-red countenance of a hot sunset evening, when the sea was a pink gleaming streak just under the horizon, and it was very pleasing in that sort of way. But what were the doctors going to say about all that mud, and what opportunities would a waste of slush, extending one and three-quarter miles at ebb tide, provide the local historian with when he came to write a guide-book and invent Roman and Early English names for the immediate district, and deal with the salubriousness of the climate, and give an analysis of the drinking water? And what about the bathing? There was none. And what length of pier would be wanted if the seaward end of it was to be permanently water-washed?

The reclaimed ground was divided into lots for building; but nobody built. The soil continued to be cultivated, nevertheless. Two market-gardeners did very well out of it. A butcher rented thirty acres of the pasture land; the remainder was variously dealt with in small ways for growing purposes.

Now, that stretch of land had been reclaimed some fifteen years, when a certain master mariner, whom I will call Captain Carey, arrived at the adjacent village with the intention of taking a view of the Brokers' Bay foreshore. News that good land was cheap hereabouts had reached him up at Blyth. He had unexpectedly come into a little fortune, had Captain Carey. For years he had followed the coasting trade, working his way out through the fore-scuttle into the captain's cabin, and after thirty years of seafaring, rendered more and more uncomfortable by gloomy anticipations of the workhouse in his old age, he had been enriched by the will of an Australian aunt, the amount being something between £9000 and £10,000.

Captain Carey had sprung from a West Country stock; his wife was a West Country woman, and when they came into the Australian aunt's legacy they determined to break up their little home at Blyth and settle somewhere on Western soil. So Captain Carey came to Brokers' Bay, and with him traveled his giant son, a youth of prodigious muscle, but of weak intellect. A second Titan son was at this time at sea, working his way towards the quarter-deck aboard an East Indiaman.

Captain Carey's survey of the Brokers' fore-shore determined him on purchasing a plot of land right amidships of the fine curve of reclaimed soil. He bought four acres at a very low figure indeed, and then ordered a small house to be built in the midst of his little estate. His wife and her niece joined him and the giant half-witted son at the adjacent village, and there the family dwelt at the sign of the Seven Bells whilst the house was building.

It was quickly put together, and was then gay with a green balcony, and it had motherly lubberly bay windows that made you think of a whaler's boats dangling at cranes, and the entrance was embellished with a singular porch after the design of the retired master mariner. who had recollected seeing something of the sort at Lisbon when he had gone as a boy on a voyage to Portugal.

Captain Carey loved seclusion. Like most retired mariners, he hated to be overlooked. This fondness for privacy, which grows out of a habit of it, may be owing to there being no streets at sea, and no over-the-way. The master of a vessel lives in a cabin all alone by himself—the Crusoe of the after part of the ship. He measures his quarter-deck in lonely walks; no eyes glittering above the bulwark rail watch his movements; his behavior as a man, his judgment as a seaman, but not his mode of life as a private individual, are criticized by his crew. Hence, when a man steps ashore after a long period of command at sea, he carries with him a strong love of privacy, and much resolution of retirement. A great number of little cottages by the ocean are occupied by solitary seamen, who pass their time in looking through a telescope at the horizon, in arguing with lonesome men of their own cloth, in smoking pipes at the Lugger Inn or at the sign of the Lord Nelson, and turning in at night and turning out in the morning.

To provide against being overlooked in case others should build hard by, Captain Carey walled his little estate of four acres with a regular bulkhead of a fence, handsomely spiked on top, and too tall even for his giant son to peer over on tiptoe. In a few months the house was built, papered, and in all ways completed; it was then furnished and the ground fenced. Captain Carey and his family now took possession of their new home. There was, first of all, Captain Carey, then Mrs. Carey, next the giant young Carey (who had been known up in Blyth by the name of Mother Carey's chicken), and last, Mrs. Carey's niece, a stout, active girl of twenty, who helped Mrs. Carey in cooking and looking after the house; for Carey, having been robbed, whilst absent on a coasting voyage, of a new coat, a soft hat, a meerschaum pipe, and a few other trifles by a maid-of-all-work, had sworn in hideous forecastle language never again to keep another servant.

This happy family of Careys were very well pleased with their new home. Old Carey was never weary of stepping out of doors to look at his house. He seemed to find something fresh to admire every time he cast his eyes over the little building. He and his son planted potatoes, onions, cabbages, and other homely vegetables, and dug out and cultivated a very considerable area of kitchen garden. They had not above three miles to walk to attend divine worship. There were several convenient shops in the adjacent village, not more than two miles and a half distant. There was no roadway to speak of to Carey's house, but in a very few weeks the feet of the family and the tread of the tradespeople tramped out a thin path over the reclaimed land to the village roadway, where it fell with the sweep of the cliff to the level of the reclaimed soil. And the view, on the whole, from Carey's windows was fairly picturesque and pleasing, even when the water was out and the scene was a sweeping flat of mud. Afar on the dark blue edge of the sea hovered the feather-white canvas of ships, easily resolved into denominationable fabrics by Carey's powerful telescope. The western sun glowed in the briny ooze till the whole stretch of the stuff resembled a vast surface of molten gold. Here and there, confronting Carey's house, stood some scores of fangs of rock, and when there was a flood-tide and a fresh in-shore gale the sea snapped and beat and burst upon the beach with as much uproar as though it were all fathomless ocean, instead of a dirty stretch of water with an eighteen-foot rise of tide, and foam so dark and thick with dirt that, after it had blown upon you and dried, it was as though you had ridden through some dozen miles of muddy lanes.

The family had been settled about three months when the eldest son arrived home from the long voyage he had made to China and the East Indies. He was a tall, powerfully-built young man; but his education in his youth had been neglected. Captain Carey, indeed, had not in those days possessed the means to put him to school. Now, however, that the skipper had come into a little fortune of, call it, £10,000, he resolved to qualify his son for a position on the quarter-deck.

"Navigation I can teach him," he said to his wife, "and if he was a master-rigger he couldn't know more about a ship. What he wants is the sort of larning which you and me's deficient in: the being able to talk and write good English, with some sort of knowledge of history and the likes of that; so that, should he ever get command of a passenger ship, why, then, sitting at the head of the cabin table, he won't be ashamed of addressing the ladies and joining in the general conversation."

So when this son arrived from China and the East Indies, the father, instead of sending him to sea again, put him to read and study with a clergyman who lived in the adjacent village, a gentleman who could not obtain a living and who disdained a curacy.

Thus it came to pass that Captain Carey lived at home with his two sons and wife and wife's niece.

He stood in a bay window one day, and it entered his head to dig out a pond and place a fountain in the middle of it.

"It'll improve the property," said Captain Carey, turning to his wife and sons, who were lingering at the breakfast-table. "We'll fix a pedestal amidships of the pond and put a female statue upon it—one of them white figures who keep their right hands aloft for the holding of a whirligig fountain. There's nothing prettier than a revolving fountain a-sparkling and a-showering down aver a noode statue."

You'll be striking salt water, father, if you fall a-digging," said the sailor son named Tom.

"And what then?" exclaimed Captain Carey. "Ain't brine as bright to the eye as fresh water? And it's not going to choke the fountain either. Blessed if I don't think the fountain might be set a-playing by the rise and fall of the tide."

When breakfast was ended, the father and the two sons stepped out of doors to decide upon a spot in which to dig the pond for the fountain. After much discussion they agreed to dig in front of the house, about a hundred paces distant, within a stone's throw of the wash of the water when the tide was at its height.

The Captain's grounds lay open to the sea, though they were jealously fenced, as has been already said, at the back and on either hand. There could be no intrusion on the sea-fronting portion of the grounds. The mud came to the embankment, and the embankment was the ocean-limit of Carey's little estate. There was no path, and no right of way if there had been. Selkirk and his goats could scarcely have enjoyed greater seclusion than did Carey and his family. The father and sons proposed to dig out the pond to the shape, depth, and area decided upon, and then bring in a mason to finish it. They went to work next day; it was something to do—something to kill the time which, perhaps, now and again lay a little heavy upon this isolated family. The old skipper dug with vehemence and enjoyment. He had been bred to a life of hard work, and was never happier than when toiling. His giant half-witted son labored with the energy of steam. The sailor son stepped in when he had done with his parson and his studies for the day, and drove his spade into the reclaimed soil with enthusiasm. This went on for several days, and something that resembled the idea of a pond without any water in it began to suggest itself to the eye.

It was on a Friday afternoon in the month of April, as the Captain whom I am calling Carey himself informed me, that this retired skipper, who had not felt well enough that day to dig, was seated in his parlor reading a newspaper and smoking a pipe. Suddenly the door was flung open, and the giant half-witted youth whose name was Jack walked in.

"Father," said he, "ain't gold found in the earth?"

"Nowhere else, sonny," answered the Captain, looking at the giant over the top of the newspaper.

"There's gold in the pond, father," said Jack "Gold in your eye!" exclaimed the Captain, putting dawn his pipe and his newspaper. "What saint of gold?" said he, smiling.

"Shiny gold, like the half-sovereign you wance gave me for behavin' myself when you was away."

On this, Captain Carey, without another word, put on his hat and walked with his son to the diggings, which were by this time a pretty considerable trench.

"There," said Jack, pointing, "my spade drove upon him, and I've scraped that much clear." The Captain looked, and perceived what resembled a fragment of a shaft of metal, dull and yellow, with lines of brightness where Jack's spade had scraped the surface. He at once jumped into the trench and bade Jack fetch his spade. They then dug together, and in about a quarter of an hour succeeded in laying bare a small brass cannon of very antique pattern and manufacture. It was pivoted. They dug a little longer and deeper, and exposed a portion of woodwork. The scantling was extraordinarily thick, and the gun was pivoted to it. The Captain's face was red with excitement.

"Run and see if Tom's in," he cried, "and if he ain't leave word that he's to join us with his spade as soon as he arrives, and then come you back, Jack By the great anchor, if here ain't a foundered ship call me a guffy!"

The sailor son, armed with a spade, appeared on the scene within twenty minutes.

"It's an old brass swivel, father," he shouted. "Jump in," cried the Skipper, "and len's a hand to clear away more of this muck."

The three plied their spades with might and main, and before sundown they had laid bare some eight feet of ship's deck, with about five feet breadth of bulwark, measuring four feet high from the plank. Mrs. Carey and the niece came to the edge of the pit to look. The three diggers, covered with sweat and hot as fire, climbed out, threw down their spades, and the family stood gazing.

"Whatever is it?" cried Mrs. Carey. "A foundered ship," answered her husband. "A whole ship, uncle?" exclaimed the niece.

"A three-hundred-ton ship," answered the Skipper. "D'ye

want to know if she's all here? I can't tell you that; but if there ain't solidness enough for a *Ryle Jarge* running fore and aft in this unearthed piece, I'm no sailor man."

"What sort of ship will she be?" said the half-witted Jack.

"Something two hundred year old, if the whole job hain't some antiquarian roose like to the burying of Roman baths for the digging of 'em up again as an advertisement for the place. Who was a-reigning two hundred year ago?"

Here every eye was directed at the sailor son, who, after rubbing his nose and looking hard at the horizon, answered, "Crummell."

"Then it's a ship of Crummell's time," cried the Captain, to whom the name of Crummell did not seem familiar, "and if so be she's all here and intact, bloomed if she won't be a fortune to us as a show."

That night, both at and after supper, all the talk of the family was about the foundered ship in the garden. The giant lad's excitement was such that even the mother owned to herself he had never been more fluent and imbecile.

D'ye think it's a whole ship, father?" said Tom the sailor.

"More'n likely. That there brass cannon ought to give us her age. Haven't I heered tell of a Spanish invasion of this country in bygone years, when the Dons was blowed to the nor'rad, and a score of their galleons cast away upon the British coasts? At a time like this a man feels not being a scholard. Tom, fetch down your history book, and see if there's a piece wrote in it about that there Spanish job."

The sailor brought a history of England to the lamp, and with fingers square-ended as broken carrots, and with palms dark with dragging upon tarry ropes, groped patiently through the pages till he came to a part of the story that told of the Spanish Armada. This was read aloud, and the family listened with attention.

"Well, she may prove to be one of them Spanish galleons after all," said Captain Carey. "She'll not be the first ship that's been dug up out of land which the sea's flowed over in its day. There was Jimmy Perkins of Sunderland—" And here he spun them a yarn.

"What'll be inside the ship, I wonder?" exclaimed the niece.

"Ah!" said the young giant Jack, opening his mouth.

"Them galleons went pretty richly freighted, I've heered," said the Skipper. "When I was a boy they used to tell of their going afloat with a store of dollars in their holds, their bottoms flush to the hatches with the choicest goods, gold and silver candle-sticks and crucifixes in the cabins for the captains and mates to say their prayers afore."

"Jacky thought the cannon gold," said Mrs. Carey. "He may be right, Thomas, though a little quick in finding out. There may be gold deeper down."

Well, now," cried the Skipper. "I'll tell you what I've made up my mind to do. We'll keep this here find a secret. Tom, you, me, and Jack'll go to work day arter day until we see what lies buried. There's no call for any of us to say a word about this discovery. We're pretty well out of sight, the fence stands high, and if so be as any visitor or tradesman should catch a view of the trench they'll not be able to see what's inside without drawing close to the brink, which, of course, won't be permitted. If that foundered craft," he cried, with great excitement, pointing towards the window, "is intact, as I before observed, then let her hold contain what it may, all mud or all dollars, all slush or all silk, as a show she ought to be worth a matter of a thousand pound to us. But not a word to anybody till we've looked inside of her. If there's treasure, why, it's to be ourn. There's to be no dividing of it with the authorities, and so I says plainly, let the law be what it will. Here's this house and grounds to be paid for, Tom to be eddicated and sent to sea in a ship he holds a share in, Jack to be made independent of me, and Eliza to be provided for; and we'll see," he shouted, hitting the table a blow with his clenched fist, "if that there foundered ship ain't a-going to work out this traverse the same as if she was chock-a-block with bullion."

Thus was the procedure settled, and next morning early the father and two sons went to work with their spades.

It was to prove a long, laborious job; they knew *that*, but were determined all the same to keep the strange business in the family, and to solve the secret of the buried craft as darkly and mysteriously as though they were bent on perpetrating some deed of horror. The quantity of soil they threw up formed an embankment which concealed the trench and their own laboring figures as they progressed. Tom went away to his studies for two or three hours in the day; saving this and the interruption of meal-times their toil was unintermittent. In three weeks they had disclosed enough of the poop-royal, poop, and quarter-deck of the strangely shaped craft to satisfy them that, at all events, a very large portion of the after part of the vessel lay solid in its centuries-old grave of mud.

In this time they had exhumed and scraped the whole breadth or beam of her upper decks to a distance of about twenty-two feet forward from the taffrail. Their notion was to clear her from end to end betwixt the lines of her bulwarks only to satisfy themselves that she was a whole ship. Day after day they labored in their secret fashion, and the people of the district never for an instant imagined that they were at work on anything more than an entrenchment of extraordinary size, depth and length, for some purpose known only to themselves.

It took them to the middle of July to expose the upper decks of the vessel; and then there lay, a truly marvellous and even beautiful sight, buried some ten feet below the level of the soil, the complete and quite perfect fabric of a little antique ship of war, about one hundred feet long and thirty feet broad, with two after decks or poops descending like steps to the quarter-deck, and the bows shelving downwards like the slope of a beach into what promised to prove a complicated curling of headboards and some nightmare device of figurehead. Four little brass cannons were pivoted on the poop rails, and on her main deck she mounted eight guns of that ancient sort called sakers. The wood of her was as hard as iron, and black as old oak with the saturation of soil and brine and time's secret hardening process. The masts were clean gone from the deck, and there was no sign of a bowsprit. Never was there a more wonderful picture than that ancient ship as she lay in her grave with her grin of old-world artillery running the fat squab length of her, the whole structure, flat still in the soil to the level of the bulwark rails, affecting the eye as some marvellous illusion of nature; as some wild, romantic vegetable or mineral caprice of the drained but sodden soil.

Our little family of diggers, having disentombed the decks and bulwarks to the whole length of the giant Jack's extraordinary discovery, next proceeded, all as secretly as though they were preparing for some hideous crime, to uproot the covers of the main-hatch, which were as hard-fixed as though they had been of Portland stone cemented into a pier. With much hammering, however—and they were three powerful men—they succeeded in splitting the cover, and the stubborn, wonderful old piece of timber-frame was picked out of the eye of the hatch in splinters.

And now they looked down into a black well, from which Captain Carey speedily withdrew his head, sniffing and spitting.

"Run for a candle, Jack," said he.

A candle was lighted and lowered, and when it had sunk half a dozen feet the flame went out as though the wick had been suddenly pinched by the fingers of a spirit. So that a current of air should sweeten the hold, they went aft with their hatchets and hammers, and, after prodigious labor, splintered and cleared away the cover of a little booby hatch just under the break of the lower poop. They next got open the small fore hatch, and at the end of two days, when they lowered a lighted candle, the flame burnt freely.

Now what did they find inside this buried ship? Carey had counted upon mud to the hatchways, and scores of curios and amazing relics of Crummell's or another's period to be dug out of the solid mass. Instead, the interior was as dry as a nut whose kernel has rotted into dust. *This* was as extraordinary as any other feature of the discovery. The three men, each bearing a lighted lantern, descended the ladder they had lowered through the hatch, and gained the bottom of the ship, where they walked upon what had undoubtedly been cargo in its time, though it might now have passed for a sort of dunnage of lava, dry, harsh, and gritty, and powdering under the tread. A basket was loaded with the stuff, and hoisted into the daylight and examined, but the family could make nothing of it. As far as could be gathered the original freight of the ship had been bale goods, skins, fine wool, and the like, East India or Spice Island commodities, which some sort of chemical action had transformed into a heap of indistinguishable stuff, as slender in comparison with its radical bulk as the cinders of a rag to the rag that is burnt.

"Nothing to make our fortunes with here," said Captain Carey, as he stood in the bottom of this wonderful old ship's hold with his two sons, the three of them holding up their lanterns and glancing with gleaming eyes and marvelling minds around. "What's abaft that bulkhead? We'll see to it arter dinner."

They went to dinner, and then returned to the ship, and applied themselves to hacking at the bulkhead so as effect an entry. This bulkhead, which partitioned the after from the main and fore holds, was of the hardness of steel. They let fly at it in vain. The hollow hold reverberated the blows of axe and chopper with the clangor of an iron ship-building yard.

"We must enter by an after-hatch of it's to be done," said Captain Carey.

With infinite labor, which expended the day and ran into the whole of the following morning, they contrived to break their way through the front of the lower poop. Here the air was as foul as ever it had been in the hold. They could do nothing for many hours. When at last the atmosphere was sweet enough to breathe they entered, and found themselves in a cabin that was unusually lofty owing to the superstructure of the poop-royal. The interior was as dry as the hold had been. So effectually had accident or contrivance, or the secret processes of the ship's grave, sealed every aperture that, standing in this now wind-swept cabin, you might have supposed the little fabric had never shipped a bucketful of water from the hour of her launch. Several human skeletons lay upon the deck. The Captain and his sons held the lanterns to the bones, and handled the rags which had been their raiment, but the colorless stuff went to pieces. It mouldered in the grasp as dry sand streams from the clenched fist.

Five cabins were bulkheaded off this black, long-buried interior. The Captain and his sons searched them, but everything that was not of timber appeared to have undergone the same transformation that was visible in what had doubtless been the cargo in the hold. They found chairs of a venerable pattern, cressetlike lamps, such as Milton describes, bunk bedsteads, upon which were faintly distinguishable the tracings of what might have been paintings and gilt-work.

"What d'ye think of this, boys, for a show?" cried Captain Carey, whose voice was tremulous with excitement and astonishment. "If there ain't two thousand pound in the job as a sight-going consarn, tell me we're all a-dreaming, and that the whole boiling's a lie. And now to see what's under hatches here."

A small square of hatchway was visible just abaft the black oblong table that centred the interior. They opened this hatch without labor. The cementing process of the ship's grave had not apparently worked very actively in this cabin, yet the foul air of the after-hold forced them once more upon no less than three days of inactivity; for to sweeten the place they were obliged to construct a windsail, whose breezy heel rendered the atmosphere fit for human respiration in a few hours.

On descending they found just such another accumulation of lavalike remains of freight as they had met with in the main-hold. But they also noticed a bulkhead ten feet abaft the sternpost. They chopped their way through it and stood for awhile peering around them under the lanterns which they held above their heads. The gleams illuminated a quantity of ancient furniture—sofas and chairs and little tables, and framed squares and ovals of obliterated paintings. Captain Carey put his hand upon a couch and drew away his fist full of pale and rotted upholstery.

"Are those things cases yonder?" said the sailor son, and the three of them made their way to a corner of the hold and stood looking for a moment or two at four square chests heavily clamped with iron.

"What's here?" said Captain Carey.

The giant Jack stooped and strove to stir one of the boxes.

"Stand aside!" roared the Skipper, and with half a dozen strokes of his axe, he split open the lid of one of the chests.

The three faces came together in a huddle, and the light shone upon lines of linked and minted metal.

"Pick out one of 'em, Tom," said Captain Carey, in a faint voice, "my hands are a-trembling too much to do it."

They were Spanish silver coins, subsequently ascertained

to have been minted in times which proved the age of this sunken and recovered ship contemporaneous with the early years of the reign of our Second Charles. Captain Carey told me that he realized £6400 on them.

But this lucky family did better yet with their incredible discovery; for after the Captain had secreted the money in his house, he called in workmen, who dug away the soil from the buried ship until she was exposed to the bilge on which she rested. This done, he carried out his resolution to make a show of her by erecting a shed for the fabric, stationing a doorkeeper at the entrance, and charging sixpence for admission. Many hundreds, indeed many thousands, came from all parts to view the wonderful ship, that was ascertained, by what is called an "expert" in naval affairs, to have been the *Sancte Ineas*, captured by the privateer Amazon, and lost whilst proceeding in charge of a prize crew to an English port. It was further discovered that her lading had consisted of coffee, cochineal, indigo, hides in the hair, bales of fine wool and fur. But down to this hour it was never known that Captain Carey had found hidden, and, in course of time, cleverly turned into good English money, four chests, of Spanish silver, worth, at all events to this happy family of Brokers' Bay, £6400. For my own part, I have honorably kept my worthy friend's secret.

THE LAZARETTE
OF THE *HUNTRESS*

I stepped into the Brunswick Hotel in the East India Docks for a glass of ale. It was in the year 1853, and a wet, hot afternoon. I had been on the tramp all day, making just three weeks of a wretched, hopeless hunt after a situation on shipboard, and every bone in me ached with my heart. My precious timbers, how poor I was! Two shillings, and three-pence—that was all the money I possessed in the wide world, and when I had paid for the ale, I was poorer yet by twopence.

A number of nautical men of various grades were drinking at the bar. I sat down in a corner to rest, and abandoned myself to the most dismal reflections. I wanted to get out to Australia, and nobody, it seems, was willing to ship me in any situation on any account whatever. Captains and mates howled me off if I attempted to cross their gangways. Nothing was to be got in the shipping yards. The very crimps sneered at me when I told them that I wanted a berth. "Shake your head, my hawbuck," said one of them, in the presence of a crowd of grinning seamen, "that the Johns may see the hayseed fly."

What was I, do you ask? I'll tell you. I was one of ten children whose father had been a clergyman, and the income "from all sources" of that same clergyman had never exceeded £230 a year. I was a lumbering, hulking lad, without friends, and, as I am now perfectly sensible, without brains, without any kind of taste for any pursuit, execrating the notion of clerkships, and perfectly willing to make away with myself sooner than be glued to a three-legged stool. But enough of this. The long and short is, I was thirsting to get out to Australia, never doubting that I should easily make my fortune there.

I sat in my corner in the Brunswick Hotel, scowling at the floor, my long legs thrust out, and my hands buried deep in my breeches pockets. Presently, I was sensible that someone stood beside me, and looking up, I beheld a young fellow staring with all his might, with a slow grin of recognition wrinkling his face. I seemed to remember him.

"Mr. William Peploe, ain't it?" said he. "Why yes," said I, "and you—and you—?"

"You don't remember Jem Back then, sir?"

"Yes I do, perfectly well. Sit down, Back. Are you a sailor? I am so dead beat that I can scarcely talk."

Jem Back brought a tankard of ale to my table, and sat down beside me. He was a youth of my own age, and I knew him as the son of a parishioner of my father. He was attired in nautical clothes, yet somehow he did not exactly look what is called a sailor man. We fell into conversation. He informed me that he was an under-steward on board a large ship called the *Huntress*, that was bound out of the Thames in a couple of days for Sydney, New South Wales. He had sailed two years in her, and hoped to sign as head steward next voyage in a smaller ship.

"There'll be a good deal of waiting this bout," said he; "we're taking a cuddy full of swells out. There's Sir Thomas Mason—he goes as Governor; there's his lady and three daughters, and a sort of suet" (he meant suite) "sails along with the boiling." So he rattled on.

"Can't you help me to find a berth in that ship?" said I.

"I'm afraid not," he answered. "What could you offer yourself as, sir? They wouldn't have you forward, and aft we're chock-a-block. If you could manage to stow yourself away—they wouldn't chuck you overboard when you turned up at sea; they'd make you useful and land you as safe as if you was the Governor himself."

I thought this a very fine idea, and asked Back to tell me how I should go to work to hide myself. He seemed to recoil, I thought, when I put the matter to him earnestly, but he was an honest, kindly-hearted fellow, and remembered my father with a certain degree of respect, and even of affection; he had known me as a boy; there was the sympathy of association and of memory between us; he looked at the old suit of clothes I sat in, and at my hollow, anxious face, and he crooked his eyebrows with an expression of pain when I told him that all the money I had was two and a penny, and that I must starve and be found floating a corpse in the dockyard basin if I did not get out to Australia. We sat for at least an hour over our ale, talking very earnestly, and when we arose and bade each other farewell I had settled with him what to do.

The *Huntress* was a large frigate-built ship of 1400 tons. On the morning of the day on which she was to haul out of dock I went on board of her. Nobody took any notice of me. The vessel was full of business, clamorous with the life and hurry of the start for the other side of the world. Cargo was still swinging over the main hold, down whose big, dark square a tall, strong, red-bearded chief mate was roaring to the stevedore's men engulfed in the bowels of the ship. A number of drunken sailors were singing and cutting capers on the forecastle. The main-deck was full of steerage, or, as they were then termed, 'tweendeck passengers—men, and seedy women and wailing and frightened, staring children. I did not pause to muse upon the scene, nor did I gaze aloft at the towering spars, where, forward, up in the dingy sky of the Isle of Dogs, floated that familiar symbol of departure, Blue Peter. I saw several young men in shining buttons and cloth caps with gold badges, and knew them to be midshipmen, and envied them. Every instant I expected to be ordered out of the ship by someone with hurricane lungs and a vast command of injurious language, and my heart beat fast. I made my way to the cuddy front, and just as I halted beside a group of women at the booby hatch, James Back came to the door of the saloon. He motioned to me with a slight toss of his head.

"Don't look about you," he whispered; "just follow me straight." I stepped after him into the saloon. It was like entering a grand drawing-room. Mirrors and silver lamps sparkled; the panelled bulkheads were rich with hand paintings; flowers hung in plenty under the skylight; goldfish gleamed as they circled in globes of crystal. These things and more I beheld in the space of a few heart-beats.

I went after James Back down a wide staircase that sank through a large hatch situated a dozen paces from the cuddy front. When I reached the bottom I found myself in a long corridor, somewhat darksome, with cabins on either hand.

Back took me into one of those cabins and closed the door.

"Now listen, Mr. Peploe," said he. "I'm going to shut you down in the lazarette." He pulled a piece of paper from his pocket, on which was a rude tracing. "This is the inside of the lazarette," he continued, pointing to the tracing. "There are some casks of flour up in this corner. They'll make you a safe hiding-place. You'll find a bag of ship's biscuit and some bottles of wine and water and a pannikin stowed behind them casks. There's cases of bottled ale in the lazarette, and plenty of tinned stuffs and grub for the cabin table. But don't broach anything if you can hold out."

"When am I to show myself?"

"When we're out of Soundings."

"Where's that?" said I.

"Clear of the Chops," he answered." If you come up when the land's still in sight the captain'll send you ashore by anything that'll take you, and you'll be handed over to the authorities and charged."

"How shall I know when we're clear of the Chops?" said I.

"I'll drop below into the lazarette on some excuse and tell you," he answered. "You'll be very careful when you turn up, Mr. Peploe, not to let them guess that anybody's lent you a hand in this here hiding job. If they find out I'm your friend, then it's all up with Jem Back. He's a stone-broke young man, and his parents'll be wishing of themselves dead rather than they should have lived to see this hour."

"I have sworn, and you may trust me, Back."

"Right," said he. "And now, is there e'er a question you'd like to ask before you drop below?"

"When does the ship haul out?"

"They may be doing of it even whilst we're talking," he said.

"Can I make my escape out of the lazarette should I feel very ill, or as if I was going to suffocate?"

"Yes, the hatch is a little 'un. The cargo sits tall under him, and you can stand up and shove the hatch clear of its bearings should anything go seriously wrong with you. But don't be in a hurry to feel ill or short o' breath. There's no light, but there's air enough. The united smells, perhaps, ain't all violets, but the place is warm."

He paused, looking at me inquiringly. I could think of nothing more to ask him. He opened the door, warily peered out, then whispered to me to follow, and I walked at his heels to the end of the corridor near the stern. I heard voices in the cabins on either hand of me; some people came out of one of the after berths, and passed us, talking noisily, but they took no heed of me or of my friend. They were passengers, and strangers to the ship, and would suppose me a passenger also, or an under-steward, like Jem Back, who, however, now looked his vocation, attired as he was in a camlet jacket, black cloth breeches, and a white shirt.

We halted at a little hatchlike trap-door a short way forward of the bulkheads of the stern cabins. Back grasped the ring in the center of the hatch, and easily lifted the thing, and laid open the hold.

"All's clear," said he, looking along the corridor. "Down with you, Mr. Peploe." I peered into the abyss, as it seemed to me; the light hereabouts was so dim that but little of it fell through the small square of hatchway, and I could scarcely discern the outlines of the cargo below. I put my legs over and sank, holding on with a first voyager's grip to the coaming of the hatch; then, feeling the cargo under my feet, I let go, and the instant I withdrew my hands, Back popped the hatch on.

The blackness was awful. It affected me for some minutes like the want of air. I thought I should smother, and could hardly hinder myself from thrusting the hatch up for light, and for the comfort of my lungs. Presently the sense of suffocation passed. The corridor was uncarpeted; I heard the sounds of footsteps on the bare planks overhead, and, never knowing but that at any moment somebody might come into this lazarette, I very cautiously began to grope my way over the cargo. I skinned my hands and my knees, and cut my small clothes against all sorts of sharp edges in a very short time. I never could have realized the like of such a blackness as I was here groping through. The deepest midnight overhung by the electric cloud would be as bright as dawn or twilight compared to it.

I carried, however, in my head the sketch Back had drawn of this interior, and remembering that I had faced aft when my companion had closed me down, I crawled in the direction in which I imagined the casks and my stock of bread and wine lay; and to my great joy, after a considerable bit or crawling and clawing about, during which I repeatedly wounded myself, I touched a canvas bag, which I felt, and found full of ship's bread, and on putting my hand out in another direction, but close by where the bag was, I touched a number of bottles. On this I felt around, carefully stroking the blackness with my maimed hands, and discovered that I had crawled into a recess formed by the stowage of a number of casks on their bilge; a little space was left behind them and the ship's wall; it was the hiding-place Back had indicated, and I sat down to breathe and think, and to collect my wits.

I had no means of making a light; but I don't believe that in any case I should have attempted to kindle a flame, so great would have been my terror of setting the ship on fire. I kept my eyes shut, fancying that that would be a good way to accustom my vision to the blackness. And here I very inopportunely recollected that one of the most dreadful prison punishments inflicted upon mutinous and ill-behaved felons is the locking of them up in a black room, where it is thought proper not to keep them very long lest they should go mad; and I wondered how many days or hours it would take to make a lunatic of me in this lazarette, that was as black certainly as any black room ever built for refractory criminals.

I had no clothes save those I wore. Stowaways as a rule do not carry much luggage to sea with them. I had heard tell of ships' slop-chests, however, and guessed when I was enlarged and put to work, the captain would let me choose a suit of clothes and pay for them out of my wages. I did not then know that it is not customary for commanders of ships to pay stowaways for their services. Indeed, I afterwards got to hear that far better men than the average run of stowaway were, in their anxiety to get abroad, very willing to sign articles for a shilling a month, and lead the lives of dogs for that wage.

I had come into the ship with a parcel of bread and cheese in my pocket: feeling hungry I partook of this modest refreshment, and clawing round touched a bottle, pulled the loosely-fitted cork out, and drank. This small repast heartened me, I grew a little less afraid of the profound blackness, and of the blue and green lights which came and went upon it, and began to hope I should not go mad.

The hours sneaked along. Now and again a sort of creaking noise ran through the interior, which made me suppose that the ship was proceeding down the river in tow of a tug. Occasionally I heard the tread of passengers overhead. It pleased me to hear that sound. It soothed me by diminishing the intolerable sense of loneliness bred by the midnight blackness in which I lay. The atmosphere was warm, but I drew breath without difficulty. The general smell was, indeed, a complicated thing; in fact, the lazarette was a storeroom. I seemed to taste ham, tobacco, cheese, and fifty other such matters in the air.

I had slept very ill on the preceding night, and after I had been for some hours in the lazarette I felt weary, and stretched myself along the deck between the casks and the ship's wall, and pillowed my head on my coat. I slept, and my slumber was deep and long. My dreams were full of pleasing imaginations—of nuggets of extraodinary size, chiefly, and leagues of rich pasture land whitened by countless sheep, all branded with the letter P. But after I had awakened and gathered my wits together, I understood that I had lost all count of time, that I should not know what o'clock it was, and whether it was day or night, until I had got out. I was glad to find that the blackness was not so intolerable as I had dreaded. I felt for the biscuits and bottles, and ate and drank as appetite dictated. Nobody in all this while lifted the hatch. No doubt the steward had plenty of stores for current use in hand, and there might be no need to break out fresh provisions for some weeks.

I had lain, according to my own computation, very nearly two days in this black hole, when I felt a movement in the ship which immediately upset my stomach. The vessel, I might suppose, was in the Channel; her pitching grew heavier, the lazarette was right aft, and in no part of the vessel saving the bows could her motion be more sensibly felt. I was speedily overcome with nausea, and for many long hours lay miserably ill, unable to eat or drink. At the expiration of this time the sea ran more smoothly; at all events, the ship's motion grew gentle; the feeling of sickness suddenly passed, leaving me, indeed, rather weak, yet not so helpless but that I could sit up and drink from a bottle of wine and water, and eat a dry ship's biscuit.

Whilst I was munching the tasteless piece of sea bread, sitting in the intense blackness, pining for the fresh air and the sunshine, and wondering how much longer I was to wait for Back's summons to emerge, the hatch was raised. I shrank and held my breath, with my hand grasping the biscuit poised midway to my mouth, as though I had been withered by a blast of lightning. A faint sheen floated in the little square. It was the dim lustre of distant lamplight, whence I guessed it was night. The figure of a man cautiously dropped through the hatchway, and by some means, and all very silently, he contrived to readjust the hatch, shutting himself down as Back had shut me down. The motion of the ship, as I have said, was gentle, the creaking noises throughout the working fabric were dim and distant; indeed, I could hear the man breathing as he seemed to pause after bringing the hatchway to its bearings over his head. I did not suppose that the captain ever entered this part of the ship. The man, for all I could conjecture, might be one of the mates, or the boatswain, or the head steward, visiting the lazarette on some errand of duty, and coming down very quietly that the passengers who slept in the cabins on either hand the corridor should not be disturbed. Accordingly, I shrank into the compactest posture I could contort myself into, and watched.

A lucifer match was struck; the flame threw out the figure of a man standing on the cargo just under the hatch; he pulled out a little bull's-eye lamp from his pocket and lighted it, and carefully extinguished the match. The long, misty beam of the magnified flame swept the interior like the revolving spoke of a wheel as the man slowly turned the lens about in a critical search of the place, himself being in blackness. The line of light broke on the casks behind which I crouched, and left me in deep shadow unperceived. After some minutes of this sort of examination, the man came a little way forward and crouched down upon a bale or something of the sort directly abreast of the casks, through whose cant-lines I was peering. He opened the lamp and placed it beside him; the light was then full upon his figure.

He might have been an officer of the ship for all I knew. His dress was not distinguishable. but I had his face very plain in my sight. He was extremely pale; his nose was long and aquiline; he wore moustaches, whiskers, and a short beard, black, but well streaked with grey. His eyebrows were bushy and dark; his eyes were black, and the reflected lamplight shot in gleams from them, like to that level spoke of radiance with which he had swept this lazarette. His hair was unusually long, even for that age of the fashion, and his being without a hat made me guess he was not from the deck, though I never doubted that he was one of the ship's company.

When he opened the bull's-eye lamp and put it down, he drew something out of his pocket which glittered in his hand. I strained my sight, yet should not have managed to make out what he grasped but for his holding it close to the light; I then saw that it was a small circular brass box; a kind of little metal cylinder, from whose side fell a length of black line, just as tape draws out of a yard measure. He talked to himself, with a sort of wild, scowling grin upon his face, whilst he inspected his brass box and little length of line; he then shut the lamp and flashed it upon what I saw was a medium-sized barrel, such, perhaps, as a brewer would call a four-and-a-half gallon cask. It rested on its bilge, after the manner in which the casks behind which I lay hidden were stowed.

I now saw him pull a spile or spike of wood out of the head of the barrel, and insert the end of the black line attached to the small brass piece in the orifice. This done he fitted a key to the brass box and wound it up. He may have taken twenty turns with the key; the lazarette was so quiet that I could distinctly hear the harsh grit of the mechanism as it was revolved. All the while he was thus employed he preserved his scowling smile, and whispered to himself. After he had wound up the piece of clockwork he placed it on the bale where his lamp had stood, and taking the light made for the hatchway, under which he came to a stand whilst he extinguished the bull's-eye. I then heard him replace the hatch, and knew he was gone.

The arrangement he had wound up ticked with the noise of a Dutch clock. I had but little brains in those days, as I have told you, and in sad truth I am not overloaded with that particular sort of cargo at this hour; but I was not such a fool as not to be able to guess what the man intended to do, and what that hollow, desperate ticking signified. Oh, my great God, I thought to myself, it is an infernal machine! and the ship will be blown up!

My horror and fright went far beyond the paralyzing form; they ran a sort of madness into my blood and vitalized me into desperate instant action. Utterly heedless now of hurting and wounding myself, I scrambled over the casks, and directed by the noise of the ticking, stretched forth my hand and grasped the brass machine. I fiercely tugged it, then feeling for the slow match, as I guessed the line to be, I ran it through my fingers to make sure I had pulled the end out of the barrel. The murderous thing ticked in my hand with the energy of a hotly-revolved capstan, whilst I stood breathing short, considering what I should do, whilst the perspiration soaked through my clothes as though a bucket of oil had been upset over me. Heavens! the horror of standing in that black lazarette with an infernal machine ticking in my hands, and a large barrel of gunpowder, as I easily guessed, within reach of a kick of my foot! I trembled in every limb and sweated at every pore, and seemed to want brains enough to tell me what ought next to be done!

How long I thus stood irresolute I don't know; still clutching the hoarsely-ticking piece of clockwork. I crawled in the direction in which I supposed lay the casks behind which I had hidden. I had scarcely advanced half a dozen feet when the mechanism snapped in my fingers; a bright flash, like to the leap of a flame in the pan of a flint musket, irradiated the lazarette; the match was kindled, and burnt freely. The first eating spark was but small; I extinguished the fiery glow between my thumb and forefinger, squeezing it in my terror with the power of the human jaw. The ticking ceased; the murderous thing lay silent and black in my hand. I waited for some minutes to recover myself, and then made up my mind to get out of the lazarette and go on deck, and tell the people that there was a barrel of gunpowder in the after-hold, and that I had saved the ship from having her side or stern blown out.

I pocketed the brass box and match, but it took me above half an hour to get out of the infernal hole. I fell into crevices, went sprawling over pointed edges, and twice came very near to breaking my leg. Happily, I was tall, and when I stood on the upper tier of cargo I could feel the deck above me, and once, whilst thus groping, I touched the edge of the hatchway, thrust up the cover, and got out.

I walked straight down the corridor, which was sown with passengers' boots, mounted the wide staircase, and gained the quarter-deck. I reeled and nearly fell, so intoxicating was the effect of the gushing draught of sweet, fresh night-wind after the stagnant, cheesy atmosphere of the lazarette. A bull's eye shone on the face of a clock under the break of the poop; the hour was twenty minutes after two. Nothing stirred on the main deck and waist; the forward part of the ship was hidden in blackness. She was sailing on a level keel before the wind, and the pallid spaces of her canvas soared to the trucks, wan as the delicate curls and shreds of vapor which floated under the bright stars.

I ascended a flight of steps which led to the poop, and saw the shadowy figures of two midshipmen walking on one side the deck, whilst on the other side, abreast of the mizzen rigging, stood a third person. I guessed by his being alone that he was the officer of the watch, and stepped over to him. He drew himself erect as I approached, and sang out, "Hallo! who the devil are you?"

"I'm just out of your lazarette," said I, "where I've saved this ship from having her stern blown out by an infernal machine!"

He bent his head forward and stared into my face, but it was too dark for him to make anything of me. I reckoned he was the second mate; his outline against the stars defined a square, bullet-headed, thick-necked man. On a sudden he bawled out to the two midshipmen, who had come to a stand on t'other side the skylight—

"Mr. Freeling, jump below and call the captain. Beg him to come on deck at once, young gentleman."

The midshipman rushed into the cuddy.

"What's this yarn about blowing out the ship's stern?" continued the second mate, as I rightly took him to be.

I related my story as straightforwardly as my command of words permitted. I told him that I had wanted to get to Australia, that I was too poor to pay my passage, that I had been unable to find employment on board ship, that I had hidden myself in the lazarette of the *Huntress*, and that whilst there, and within the past hour, I had seen a man fit a slow match into what I reckoned was a barrel of gunpowder and disappear after setting his infernal machine a-going. And thus speaking, I pulled the machine out of my pocket, and put it into his hand.

At this moment the captain arrived on deck. He was a tall man, with a very deep voice, slow, cool, and deliberate in manner and speech.

"What's the matter?" he inquired, and instantly added, "Who is this man?" The second mate gave him my story almost as I had delivered it.

The captain listened in silence, took the infernal machine, stepped to the skylight, under which a lamp was dimly burning, and examined the piece of mechanism. His manner of handling it by some means sprang the trigger, which struck the flint, and there flashed out a little sun-bright flame that fired the match. I jumped to his side and squeezed the fire out between my thumb and forefinger as before. The captain told the two midshipmen to rouse up the chief mate and send the boatswain and carpenter aft.

"Let there be no noise," said he to the second mate. "We want no panic aboard us. Describe the man," said he, addressing me, "whom you saw fitting this apparatus to the barrel." I did so. "Do you recognize the person by this lad's description?" said the captain to the second mate.

The second mate answered that he knew no one on board who answered to the likeness I had drawn.

"Gentlemen, I swear he's in the ship!" I cried, and described him again as I had seen him when the open bull's-eye allowed the light to stream fair upon his face.

But now the arrival of the chief officer, the boatswain, and the carpenter occasioned some bustle. My story was hastily re-told. The carpenter fetched a lantern, and the whole group examined the infernal machine by the clear light.

"There's no question as to the object of this piece of

clockwork, sir," said the chief officer.

"None," exclaimed the captain; "it flashed a few minutes ago in my hand. The thing seems alive. Softly now. The passengers musn't hear of this: there must be no panic. Take the boatswain and carpenter along with you, Mr. Morritt, into the lazarette. But mind your fire." And he then told them where the barrel was stowed as I had described it.

The three men left the poop. The captain now examined me afresh. He showed no temper whatever at my having hidden myself on board his ship. All his questions concerned the appearance of the man who had adjusted the machine, how he had gone to work, what he had said when he talked to himself—but this question I could not answer. When he had ended his inquiries he sent for the chief steward, to whom he related what had happened, and then asked him if there was such a person in the ship as I had described. The man answered there was.

"What's his name?"

"He's booked as John Howland, sir. He's a steerage passenger. His cabin's No. 2 on the starboard side. His meals are taken to him into his cabin, and I don't think he's ever been out of it since he came aboard."

"Go and see if he's in his cabin," said the captain.

As the steward left the poop the chief mate, the boatswain, and carpenter returned. "It's as the young man states, sir," said Mr. Morritt. "There's a barrel of gunpowder stowed where he says it is with a hole in the head ready to receive the end of a fuse."

"Presently clear it out, and get it stowed away in the magazine," said the captain, calmly. "This has been a narrow escape. Carpenter, go forward and bring a set of irons along. Is there only one barrel of gunpowder below, d'ye say, Mr. Morritt?"

"No more, sir."

"How could such a thing find its way into the lazarette?" said the captain, addressing the second mate.

"God alone knows!" burst out the other. "It'll have come aboard masked in some way, and it deceived me. Unless there's the hand of a lumper in the job—does *he* know no more about it than what he says?" he cried, rounding upon me.

At this moment the steward came rushing from the companion way, and said to the captain, in a trembling voice, "The man lies dead in his bunk, sir, with his throat horribly cut."

"Come you along with us," said the captain, addressing me, and the whole of us, saving the carpenter and second mate, went below.

We walked along the corridor obedient to the captain's whispered injunction to tread lightly, and make no noise. The midnight lantern faintly illuminated the length of the long after passage. The steward conducted us to a cabin that was almost right aft, and threw open the door. A bracket lamp filled the interior with light. There were two bunks under the porthole, and in the lower bunk lay the figure of the man I had beheld in the lazarette. His throat was terribly gashed, and his right hand still grasped the razor with which the wound had been inflicted.

"Is that the man?" said the captain.

That's the man," I answered, trembling from head to foot, and sick and faint with the horror of the sight.

"Steward, fetch the doctor," said the captain, "and tell the carpenter we shan't want any irons here."

The narrative of my tragic experience may be completed by the transcription of two newspaper accounts, which I preserve pasted in a commonplace book. The first is from the *Sydney Morning Herald*. After telling about the arrival of the *Huntress*, and the disembarkation of his Excellency and suite, the writer proceeds thus:—

"When the ship was five days out from the Thames an extraordinary incident occurred. A young man named William Peploe, a stowaway, whilst hidden in the lazarette of the vessel, saw a man enter the place in which he was hiding and attach a slow match and an infernal machine to a barrel of gunpowder stored amidships of the lazarette, and, from what we can gather, *on top of the cargo!* When the man left the hold young Peploe heroically withdrew the match from the powder and carried the machine on deck.

The youth described the man, who proved to be a second-class passenger, who had embarked under the name of John Howland. When the villain's cabin was entered he was found lying in his bunk dead, with a severe wound in his throat inflicted by his own hand. No reason is assigned for this dastardly attempt to destroy a valuable ship and cargo and a company of souls numbering two hundred and ten, though there seems little reason to doubt that the man was mad. It is certain that but for the fortunate circumstance of young Peploe lying hidden in the lazarette the ship's stern or side would have been blown out, and she must have gone down like a stone, carrying all hands with her. On the passengers in due course being apprised of their narrow escape, a purse of a hundred guineas was subscribed and presented by his Excellency to young Peploe. The captain granted him a free passage and provided him with a comfortable outfit from the ship's slop-chest. It is also understood that some situation under Government has been promised to Mr. William Peploe in consideration of the extraordinary service rendered on this memorable occasion."

My next quotation is from the pages of the Nautical Magazine, dated two years subsequent to the publication of the above in the Australian paper:—

"A bottle was picked up in March last upon the beach of Terceira, one of the Azores, containing a paper bearing a narrative which, unless it be a hoax, seems to throw some light on the mysterious affair of the *Huntress*, for the particulars of which we refer our readers to our volume of last year. The paper, as transmitted by the British Consul, is as follows:—

"Ship *Huntress*. At sea, such and such a date, 1853.

"I, who am known on board this vessel as John Howland, am the writer of this document. Twenty years ago I was unjustly sentenced to a term of transportation across seas, and my treatment at Norfolk

Island was such that I vowed by the God who made me to be revenged on the man who, acting on the representation of his creatures, had caused me to be sent from Hobart Town to that hellish penal settlement. That man, with his wife and children, attended by a suite, is a passenger in this ship, and I have concerted my plan to dispatch him and those who may be dear to him to that Devil to whom the wretch consigned my soul when he ordered me to be sent as a further punishment to Norfolk Island. The destruction of this ship is ensured. Nothing can avert it. A barrel of gunpowder was stowed by well-bribed hands in the East India Docks in the lazarette, to which part of the bold access is easy by means of a small trap door. I am writing this three-quarters of an hour before I proceed to the execution of my scheme, and the realization of my dream of vengeance. When I have completed this document I will place it in a bottle, which I shall carefully cork and seal and cast into the sea through my cabin porthole. I am sorry for the many who must suffer because of the sins of one; but that one must perish, and immediately, in which hope, craving that, when this paper is found it may be transmitted to the authorities at home, so that the fate of my bitter enemy may be known, I subscribe myself,

    "ISRAEL THOMAS WILKINSON,
      "Ex-Convict and Ticket-of-Leave Man."

A MEMORY OF THE PACIFIC

It was in December, 1858, that the ship *Walter Hood* shifted her berth to the woolsheds at Sydney to load a cargo for London. I was chief officer of the vessel; my name, let me say here, is Adam Chichester.

I was standing on the wharf near the ship, waiting for the arrival of some wagons of wool, when the master of a German vessel that lay just astern of us came up to me, and said—

"Dot vhas a bad shob last night."

"What was?" said I.

"Haf not you heard of der brudal murder in Shorge Street?"

"I have not seen a morning paper."

"She vhas dot small chop vhere dey sells grocery und odder tings on der left going oop. She vhas a Meester Abney, dey say. Der murderer vhas a beastly rogue called Murray; she helped in der shop; she hod been a soldier. Dis morning poor Abney vhas found dead in her bedt mit her troat cut und her skull sphlit."

"Have they got the murderer?"

"No. Dot vhas der pity. He make clean off mit sixty pound." Throughout the day people coming and going talked of this murder. The yarn ran thus:—Mrs. Abney occupied a room next to the murdered man's; the son, Thomas, a youth of about eighteen, used an apartment at the back of the shop; the servant lay in the attics; the assistant, Murray, lodged out. Neither Mrs. Abney, her son, nor the servant had heard a sound in the night; Murray had broken into the house, passed into Abney's room, and murdered him; then from a safe, whose key Abney kept under his pillow, he had taken about sixty sovereigns; all so noiselessly, the footfalls of a cat are not stiller. The family slept on, and the murder was not discovered till half-past seven in the morning.

It was known by these damning tokens that Murray was the murderer: first, the knife Abney's throat had been cut with was Murray's; after using it he had dropped it behind some paper in the bedroom grate. Next, when he had shifted himself at his lodgings he had buried the clothes in the back garden; a dog belonging to the woman of the house was observed to run into the garden with its nose stooped as though on a trail, and stopping where the bundle was buried, it began to scratch and howl. The woman called a neighbor; they went to the place with a spade and found Murray's clothes, covered with bloodstains.

The man himself was off, and the people who from time to time during the day gave me news of this thing told me he was still at large, that the police were in hot pursuit, and there was no hope for him.

That evening I strolled up George Street for a walk, and saw a great crowd at the Abney's shop. I stopped to stare with the rest of them. They call this sort of curiosity vulgar and debasing. But crime puts the significance of human emotion, misery, and remorse into stocks and stones. Human passion gives the vitality of romance, tragic, or comic, to the most sordid and contemptible aspects of the common-place. I had passed that grocer's shop twenty times, and often looked at the house. I looked at it again now, and found the matter-of-fact structure as strange, grotesque, repulsive as a nightmare.

The days rolled on; Murray remained at large. His escape, or at least his marvellous manner of hiding, was the source of more excitement than the murder itself had proved. Most people supposed he had got clean away and was lurking among the islands, unless he was halfway on the road to Europe or America; others that he had struck inland and had perished in the wilds.

But by degrees of course the matter went out of one's head; out of mind certainly. Before the ship sailed I could walk up George Street and look at the shop and think of other things than the murder. Yet the memory of it was freshened a day or two before the tug got hold of us by the commander of the ship, Captain Charles Lytton, telling me that amongst those who had taken berths in the steerage were the widow and son of the murdered man.

"I'm almost sorry they chose this ship," said he, with an uneasy half-laugh. "For my part I'd as lief sail on a Friday as carry anything with such a shadow upon it as murder."

"They're long in catching Murray," said I.

"It's no fault of the police," he answered. "We're not in England here. A brisk walk takes a man into desolation. When you talk of catching a murderer, you think of beadles and fire-engines, and the electric telegraph. But the black man is still in this country; there's never a village pump betwixt Wooloomooloo and the Antarctic circle. Small wonder your bushranger flourishes."

We sailed on a Monday in the beginning of February, having been belated by the breakdown of some transport machinery in the interior. There went about a dozen people to the steerage company, and we carried ten passengers in the saloon. The *Walter Hood* was a smart and beautiful clipper of a vanished type; elliptical stern, a swelling lift of head with an exquisite entry of cut-water, coppered to the bends, a green hull, yards as square as a frigate's, with a noble breast of topsail and royal yards hoisting close under the trucks, man-of-war style. On a wind, one point free, she could have given her tow-rope to any Blackwall liner then afloat and not known there was anything in her wake.

When we were clear of the Heads, I came aft after seeing to the ground tackle, and in the waist saw a woman in deep mourning, looking over the rail at the receding land. A young fellow stood beside her. He too was in black. I cannot recall a finer specimen of a young man than that youth. His height was about six feet. He held himself erect as a soldier. His breadth of shoulder warranted in him the hurricane lungs of a boatswain. He was looking at the land, and his face was hard with a fixed and dark expression of grief.

The third mate was near. I whispered to him to say if those two were the Abney's. He answered they were. When some time later on I had leisure to look about me, I observed that the widow of the murdered man and her son held aloof from their fellow-passengers down on the main-deck. She always appeared with a veil on. She and the youth would get together in some corner or recess, and there sit, talking low. The steerage folks treated them with a sort of commiserative respect, as though affliction had dignified the pair. The steward told how he had picked up that, after the murder of Abney, the widow had sold off the contents of the shop and her furniture; she was going home to live with her sister, the wife of a tradesman at Stepney. He told me that the son often spoke of his father's murder.

"His notion is," said the steward, "that Murray's out of the colony, and's to be found in England. That's his 'ope. He's a bit crazed, I think, with some queer dream of meeting of him, and talks, with his eyes shining, of a day of reckoning. Otherwise he'd have stayed in Sydney, where he's got friends, and where his father's murder was likely to have improved his prospects by bringing him pity and business."

When the Australian coast was out of sight, the wind chopped from the westward into the south, and blew a wonderful sailing breeze, bowling a wide heave of sea from horizon to horizon in lines of milky ridges and soft, dark blue valleys, freckled as with melting snow, and along this splendid foaming surface rushed the ship with the westering sunlight red as blood in every lifting flash of her wet sheathing. So through the night; the white water full of fire poured away on either hand the thunderous stem; the purely-shining stars reeled above our phantom heights of sail faint as steam.

At ten a corner of crimson moon rose over our bows, to be eclipsed for awhile by the shadowy square of a ship's canvas right ahead; but before the moon had brightened into silver we had the stranger abeam of us, and were passing her as though she were at anchor—a lubberly, blubberly whaler, square-ended, with stump topgallant-masts—a splashing grease-box gamely tumbling in our wake with a convulsive sawing and shearing of her masts and yardarms, as though, sentient but drunken too, the lonely fabric sought to foul the stars with her trucks, and drag the stellar system out of gear.

So through next day, and a whole week of days and nights following; then the breeze scanted one afternoon, and at sundown it was a glassy calm, with a languid pulse of swell out of the southeast, and a sky of red gold, shaded with violet cloud, brighter eastwards when the sun was set than astern where the light had been.

The middle watch was mine that night. I turned out with a yawn at midnight, and going on deck found the reflection of the moon trembling with the brushing of a delicate warm cats-paw of wind; the sails were asleep, and the shin was wrinkling onwards at two knots. The moon was over our port main-topsail yardarm, and being now hard upon her full, and hanging in a perfectly cloudless sky, she filled the night with a fine white glory till the atmosphere looked to brim to the very stars with her light; the Southern Cross itself in the south shone faint in that spacious firmament of moonlight.

I never remember the like of the silence that was upon that sea; the sense of the solitude of the prodigious distances worked in one like a spirit, subduing the heart with a perception of some mysterious inaudible *hush!* floating to and meeting *in* the ship out of every remote pale ocean recess. I had used the sea for years, and knew what it was to lie motionless under the Line for three weeks, stirless as though the keel had been bedded in a sheet-flat surface of ice or glass; but never before had the mystery, the wonder, the awe which dwell like sensations of the soul itself in any vast scene of ocean night that is silent as death, and white as death too with overflowing moonlight, affected and governed me as the beauties and sublime silence of this midnight did.

The second mate went below, and I paced the deck alone. Saving the fellow at the helm, I seemed to be the only man in the ship. Not a figure was visible. But then I very well knew that to my call the deck would be instantly clamorous and alive with running shapes of seamen.

After I had walked a little while, I crossed to the port side where the flood of moonshine lay shivering upon the ocean, and looked at the bright white rim of the sea under the moon, thinking I saw a sail there. It was then I heard a faint cry; it sounded like a halloaing out upon the water on the port bow. I strained my ears, staring ahead with intensity. Then hearing nothing, I supposed the sound that had been like a human voice hailing was some creaking or chafing noise aloft, and I was about to resume my walk when I heard it again, this time a distinct, melancholy cry.

"Did you hear that, sir?" cried the fellow at the wheel.

I answered "Yes," and sung out for some hands to get upon the forecastle and report anything in sight. The halloaing was repeated; in a few minutes a man forward hailed the poop and told me there was a boat or something black two points on the port bow; on which I shifted the helm for the object, which the night-glass speedily resolved into the proportions of a small open boat, with a man standing up in her.

By this time the captain, who had been aroused by our voices, was on deck. We floated slowly down upon the little boat, and the captain hailed to know if the man had strength to scramble aboard alone.

"Yes, sir," was the answer. "Then look out for a line."

The boat came under the bow; a rope's end was thrown and caught. The man languidly climbed into the fore-channels, omitting to secure the boat, which drove past and was already in our wake whilst the fellow was crawling over the side. Some of our seamen helped him over the rail, and he then came aft, walking very slowly, with an occasional reel in his gait, as though drunk or excessively weak.

He mounted the poop ladder with the assistance of a seaman. The moonlight was so bright it was almost the same as seeing things by day. He was a short, powerfully built man, habited in the Pacific beachcomber's garb of flannel shirt and dungaree breeches, without a hat or shoes; his hair was long and wild, his beard ragged; he was about thirty years of age, with a hawksbill nose, and large protruding eyes, hollow cheeked, and he was of the color of a corpse as he faced the moon.

He begged for a drink and for something to eat, and food and a glass of rum and water were given to him before he was questioned.

He then told us he had belonged to the Colonial schooner *Cordelia* that had been wrecked five days before on a reef, how far distant from the present situation of our ship he did not know. The master and Kanaka crew left the wreck in what he called the long-boat. He said he was asleep when the schooner grounded. He did not apparently awaken until some time after the disaster; when he came on deck he found the schooner hard and fast and deserted. A small boat was swinging in davits; he lowered her and left the wreck, unable to bring away anything to eat or drink with him, as the hold was awash and the vessel quickly going to pieces and floating off in staves.

He delivered this yarn in a feeble voice, but fluently; undoubtedly he had suffered; but somehow, as I listened, I could not satisfy myself that what had befallen him had happened just as he stated.

He asked what ship ours was, and looked round quickly when he was told she was the *Walter Hood* from Sydney bound to London. The captain asked him what his rating had been aboard the schooner; he answered, "Able seaman." He was then sent forward into the forecastle.

I went below at four, and was again on deck at eight, and learned that the man we had rescued was too ill to "turn to," as we call it. The ship's doctor told me he was suffering from the effects of privation and exposure, but that he was a hearty man, and would be fit for work in a day or two. He had told the doctor his name was Jonathan Love, and that the *Cordelia* belonged to Hobart Town, at which place he had joined her. The doctor said to me he did not like his looks.

"I make every allowance," he went on, "for hairiness and color, and for the expression which the sufferings a man endures in a dry, starving, open boat at sea will stamp upon his face, sometimes lastingly. There's an evil memory in the eyes of that chap. He glances at you as though he saw something *beyond*."

"Men of a sweet and angelic expression of countenance are rarely met with in these seas," said I.

"Likely as not he will prove an escaped convict," said the doctor. Three days passed, and Love still kept his hammock. But now the doctor reported him well, and the captain sent orders to the boatswain to turn the man to and find out what he was fit for. This happened during a forenoon watch which was mine. The day had broken in splendor. Masses of white cloud were rolling their stately bulk, prismatic as oyster shells, into the northeast, and the blue in the breaks of them was of the heavenly dye of the Pacific. The ship was curtsying forwards under breathing topsails and studding-sails, and the cuddy breakfast being ended, all the passengers were on deck.

I stood at the head of the starboard poop ladder watching the steerage passengers on the main deck. I took particular notice, I recollect, on this occasion, of the Abneys, widow and son, as they sat on the coaming of the main-hatch, the youth reading aloud to his mother. It was the contrast, I suppose, of the heavy crape and thick veil of the woman with the light tropic garments of the rest of the people which invited my eyes to the couple. I found my mind recalling as best my memory could the particulars of the horrible crime the widow's sombre clothes perpetuated.

Then it was, and whilst I was recreating the picture of the shop in George Street, that I observed the young fellow lift his gaze from the page it had been fastened to, violently start, then leap to his feet with a sudden shriek. He was looking at the man we had rescued; *he* stood in the waist, trousers upturned, arms bared, posture as erect as a soldier's; a formidable iron figure of a fellow of medium height, ragged with hair about the head and face—

"Mother," yelled the young fellow almost in the instant of his first shriek, whilst the rescued man turned to look at him. "Father's murderer!—James Murray!—There he is!"

"Not by the son—not by the son!" shouted Murray, holding out his arms as the other rushed towards him. "Not by *you!* He's got his father's looks! Any man else—but—"

Before the young fellow could grasp him, Murray, in a single leap, swift and agile as a goat's, had gained the fore-rigging, and was halfway up the shrouds, the young fellow after him.

"Not you!" roared the murderer, "not with your father's face on you! S'elp me God, it *shan't* be, then!" and rounding to the sea, he put his hands together and shot overboard, brushing the outstreched hand of his pursuer as he flashed past him.

"Pick us up! He must hang for it. Drowning's too easy! He murdered my father!" and thus shouting the lad sprang into the water.

Such a scene of confusion as now followed defies my pen. The ceaseless screaming of the poor widow complicated the uproar. I bawled to the man at the wheel to put the helm down, then for hands to lay aft to clear away and lower a boat. All our passengers were from Sydney; most of the crew had shipped at that port; everyone there had heard of the murder of Mr. Abney; and the effect of the discovery that we had fallen in with the murderer who had so long and successfully eluded justice, that he had been on board the ship three days, that he was yonder floating on our quarter, with the murdered man's son making for him with bold furious sweeps of his arms—was electrical! Women shrieked and men roared; overhead the sails flapped as the ship came to the wind, and there was the further noise of the heavy tread of seamen, the flinging down of ropes, my own and the captain's sharp commands.

When I had time to look, I beheld a death struggle in the sea some quarter of a mile distant. They had grappled. God knows what intention was in the young fellow's mind; it may be he hoped to keep the murderer afloat till the boat reached them. They churned up the foam as though it was white water there boiling on some fang of rock.

The moment the boat put off, an awful silence fell upon the ship.

"Pull, men, pull!" the captain shouted, and the brine flew in sheets from the oars as the little fabric sprang forward. But though the crew with the second mate in the stern-sheets toiled like demons, they were too late. The boat was within three of her own lengths of the spot, when the two men disappeared. We watched breathless, with a very madness and anguish of expectation, for a sight of the head of one or the other of them; but idly: and after the boat had hung some three-quarters of an hour about the place where they had vanished, with the second mate standing up in her, eagerly looking around, she was recalled, hoisted, and we proceeded on our voyage.

"SO UNNECESSARY!"

In 1851 (he began—and who it was that began will quickly appear) I was in command of a small but well-known East Indiaman. She was loading for Bombay in the West India Docks in the month of August, and on returning home one afternoon I found a letter from an old friend whom I had not set eyes on for above three years. His name was Mills—Captain Francis Mills.

He had just heard (he wrote) that I was in command of the *Hecla*, and that she was to sail for Bombay in the middle of September. He wanted to send his daughter to India in charge of a trustworthy friend. Would I dine with him and talk the matter over?

I was then living in Shadwell, and Mills hailed from the other end of London. However, I promised to dine with him on the following Sunday, and with the help of the Blackwall railway and omnibuses I kept my word.

Mills was about sixty years old, a white-haired, red-faced man; he had used the sea for above thirty years, had built, owned, and commanded ships, and was now moored in a plain, comfortable house out of Westbourne Grove. His wife had long been dead. He had one child, a daughter, to whom I had supposed him so deeply attached, that I was surprised on reading his letter to find him willing to part with her. I recollected her as a pretty girl; but after three years of ocean and travel one's memory of a person grows dim.

Miss Minnie Mills was not at home when I arrived. The old skipper and I found many things to talk about before we came to the point; by-and-by he said—

"My daughter—do you remember her, Cleaver?"

"I do."

"She is engaged to be married. She got in tow with a parson two years ago. He was home from India, and we met him at the house of a clergyman whose church we attend. He's chaplain at Junglepore, in a corner of the Punjaub, and is now ready to marry her. He's come into a trifle of money, and I want to send her out to him."

"I wonder you can part with her."

"Why, yes, and so do I wonder. But I'm getting on in years. I wish to see her settled with someone to look after her before my life-lines are unrove. She has no mother. Then, again, I don't mind owning she's a bit uneasy, and she makes me so too; hankers a trifle too much after pleasure; wants to go to the theatre when there's nobody to take her; pines for a few friends when I don't feel well. She's young, and her animal spirits run high, and custom, I dare say, is beginning to sicken the sympathy in her," said he, looking at his left hand, which was rugged with gout, every finger with a "list to port."

"Parting with her will be like parting with half my heart; but it's for her good, and the man she's going to is as worthy, sober, straight-headed and pious a person as the most anxious parent could wish to see his daughter in charge of."

"You want to send her out by the *Hecla?*"

"I want to send her out with you."

"I suppose you know I'm a bachelor?" said I.

"Pah!" he exclaimed, grinning. "An old ape hath an old eye. You are to windward now, Cleaver. Keep so, my lad, keep so."

"I was never commissioned in this way before," said I; "but I shall be happy to oblige you in anything. If your daughter goes as passenger in my ship, she shan't lack care and kindness. No man better than you knows a skipper's duties. A captain's eyes aren't like a cod's. He can't see round corners without a shift of nose—scarcely more than straight ahead, mostly. But I'll do my best, and that best shall be a pleasure to me."

We shook hands. Soon after this Miss Minie Mills came into the room. I stood up and bowed to as handsome a young creature as ever flashed an eye at a man. Indeed, the instant impression of her beauty was disheartening; it flung a sudden weight into my obligation, and I bowed a little nervously over the hand I held. At seventeen she had been pretty merely, slight in form, reserved in manner; now she was a woman, very handsomely clothed with her sex's charms. Her face was full of life; vivacity and spirit were in every turn and move of her. She had dark brown eyes, deep, bland, and eloquent with light; her hair was a dark red, like bronze, and she had

plenty of it; her complexion was of a charming soft whiteness, tinged with color, as though either cheek reflected the
shadow of a rose; and my bachelor eyes found a particular
beauty in a very delicate spangling of golden freckles—they
gave a summer sunny look to her beauty, ripening it till
somehow you thought of orchards, and a prospect of corn
fields reddened with poppies.

At dinner our talk was mainly of India and the voyage to
it, of Junglepore and the duties of the Reverend Joseph
Moxon. Miss Minnie did not flush, nor did her eyes sparkle,
nor did she manifest any particular emotion of any sort when
we talked of India and Mr. Moxon. I thought she tried to di-
vert the conversation from those topics: she asked me what
theatres I had been to since my arrival in England; if I did
not love dancing; for her part she adored it, she said—
dancing and music. Old Captain Mills stuck stoutly in his
talk to India and Moxon. When I asked Miss Minnie how
she liked the notion of a residence in India she pouted her
lips kissingly, and glanced at her father, but not wistfully.

"You'll get plenty of dancing out in India," said I. "At
most of the stations a man, I understand, has little more to do
than cut capers."

"Moxon won't have it," said Captain Mills. "He shan't
prevent me from enjoying myself," exclaimed the girl, with a
note of mutiny. Captain Mills, with one eye closed, viewed
me steadfastly with the other over the top of the wine-glass
he poised.

It was arranged that he should bring his daughter to the
ship on the following Tuesday to look at the vessel and
choose a cabin. I turned the fancy of her marriage over in my
head from time to time till she came to the ship with her father, wondering that the old skipper did not see what would
be plain to everybody:

I mean that he was sending the girl out to be married to a
man she had no liking for, who did not dance and would not
allow his wife to dance; who did not sing, and possibly ob-
jected to profane music; who, as my imagination figured, and
as, indeed, I had gathered from what Mills had let fall, was
just a plain, homely clergyman of decided views, without title
to a bride of beauty and gaiety. His choice would have been

well enough in a captain of Dragoons; in a parson it was highly improper. I suppose Mills counted upon association doing the work of sentiment. It might end in the girl making a devoted wife, and in the clergyman looking coldly upon her. I had sailed with some romantic commodities in my time, and had lived to see more than one surprising, unexpected issue.

Father and daughter came to the ship, and I was on board when they arrived. The *Hecla* was a comfortable, handsomely equipped vessel. She carried a cuddy, or saloon, with sleeping-berths on either hand; the furniture and fittings were of the old-world sort; strips of mirror panelled the bulkheads; the shaft of mizzenmast was hand-painted; a pianoforte was secured to the back of it; the skylights were large and handsome.

I had supposed that the girl would take some interest in, or show some pleasure at, the sights about her. She glanced languidly, and exhibited a spiritlessness of manner, as though the thought of leaving her father was beginning to sit very heavily upon her heart.

I observed, however, that, whilst she barely had eyes for the ship, she did not neglect to look at the chief mate, Mr. Aiken, who stood at the main-hatch superintending some work that was going on. He was a good-looking man, and it was therefore intelligible that the girl should notice him. He was a smart officer, and understood his duty, and continued to shout orders and sing down instructions to the fellows in the hold, insensible of our presence. Aiken was about thirty years of age; his face was colored by weather into the manly hue of the ocean calling; he had white teeth, a finely chiselled profile, an arch, intelligent, dark grey eye. Captain Mills looked at him whilst we stood on the quarter-deck after coming out of the cuddy, but seemed more struck by the smartness of his demeanor and general air than by the beauty of his face. The old salt was full of the ship, and could think of little else. All sorts of memories crowded upon him now that he was in the docks.

I wouldn't go to it again," he exclaimed in a broken voice; "yet I love the life—I love the life!" Miss Minnie chose a berth on the port side. I asked if she meant to bring a maid with her.

"No," says Captain Mills. "She can do without a maid. What scope of purse, Cleaver, do you suppose I ride to?"

"If I can do without a maid on shore," said Miss Minnie, "I can do without one at sea." A note of complaint ran through her sentences, as though she had a mind to make a trouble of things.

"A maid," said Captain Mills, "will be seasick till you're up with the Cape, and idle and useless and carrying on with the steward for the rest of the time till you go ashore, and then she'll leave you to get married."

As we went to the gangway the mate made a step to let us pass. Miss Minnie looked at him again, and went over the side holding her father's arm with a sudden life in her movements, as though the sight of a handsome man had worked up the whole spirit of the coquette in her.

I felt rather sorry for the Reverend Joseph Moxon as I followed the couple on to the quay, hugely admiring the fine floating grace of the girl's figure, the sparkle of her dark eye as she turned her head to look at the ship, the rich tinge her hair took from the sun. In fact, I seemed to find an image of the Reverend Joseph Moxon in old Mills' square, lurching figure alongside the sweet shape of his daughter; and *that* set me thinking of well-bred, jingling, handsome young officers at Moxon's station, where life would provide plenty of leisure for looking and for sighing.

We towed down to Gravesend on a wet morning. Nature is incapable of a gloomier exhibition of wretchedness than the scene she will paint you of the Isle of Dogs and Bugsby's Reach and the yellow stretch of water past Woolwich on a wet day. We had convict hulks moored in the river in those times, and they fitted the dark weeping weather as though they were creations of the spirit of the stream in its sulkiest and most depraved temper of invention. Their influence, too, as a spectacle was a sickness to the soul of the outward bound, whilst the decks streamed and the scuppers gushed and the rigging howled to the whipping of the wet blast, and the greasy water washed into the wake in a sort of oily ironic chuckling, as though the filthy god of the flood was in tow, and laughing under the ship's counter at the general misery aboard.

We moored to a buoy off Gravesend in the afternoon, and next morning, whilst it was still raining, the passengers arrived. Amongst the first to mount the gangway ladder were Captain Mills and his daughter. I received them and took them into the cuddy, and did my best to cheer up the old man, but to no purpose. He broke down when the three of us were by ourselves, and sobbed in a strange, dry-eyed, most affecting manner, often turning to his daughter and bringing her to his heart and blessing her in tones which I confess made my own vision dim. She was pale with weeping.

She cried out once when he turned to fondle her— "Father. I don't want to go! I don't love him enough to leave you. Let me remain with you; we will return home together. It is not too late. Captain Cleaver will send my baggage ashore."

This, I think, served to rally the old chap somewhat. He pulled his faculties together, and in a trembling voice bade his daughter remember that the man she was going to loved her, and was worthy to be loved in return. He himself was getting old, he said, and his closing days would be miserable if he believed he should die and leave her without a protector. A year is quickly lived through: she would soon be coming on a visit to England; or perhaps—who could tell?—he might himself go out the next voyage in this very identical ship, with his friend Cleaver, if he then commanded her.

When he was gone I called to the stewardess and bade her see to Miss Mills' comfort in every direction of the cabin life. The rest of the cuddy passengers arrived quickly from Gravesend. I forget how many they were in all. I believe that every cabin was occupied. The people were of the usual sort in those days of the voyage to India by way of the Cape: a colonel and his wife, the colonel a black-faced man, with gleaming eyes that followed you to the extremities of their sockets; the wife a vast, shapeless bulk of a woman, her head covered by a wig of scarlet curls and her fingers with flashing rings, sheathing them to the first joints; several military officers of various ages; a parson; two merchants of Bombay; five or six ladies, and as many children.

We met with heavy weather down Channel. In this time I

saw nothing of Miss Mills, though I was constant in my inquiries after her. She was not very ill, the stewardess told me. She ate and drank, but she chose to keep her cabin. One morning, when the ship was flapping sluggishly over a wide heave of swell, clothed to the trucks in misty sunshine, which poured like pale steam into the recesses of the ocean, the girl came on deck. She was charmingly attired (I thought); her dark red hair glowed like bronze under the proudly feathered hat. Her complexion was raised; her eyes shone; the Channel dusting had done her good, and I told her so, looking with helpless admiration into her beautiful face as I gave her my arm for a turn.

After this she was punctual at table and constantly on deck. I then considered it fortunate for the Rev. Joseph Moxon that our military passengers should be, without exception, married men; the two or three who were going out alone were either leaving or joining their wives: hence the attention the girl received was without significance. They hung about her; they ran on errands; they were full of business when she hove in sight, so as to plant a chair for her and the like: but it never could come to more than that. The wives looked on, and were civil and kind in a ladylike way to the girl; but I guess she was too pretty to please them; her looks and coquettish vivacity were too conquering; whenever she spoke at table there was an eager sweep of moustache, a universal rounding of Roman and other noses in the direction of her chair. I don't think the wives liked it; but, as I have said, they were all very kind in a genteel way.

I had made up my mind, judging from the glances the girl had directed at the handsome mate Aiken in dock, that she would, though perhaps without losing her heart, yield to the influence of his manly beauty, and be very willing to carry on an aimless flirtation when I was out of sight and the man in charge of the ship. I had also made up my mind if I caught the mate attempting to fool with the girl to bring him up with a "round turn." In fact, I chose to be a taut hand in those matters, quite irrespective of private feelings. Apparently, however, I was to be spared the trouble of bidding my handsome mate keep himself to himself and his weather-eye lifting for the ship and his duties only. Day after day passed, and I never caught him speaking to her.

Once only, and this was at some early date, when she and I were pacing the deck together, and Aiken was standing at the head of the weather-poop ladder, she asked me to tell her about him. Was he married? I said I believed not—I happened to *know* he was not. Who and what was his father? How long had he been at sea? When was he likely to get command? The subject was then changed, and afterwards, though I watched them somewhat jealously, I never detected so much as a glance pass between them.

The long and short of it was—I am bound to confess it—before we had struck the Canary parallels, I—myself—I—Captain Cleaver, commander of the ship *Hecla*—was seriously in love with the girl, and making my days and nights uneasy by contemplation of a proposal of marriage based on these considerations: first, that I was in love with her; next, that she was not in love with the Rev. Joseph Moxon; third, that I could give her a home in England; and then, again, her father was my friend, one of my own cloth, and I had no doubt he would be delighted if I brought her home with me as my wife.

No good, in a short yarn like this, to enter into the question of what was due from me to Joseph Moxon. Enough that I was in love with the girl, and that I had quite clearly discovered she had no affection for—she did not even like or respect—Joseph. I was eight-and-thirty years of age, and a young man at that, as I chose to think; yet somehow Miss Minnie, by no means unintentionally, as I *now* know, contrived to keep sentiment at bay by making me feel that in taking the place of her father whilst we were at sea I had become her father. Never by word of lip did I give her to know that I was in love with her; but I saw she was perfectly sensible that I was her devoted admirer, and that something was bound to happen before we should climb very far north into the Indian Ocean.

One night at about eleven o'clock—six bells—I stepped on deck from my cabin to take a look round. The ship's latitude was then about 25° south. It was a cool, very quiet, dark night, with a piece of dusky-red moon dying out bulbous and distorted in the liquid blackness northwest; a few stars shone sparely; the canvas rose pale and silent; saving the lift of the fabric on the long-drawn heave of the swell, all the life in her was in a little music of ripples, breaking from her stem and tinkling aft in the noise of a summer shower upon water.

I looked into the binnacle, and not immediately seeing the officer of the watch, went a little way forward, and perceived two figures to leeward standing against the poop rail. I walked straight to them quickly. One was Mr. Aiken and the other Miss Minnie Mills. She laughed when I stepped up to her, and exclaimed, "No scolding, I beg. I was disturbed by a nightmare, and came on deck to see if I was really upon the ocean instead of at Junglepore. Mr. Aiken has reassured me. I shall be able to sleep now, I think. So good-night to you both," and with that she left us and disappeared.

I was angry, excited, exceedingly jealous. I guessed I had been tricked, and that a deal had passed between these two, for many a long day gone, utterly unobserved by me. I gave Mr. Aiken a piece of my mind.

Never had I "hazed" any man as I did that fellow as he stood before me. He said it was not his fault; the girl had come on deck and accosted him: he was no ship's constable to order the passengers about; if he was spoken to, he answered; I expected he would be civil to the passengers, he supposed.

I bestowed several sea blessings on his eyes and limbs, and bade him understand that Miss Minnie Mills was under my protection; if I caught him speaking to her I would break him for insubordination. He was mate of the ship, and his business lay in doing his duty. If he went beyond it, he should sling his hammock in the forecastle for the rest of the voyage.

I was horribly in earnest and angry; and when I returned to my cabin, I paced the floor of it as sick at heart as a jilted woman with jealousy and spleen. However, after a while I contrived to console myself with believing that their being together was an accident, and that it might have been as Aiken had put it. At all events, it made me somewhat easy to reflect that I had never observed them in company before, never even caught them looking at each other—that is, significantly.

She was in a sullen and pouting temper all next day.

"Why mayn't I go on deck at night if I choose?" said she.

"Your father would object," said I. "You are under my care. I am responsible for you," I added, with a tender look.

"Would you prohibit the other lady passengers from going on deck at night?"

"You shall have your way in anything that is good for you," said I.

She flashed an arch, saucy glance at me, then sighed, and seemed intensely miserable on a sudden. I believe but for having caught her in Aiken's company I should then and there have offered her my hand.

For a week following she was so completely in the dumps it was hard to get a word from her. Sometimes she looked as if she had been secretly crying, yet I never could persuade myself that the appearance her eyes would at such times present was due to weeping. She moped apart. Some of the passengers noticed her behavior and spoke to me about it, thinking she was ill. The ship's surgeon talked with her and assured me privately he could find nothing wrong save that she complained of poorness of spirits.

"She seems to hate the idea of India," said he, "and wants to go home." And so she shall (thought I), but she must arrive in India first, where she may leave it to me to square the yards for her with the Reverend Joseph Moxon.

We blew westwards round the Cape before a strong gale of wind. One morning, at the grey of dawn, I was aroused by a knocking on my cabin door. The second mate entered. He was a man named Wickham, a bullet-headed, immensely strong, active seaman, the younger son of a baronet: he would have held command at that time but for "the drink." He grasped a woman's hat and handkerchief, and exclaimed—

"I've just found these in the port mizzen chains, sir. I can't tell how they happen to have come there. It looks like mischief."

I sprang from my cot partially clothed, as I invariably was on turning in, and taking the hat in my hand, and bringing it to the clearer light of the large cabin window, I seemed to remember it as having been worn by Minnie Mills. I snatched the handkerchief from the man, and saw the initials

M. M. marked upon it. This sufficed. I swiftly and completely clothed myself and entered the saloon.

My first act was to send the second mate for the stewardess. The woman arrived out of the steerage, where she slept. I said—speaking softly that the people in the berths on either hand might not be disturbed—

"Go and look into Miss Mills' cabin, and report to me if all is well there." She went, vanished, was some little while out of sight, then reappeared and approached me, pale in the ashen light that was filtering through the skylights.

"Miss Mills' cabin is empty, sir."

I was prepared for this piece of news; yet my heart beat with a fast sick pulse when, without speech, I went to the girl's berth, followed by the stewardess. The bunk had been occupied—the bed-clothes lay tossed in it. My eye traveling rapidly over the interior was quickly taken by a note lying upon a chest of drawers. It was addressed to me, and ran thus:—

"I am tired of life, and have resolved to end it. The thought of living even for a short while with Mr. Moxon at Junglepore has broken my heart, and you are as tyrannical and cruel to me as life itself. Farewell, and thank you for such kindness as you have shown me, and when you see my father tell him that I died loving him and blessing him."

"Good God? She's committed suicide," cried I.

The stewardess shrieked.

I felt mad with amazement and grief. I read and re-read her letter, and then looked round the berth again, wondering if this were not some practical joke which she intended should be tragical by the fright it excited. I then went to work to make inquiries. I roused up Mr. Aiken, and showing him the girl's note asked him if he had seen her on deck during his watch—if he himself had at any time foreboded this dreadful thing—if he could help me with any suggestions or information. He read the letter and stared blankly; his handsome countenance was as pale as milk whilst he eyed me. I seemed to find the ghastly mildness of a dead man's face in his looks. He had nothing to say. No lady had come on deck in his watch. He had not exchanged a sentence with Miss Mills since that night when I threatened to break him if I found him in her company.

The men who had steered the ship throughout the night were brought out of the forecastle: no man had seen any lady jump overboard or slip into the mizzen-chains—not likely! Wouldn't the helmsman, seeing such a thing, yell out?

The morning was now advanced. The passengers came from their berths, and it was quickly known fore and aft that the beautiful young girl who had been moping apart for three weeks past as though slowly going mad with melancholy had committed suicide by jumping overboard. The doctor and I and the two mates spent a long time whilst we overhung the mizzen-chains in conjecturing how she had managed it. The cabin windows were small: she had certainly never squeezed her fine ripe figure through the porthole of her berth; therefore she had come on to the poop in some black hour of the night by way of the quarter-deck, passing like a shadow to leeward till she arrived at the mizzen-rigging, where the deep dye flung upon the blackness by the mizzen—for it had been a quiet night, the ship under all plain sail—completely shrouded her. The rest would be easy, and if she dropped from the chains, which, through the angle of the deck, were depressed to within a few feet of the water, her fall might have been almost soundless.

The blow to me was terrible, and for some days I was prostrated. So unnecessary, I kept on saying to myself. Good heavens! For weeks I had been on the verge of proposing to her. The offer of my hand would have saved her life. I could not reconcile so enormous an act with the insignificance of the occasion for it. Old Mills was no tyrant. He had not *driven* her to India. She had consented—with an ill grace perhaps, not caring for the man she was going to; but there had been an acquiescence on her part too, enough of, it at all events, to make one wonder that she should have destroyed herself. How should I be able to meet the old captain? Where was I to find the spirit to tell him the story?

The stewardess, to satisfy herself, thoroughly searched the after part of the ship. It came to my ears that she did not believe that the girl had committed suicide, having neither cause nor courage for such an act. She fancied that one or another of the passengers had hidden her. But for what purpose? The fool of a woman could not answer *that* when the question was put to her.

What end would the girl's hiding achieve? She was bound to come to light on our arrival at Bombay. What motive, then, could she have for concealing herself, for denying herself the refreshment of the deck in the Indian Ocean, ultimately to be shamefully revealed as an imposter capable of the most purposeless and idiotic of deceits?

The beauty was overboard and dead, and my heart, what with disappointed love and grieving for her and sorrow for her poor old father, weighed as lead in me when I thought of it.

We were within a fortnight's sail of Bombay, when there broke a dawn thick and dirty as smoke, with masses of sooty vapor smouldering off the edge of the sea in the west and darkening overhead till the trucks faded out in the gloom. Yet the glass stood high, and I made nothing of the mere appearance of this weather. It lasted all day, with now and again a distant groan of thunder. A weak, hot breeze held the canvas steady, and the ship wrinkled onward holding her course, but sailing through a noon that was as evening for shadow.

We dined at seven. The deck was then in charge of the second mate, Wickham. Before going below I told him to keep a bright lookout, and took myself an earnest view of the sea. The dusk lay very thick upon the cold, greasy, gleaming surface of the ocean, there was not a star overhead, and maybe a man would not have been able to see a distance of half a dozen ships' lengths.

About the middle of dinner I heard a great bawling, a loud and fearful crying out as for life or death. The mate, Aiken, who sat at the foot of the long cuddy table, caught the sound with a sailor's ear as I did, and sprang to his feet, and we rushed on deck together. I had scarcely passed through the companion hatch when the ship was struck. She heeled violently over, listing on a sudden to an angle of nearly fifty degrees, and a dismal, loud, general shriek rose through the open skylight, accompanied by the crash of timber overhead. Along with this went a wild hissing noise and an extraordinary sound of throbbing.

I rushed to the side, and saw that a large steamer had run

into us. She was a big black paddle-boat, one of the few large side-wheel steamers which formerly traded betwixt England and the East Indies by way of the Cape. The sky seemed charged with stars from the spangles of fire which floated along with the thick smoke from her chimney. She was full of light. Every cabin window looked like the lens of a flaming bull's-eye.

I sprang on to the rail, and, hailing the steamer, asked him to keep his stem into us till we found out what damage he had done, and then roared to the mate, but obtained no reply. I yelled again, then shouted to Wickham to tell the carpenter to sound the well. The passengers came crowding on to the poop. I told them there was no danger, that though it should come to our leaving the ship the steamer would stand by us and take all aboard.

The well was sounded, and two feet of water reported. On this I instantly understood that the ship was doomed, that to call the hands to the pumps would be to exhaust them to no purpose; and, hailing the steamer afresh as she lay hissing on our bow, with her looming stem-head overshadowing our forecastle, I reported our condition, and told him to stand-by to pick us up.

We immediately lowered the boats and sent away the women and as many men as there was room for; a second trip emptied the *Hecla* of her passengers. Meanwhile the steamer, at my request, kept her bows right into us. At this time there were seven feet of water in the hold. It was very black, and we worked with the help of lanterns. The mate appeared amongst my people now, and I asked him with an oath, out of the rage and distress of that hour, where he had been skulking. He answered, he was from the forecastle. I told him he was a liar, and ordered him whilst the ship swam to take a number of the hands into the cabin and save as much of the passengers' effects as they could come at.

Not much time was permitted for this: every minute I seemed to feel the ship settling deeper and deeper with a sickening, sullen lift of her whole figure to every heave of the swell, as though she rose wearily to make her farewell plunge. Now the vessels were disengaged, and the steamer lay close abreast. I lingered, almost heart-broken, scarcely yet realizing to its full height this tragic disaster to my ship and my own fortunes; and then, hearing them calling to me, I got into the mizzen-chains, thinking as I did so, of Minnie Mills, wishing to God I was at rest and out of it all where she lay, and entered one of the boats.

The commander of the steamer received me in the gangway. The decks were light as noontide with lanterns. He was a grey-haired man, tall and somewhat stately, dressed in a uniform after the pattern of the old East India Company's service. When he understood I was the captain he bowed, and said—

"It's a terrible calamity, sir. I hope to live to see the day when they will compel all masters, by Act of Parliament, to show lights at sea at night."

A lantern was sparkling on his fore-stay, but our ship was without side-lights, and when I turned to look at her the roar of her bursting decks came along in a shock hard as a blow on the ear, and the whole pale fabric of canvas melted out upon the black water as a wreath of vapor dies in the breeze.

The steamer was the *Nourmahal*, Bulstrode commander. She was half full of invalided soldiers and other folks going home, and when our own people were aboard she was an overloaded craft, humanly speaking; but after a consultation with me the captain resolved to proceed. He was flush with water and provisions, and had the security besides of paddles, which slapped an easy ten knots into the hull. And then again she lifted the yards of a ship of twelve hundred tons, and showed as big a topsail to the wind as a frigate's.

All that could be done was done for us. Men turned out of their cabins to accommodate the ladies and children, and a cot was slung for me in the chief officer's berth. But I needed no pillow for my head that first night. There was nothing in laudanum short of a death-draught that could have given me sleep.

But to pass by my own state of mind, that came very near to a suicidal posture. At eight bells next morning, the mate whose cabin I shared stepped in and exclaimed, "Did you know you had a woman dressed up as a man amongst your passengers?

"No!" I exclaimed, "not likely. I should not permit such a

thing."

"It's so, then," said he: "our doctor twigged her at once, and handed her over to the stewardess, who has berthed her aft. She's a lady, and a develish pretty woman,—mighty pale, though, with a scared, wild blind look, as though she had been dug up out of darkness, and couldn't get used to the light."

"What name does she give?" said I.

"I don't know."

I wished immediately to see her. An extraordinary suspicion worked in my head. The mate told me she was in the stewardess's berth, and directed me to it. I knocked. The stewardess opened the door, and I immediately saw standing in the middle of the berth, with her hands to her head, pinning a bronze tress to a bed of glowing coils, Miss Minnie Mills!

I stared frantically, shouted "Good God!" and rushed in. She screamed and shrank, then clasped her hands, and reared herself loftily with a bringing of her whole shape, so to speak, together.

"So," said I, breathing short with astonishment and twenty conflicting passions. "and this is how they commit suicide in your country, hey?"

The stewardess enlarged her eyes.

"I don't mean to marry Mr. Joseph Moxon," said the girl.

"In what part of the ship did you hide?" I exclaimed. She made no answer.

"Was Mr. Aiken in the secret?"

Still no reply.

"Oh, but you should answer the captain, miss," cried the stewardess. The girl burst into tears, and turned her back upon me. I stepped out and asked for Captain Bulstrode. He received me in his cabin, and then I told him the story of Miss Minnie Mills.

"I never would take charge of a young lady," said he, half laughing, though he was a good deal astonished, "after an experience I underwent in that way. I'll tell it you another time. Let's send for your mate, and see what he has to say for himself."

Presently Mr. Aiken arrived. He was pale, but he carried a

lofty, independent air; the fact was, I was no longer his captain. The ship was sunk, and Jack was as good as his master. I requested, representing Captain Mills as I did, that he would be candid with me, tell me how it stood between him and Miss Mills, if he had helped her in her plot of suicide, where he had hidden her in the ship, and what he meant to do. I thought Bulstrode looked at him with an approving eye. I am bound to repeat he was an uncommonly handsome fellow.

"Captain Cleaver," he said, addressing me with a very frank, straightforward face and air, "I am perfectly aware that I have done wrong, sir. But the long and short of it is, Miss Mills and I are in love with each other, and we mean to get married."

"Why didn't you tell me so?" I said.

He looked at me knowingly. I felt myself color.

"Well," said I, "anyhow, it was so confoundedly unnecessary, you know, for her to pretend to drown herself, and for you to hold her in hiding."

"I beg your pardon—you made it rather necessary, sir— you will remember that night—"

"So unnecessary!" I thundered out in a passion.

"Where did ye hide her?" said Captain Bulstrode.

"I decline to answer that question," replied Aiken. And the dog kept his word, for we never succeeded in getting the truth out of him, or the girl either; though if she did not lie secret in the blackness of the after-hold, then I don't know in what other part of the ship he could have kept her: certainly not in his own cabin, which the ship's steward was in and out of often, nor in any of the cuddy or steerage berths.

To end this: there was a clergyman in the ship; and Bulstrode, who, without personal knowledge of Captain Mills, had heard of him and respected him, insisted upon the couple being married that same forenoon. They were not loth, and, the parson consenting, they were spliced in the presence of a full saloon. I shook the girl by the hand when the business was over, and wished her well; but from beginning to end it was all so unnecessary!

THE MAJOR'S COMMISSION

My name is Henry Adams, and in 1881 I was mate of a ship of 1200 tons named the *Jessamy Bride*. June of that year found her at Calcutta with cargo to the hatches, and ready to sail for England in three or four days.

I was walking up and down the ship's long quarterdeck, sheltered by the awning, when a young apprentice came aft and said a gentleman wished to speak to me. I saw a man standing in the gangway; he was a tall, soldierly person, about forty years of age, with iron-grey hair and spiked mustache, and an aquiline nose. His eyes were singularly bright and penetrating. He immediately said—

"I wanted to see the captain; but as chief officer you'll do equally well. When does this ship sail?"

"On Saturday or Monday next."

He ran his eye along the decks and then looked aloft: there was something birdlike in the briskness of his way of glancing.

"I understand you don't carry passengers?"

"That's so, sir, though there's accommodation for them."

"I'm out of sorts, and have been sick for months, and want to see what a trip round the Cape to England will do for me. I shall be going home, not for my health only, but on a commission. The Maharajah of Ratnagiri, hearing I was returning to England on sick-leave, asked me to take charge of a very splendid gift for Her Majesty the Queen of England. It is a diamond, valued at fifteen thousand pounds."

He paused to observe the effect of this communication, and then proceeded—"I suppose you know how the Koh-i-noor was sent home?"

"It was conveyed to England, I think," said I, "by H. M. S. *Medea*, in 1850."

"Yes, she sailed in April that year, and arrived at Portsmouth in June. The glorious gem was intrusted to Colonel Mackieson and Captain Ramsay. It was locked up in a small box along with other jewels, and each officer had a key. The box was secreted in the ship by them, and no man on board the vessel, saving themselves, knew where it was hidden."

"Was that so?" said I, much interested.

Yes; I had the particulars from the commander of the vessel, Captain Lockyer. When do you expect your skipper on board?" he exclaimed, darting a bright, sharp look around him.

"I cannot tell. He may arrive at any moment."

The having charge of a stone valued at fifteen thousand pounds, and intended as a gift for the Queen of England, is a deuce of a responsibility," said he. "I shall borrow a hint from the method adopted in the case of the Koh-i-noor. I intend to hide the stone in my cabin, so as to extinguish all risk, saving, of course, what the insurance people call the act of God. May I look at your cabin accommodation?"

"Certainly."

I led the way to the companion hatch, and he followed me into the cabin. The ship had berthing room for eight or ten people irrespective of the officers who slept aft. But the vessel had no bid for passengers. She left them to Blackwall liners, to the splendid ships of Green, Money, Wigram, and Smith. and to the P. & O. and other steam lines. The overland route was then the general choice; few of their own decision went by way of the Cape. No one had booked with us down to this hour, and we had counted upon having the cabin to ourselves.

The visitor walked into every empty berth, and inspected it as carefully as though he had been Government surveyor. He beat upon the walls and bulkheads with his cane, sent his brilliant gaze into the corners and under the bunks and up at the ceiling, and finally said, as he stepped from the last of the visitable cabins—

"This decides me. I shall sail with you."

I bowed and said I was sure the captain would be glad of the pleasure of his company. "I presume." said he, "that no objection will be raised to my bringing a native carpenter aboard to construct a secret place, as in the case of the Koh-i-noor, for the Maharajah's diamond?"

"I don't think a native carpenter would be allowed to knock the ship about," said I.

"Certainly not. A little secret receptacle—big enough to

receive this," said he, putting his hand in his side pocket and producing a square Morocco case, of a size to berth a bracelet or a large brooch. "The construction of a nook to conceal this will not be knocking your ship about?"

"It's a question for the captain and the agents, sir," said I.

He replaced the case, whose bulk was so inconsiderable that it did not bulge in his coat when he had pocketed it, and said, now that he had inspected the ship and the accommodation, he would call at once upon the agents. He gave me his card and left the vessel.

The card bore the name of a military officer of some distinction. Enough if, in this narrative of a memorable and extraordinary incident, I speak of him as Major Byron Hood.

The master of the *Jessamy Bride* was Captain Robert North. This man had, three years earlier, sailed with me as my chief mate; it then happened I was unable to quickly obtain command, and accepted the offer of mate of the *Jessamy Bride,* whose captain, I was surprised to hear, proved the shipmate who had been under me, but who, some money having been left to him, had purchased an interest in the firm to which the ship belonged. We were on excellent terms; almost as brothers indeed. He never asserted his authority, and left it to my own judgment to recognize his claims. I am happy to know he had never occasion to regret his friendly treatment of me.

He came on board in the afternoon of that day on which Major Hood had visited the ship, and was full of that gentleman and his resolution to carry a costly diamond round the Cape under sail, instead of making his obligation as brief as steam and the old desert route would allow.

"I've had a long talk with him up at the agents'," said Captain North. "He don't seem well."

"Suffering from his nerves, perhaps," said I.

"He's a fine, gentlemanly person. He told Mr. Nicholson he was twice wounded, naming towns which no Christian man could twist his tongue into the sound of."

"Will he be allowed to make a hole in the ship to hide his diamond in?"

"He has agreed to make good any damage done, and to pay at the rate of a fare and a half for the privilege of hiding the stone."

"Why doesn't he give the thing into your keeping, sir? This jackdawlike hiding is a sort of reflection on our honesty, isn't it, captain?"

He laughed and answered. "No; I like such reflections, for my part. Who wants to be burdened with the custody of precious things belonging to other people? Since he's to have the honor of presenting the diamond, let the worry of taking care of it be his; this ship's enough for me."

"He'll be knighted. I suppose for delivering this stone" said I. "Did he show it to you, sir?"

"No."

"He has it in his pocket."

"He produced the case," said Captain North, "A thing about the size of a muffin. Where'll he hide it? But we're not to be curious in *that* direction," he added, smiling.

Next morning, somewhere about ten o'clock, Major Hood came on board with two natives one a carpenter, the other his assistant. They brought a basket of tools, descended into the cabin, and were lost sight of till after two. No, I'm wrong. I was writing at the cabin table at half-past twelve when the Major opened his door, peered out, shut the door swiftly behind him with an extraordinary air and a face of caution and anxiety, and coming along to me asked for some refreshments for himself and the two natives. I called to the steward, who filled a tray, which the Major with his own hands conveyed into his berth. Then, some time after two whilst I was at the gangway talking to a friend, the Major and the blacks came out of the cabin Before they went over the side I said—

"Is the work finished below, sir?"

"It is, and to my entire satisfaction," he answered.

When he was gone, my friend, who was the master of a barque, asked me who that fine-looking man was. I answered he was a passenger and then, not understanding that the thing was a secret, plainly told him what they had been doing in the cabin, and why.

"But," said he, "those two niggers'll know that something precious is to be hidden in the place they've been making."

"That's been in my head all the morning," said I. "Who's

to hinder them," said he," from blabbing to one or more of the crew? Treachery's cheap in this country. A rupee will buy a pile of roguery." He looked at me expressively. "Keep a bright lookout for a brace of well-oiled stowaways," said he.

"It's the Major's business," I answered, with a shrug.

When Captain North came on board he and I went into the Major's berth. We scrutinized every part, but saw nothing to indicate that a tool had been used or a plank lifted. There was no sawdust, no chip of wood: everything to the eye was precisely as before. No man will say we had not a right to look: how were we to make sure, as captain and mate of the ship for whose safety we were responsible, that those blacks under the eye of the Major had not been doing something which might give us trouble by-and-by?

"Well," said Captain North, as we stepped on deck, "if the diamond's already hidden, which I doubt, it couldn't be more snugly concealed if it were twenty fathoms deep in the mud here."

The Major's baggage came on board on the Saturday, and on the Monday we sailed. We were twenty-four of a ship's company all told: twenty-five souls in all, with Major Hood. Our second mate was a man named Mackenzie, to whom and to the apprentices whilst we lay in the river I had given particular instructions to keep a sharp lookout on all strangers coming aboard. I had been very vigilant myself too, and altogether was quite convinced that there was no stowaway below, either white or black, though under ordinary circumstances one never would think of seeking for a native in hiding for Europe.

On either hand of the *Jessamy Bride's* cabin five sleeping berths were bulkheaded off. The Major's was right aft on the starboard side. Mine was next his. The captain occupied a berth corresponding with the Major's, right aft on the port side. Our solitary passenger was exceedingly amiable and agreeable at the start and for days after. He professed himself delighted with the cabin fare, and said it was not to be bettered at three times the charge in the saloons of the steamers. His drink he had himself laid in: it consisted mainly of claret and soda. He had come aboard with a large cargo of Indian cigars, and was never without a long, black weed, bearing to me tongue-staggering, up-country name, betwixt his lips. He was primed with professional anecdote, had a thorough knowledge of life in India, both in the towns and wilds, had seen service in Burmah and China, and was altogether one of the most conversible soldiers I ever met: a scholar, something of a wit, and all that he said and all that he did was rendered the more engaging by grace of breeding.

Captain North declared to me he had never met so delightful a man in all his life, and the pleasantest hours I ever passed on the ocean were spent in walking the deck in conversation with Major Byron Hood.

For some days after we were at sea no reference was made either by the Major or myself to the Maharajah of Ratnagiri's splendid gift to Her Majesty the Queen. The captain and I and Mackenzie viewed it as tabooed matter: a thing to be locked up in memory, just as, in fact, it was hidden away in some cunningly-wrought receptacle in the Major's cabin. One day at dinner, however, when we were about a week out from Calcutta, Major Hood spoke of the Maharajah's gift. He talked freely about it: his face was flushed as though the mere thought of the thing raised a passion of triumph in his spirits. His eyes shone whilst he enlarged upon the beauty and value of the stone.

The captain and I exchanged looks: the steward was waiting upon us with cocked ears and that menial, deaf expression of face which makes you know every word is being greedily listened to. We might therefore make sure that before the first dog-watch came round all hands would have heard that the Major had a diamond in his cabin intended for the Queen of England, and worth fifteen thousand pounds. Nay, they'd hear even more than that; for in the course of his talk about the gem the Major praised the ingenuity of the Asiatic artisan, whether Indian or Chinese, and spoke of the hiding-place the two natives had contrived for the diamond as an example of that sort of juggling skill in carving which is found in perfection amongst the Japanese.

I thought this candor highly indiscreet: charged too with menace. A matter gains in significance by mystery. The Jacks would think nothing of a diamond being in the ship as a part of her cargo, which might include a quantity of specie for all they knew. But some of them might think more often about it than was at all desirable when they understood it was stowed away under a plank, or was to be got by tapping about for a hollow echo, or probing with the judgment of a carpenter when the Major was on deck and the coast aft all clear.

We had been three weeks at sea; it was a roasting afternoon, though I cannot exactly remember the situation of the ship. Our tacks were aboard and the bowlines triced out, and the vessel was scarcely looking up to her course, slightly heeling away from a fiery fanning of wind off the starboard bow, with the sea trembling under the sun in white-hot needles of broken light, and a narrow ribbon of wake glancing off into a hot blue thickness that brought the horizon within a mile of us astern.

I had charge of the deck from twelve to four. For an hour past the Major. cigar in mouth, had been stretched at his ease in a folding chair; a book lay beside him on the skylight, but he scarcely glanced at it. I had paused to address him once or twice, but he showed no disposition to chat. Though he lay in the most easy lounging posture imaginable, I observed a restless, singular expression in his face, accentuated yet by the looks he incessantly directed out to sea, or glances at the deck forward, or around at the helm, so far as he might move his head without shifting his attitude. It was as though his mind were in labor with some scheme. A man might so look whilst working out the complicated plot of a play, or adjusting by the exertion of his memory the intricacies of a novel piece of mechanism.

On a sudden he started up and went below.

A few minutes after he had left the deck, Captain North came up from his cabin, and for some while we paced the planks together. There was a pleasant hush upon the ship; the silence was as refreshing as a fold of coolness lifting off the sea. A spun-yarn winch was clinking on the forecastle; from alongside rose the music of fretted waters.

I was talking to the captain on some detail of the ship's furniture, when Major Hood came running up the companion steps, his face as white as his waistcoat, his head uncovered, every muscle of his countenance rigid, as with horror.

"Good God, captain!" cried he, standing in the companion, "what do you think has happened?" Before we could fetch a breath he cried, "Someone's stolen the diamond!"

I glanced at the helmsman who stood at the radiant circle of wheel staring with open mouth and eyebrows arched into his hair. The captain, stepping close to Major Hood, said in a low, steady voice—

"What's this you tell me, sir?"

"The diamond's gone!" exclaimed the Major, fixing his shining eyes upon me, whilst I observed that his fingers convulsively stroked his thumbs as though he were rolling up pellets of bread or paper.

"Do you tell me the diamond's been taken from the place you hid it in?" said Captain North, still speaking softly, but with deliberation.

"The diamond never was hidden," replied the Major, who continued to stare at me. "It was in a portmanteau. *That's* no hiding-place!"

Captain North fell back a step. "Never was hidden!" he exclaimed. "Didn't you bring two native workmen aboard for no other purpose than to hide it?

"It never was hidden," said the Major, now turning his eyes upon the captain. "I chose it should be believed it was undiscoverably concealed in some part of my cabin, that I might safely and conveniently keep it in my baggage, where no thief would dream of looking for it. Who has it?" he cried with a sudden fierceness, making a step full of passion out of the companion-way; and he looked with knitted brows towards the ship's forecastle.

Captain North watched him idly for a moment or two, and then with an abrupt swing of his whole figure, eloquent of defiant resolution, he stared the Major in the face, and said in a quiet, level voice—

"I shan't be able to help you. If it's gone, it's gone. A diamond's not a bale of wool. Whoever's been clever enough to find it will know how to keep it."

"I must have it!" broke out the Major. "It's a gift for Her Majesty the Queen. It's in this ship. I look to you, sir, as master of this vessel, to recover the property which someone of the people under your charge has robbed me of!"

"I'll accompany you to your cabin," said the captain; and

they went down the steps. I stood motionless, gaping like an idiot into the yawn of hatch down which they had disappeared. I had been so used to think of the diamond as cunningly hidden in the Major's berth, that his disclosure was absolutely a shock with its weight of astonishment. Small wonder that neither Captain North nor I had observed any marks of a workman's tools in the Major's berth. Not but that it was a very ingenious stratagem, far cleverer to my way of thinking than any subtle, secret burial of the thing. To think of the Major and his two Indians sitting idly for hours in that cabin, with the captain and myself all the while supposing they were fashioning some wonderful contrivance or place for concealing the treasure in! And still, for all the Major's cunning, the stone was gone! Who had stolen it? The only fellow likely to prove the thief was the steward, not because he was more or less of a rogue than any other man in the ship, but because he was the one person who, by virtue of his office, was privileged to go in and out of the sleeping-places as his duties required.

I was pacing the deck, musing into a sheer muddle this singular business of the Maharajah of Ratnagiri's gift to the Queen of England, with all sorts of dim, unformed suspicions floating loose in my brains round the central fancy of the fifteen thousand pound stone there, when the captain returned. He was alone. He stepped up to me hastily, and said—

"He swears the diamond has been stolen. He showed me the empty case."

"Was there ever a stone in it at all?" said I.

"I don't think that," he answered quickly; "there's no motive under Heaven to be imagined if the whole thing's a fabrication."

"What then sir?"

"The case is empty, but I've not made up my mind yet that the stone's missing."

"The man's an officer and a gentleman."

"I know, I know!" he interrupted. "but still, in my opinion, the stone's not missing. The long and short of it is," he said, after a very short pause, with a careful glance at the skylight and companion hatch, "his behavior isn't convincing enough. Something's wanting in his passion and his vexation."

"Sincerity!"

"Ah! I don't intend that this business shall trouble me. He angrily required us to search the ship for stowaways. Bosh! The second mate and steward have repeatedly overhauled the lazarette: there's nobody there."

"And if not there, then nowhere else," said I, "Perhaps he's got the fore-peak in his head."

"I'll not have a hatch lifted," he exclaimed warmly, "nor will I allow the crew to be troubled. There's been no theft. Put it that the stone is stolen. Who is going to find it in a forecastle full of men—a thing as big as half a bean perhaps? If it's gone, it's gone, indeed, whoever may have it. But there's no go in this matter at all," he added, with a short, nervous laugh.

We were talking in this fashion when the Major joined us; his features were now composed. He gazed sternly at the captain and said loftily—

"What steps are you prepared to take in this matter?"

"None, sir."

His face darkened, He looked with a bright gleam in his eyes at the captain, then at me: his gaze was piercing with the light in it. Without a word he stepped to the side and, folding his arms, stood motionless.

I glanced at the captain; there was something in the bearing of the Major that gave shape, vague indeed, to a suspicion that had cloudily hovered about my thoughts of the man for some time past. The captain met my glance, but he did not interpret it.

When I was relieved at four o'clock by the second mate, I entered my berth, and presently, hearing the captain go to his cabin, went to him and made a proposal. He reflected, and then answered—

"Yes; get it done."

After some talk I went forward and told the carpenter to step aft and bore a hole in the bulkhead that separated the Major's berth from mine. He took the necessary tools from his chest and followed me. The captain was now again on deck, talking with the Major; in fact, detaining him in conversation, as had been preconcerted. I went into the Major's berth, and quickly settled upon a spot for an eye-hole. The carpenter then went to work in my cabin, and in a few minutes bored an orifice large enough to enable me to command a large portion of the adjacent interior. I swept the sawdust from the deck in the Major's berth, so that no hint should draw his attention to the hole, which was pierced in a corner shadowed by a shelf. I then told the carpenter to manufacture a plug and paint its extremity of the color of the bulkhead. He brought me this plug in a quarter of an hour. It fitted nicely, and was to be withdrawn and inserted as noiselessly as though greased.

I don't want you to suppose this Peeping-Tom scheme was at all to my taste, albeit my own proposal; but the truth is, the Major's telling us that someone had stolen his diamond made all who lived aft hotly eager to find out whether he spoke the truth or not; for, if he had been really robbed of the stone, then suspicion properly rested upon the officers and the steward, which was an *infernal* consideration dishonoring and inflaming enough to drive one to seek a remedy in even a baser device than that of secretly keeping watch on a man in his bedroom. Then, again, the captain told me that the Major, whilst they talked when the carpenter was at work making the hole, had said he would give notice of his loss to the police at Capetown (at which place we were to touch), and declared he'd take care no man went ashore—from Captain North himself down to the youngest apprentice—till every individual, every sea-chest, every locker, drawer, shelf and box, bunk, bracket and crevice, had been searched by qualified rummagers.

On this the day of the theft, nothing more was said about the diamond: that is, after the captain had emphatically informed Major Hood that he meant to take no steps whatever in the matter. I had expected to find the Major sullen and silent at dinner; he was, not, indeed, so talkative as usual, but no man watching and hearing him would have supposed so heavy a loss as that of a stone worth fifteen thousand pounds. the gift of an Eastern potentate to the Queen of England, was weighing upon his spirits.

It is with reluctance I tell you that, after dinner that day, when he went to his cabin, I softly withdrew the plug and watched him. I blushed whilst thus acting, yet I was determined, for my own sake and for the sake of my shipmates, to persevere. I spied nothing noticeable saving this: he sat in a folding chair and smoked, but every now and again he withdrew his cigar from his mouth and talked to it with a singular smile. It was a smile of cunning, that worked like some baleful, magical spirit in the fine high breeding of his features; changing his looks just as a painter of incomparable skill might color a noble, familiar face into a diabolical expression, amazing those who knew it only in its honest and manly beauty. I had never seen that wild, grinning countenance on him before, and it was rendered the more remarkable by the movement of his lips whilst he talked to himself, but inaudibly.

A week slipped by; time after time I had the man under observation; often when I had charge of the deck I'd leave the captain to keep a look out, and steal below and watch Major Hood in his cabin.

It was a Sunday, I remember. I was lying in my bunk half dozing—we were then, I think, about a three weeks' sail from Table Bay—when I heard the Major go to his cabin. I was already sick of my aimless prying; and whilst I now lay I thought to myself, "I'll sleep; what is the good of this trouble? I know exactly what I shall see. He is either in his chair, or his bunk, or overhauling his clothes, or standing, cigar in mouth, at the open porthole." And then I said to myself. "If I don't look now I shall miss the only opportunity of detection that may occur." One is often urged by a sort of instinct in these matters.

I got up, almost as through an impulse of habit, noiselessly withdrew the plug, and looked. The Major was at that instant standing with a pistol-case in his hand: he opened it as my sight went to him, took out one of a brace of very elegant pistols, put down the case, and on his apparently touching a spring in the butt of the pistol, the silver plate that ornamented the extremity sprang open as the lid of a snuff-box would, and something small and bright dropped into his hand. This he examined with the peculiar cunning smile I have before described; but owing to the position of his hand,

I could not see what he held, though I had not the least doubt that it was the diamond.

I watched him breathlessly. After a few minutes he dropped the stone into the hollow butt-end, shut the silver plate, shook the weapon against his ear as though it pleased him to rattle the stone, then put it in its case, and the case into a portmanteau.

I at once went on deck, where I found the captain, and reported to him what I had seen. He viewed me in silence, with a stare of astonishment and incredulity. What I had seen, he said, was not the diamond. I told him the thing that had dropped into the Major's hand was bright, and, as I thought, sparkled, but it was so held I could not see it.

I was talking to him on this extraordinary affair when the Major came on deck. The captain said to me, "Hold him in chat. I'll judge for myself," and asked me to describe how he might quickly find the pistol-case. This I did, and he went below.

I joined the Major, and talked on the first subjects that entered my head. He was restless in his manner, inattentive, slightly flushed in the face; wore a lofty manner, and being half a head taller than I, glanced down at me from time to time in a condescending way. This behavior in him was what Captain North and I had agreed to call his "injured air." He'd occasionally put it on to remind us that he was affronted by the captain's insensibility to his loss, and that the assistance of the police would be demanded on our arrival at Cape-town.

Presently looking down the skylight, I perceived the captain. Mackenzie had charge of the watch. I descended the steps, and Captain North's first words to me were—

"It's no diamond!"

"What, then, is it?"

"A common piece of glass not worth a quarter of a farthing."

"What's it all about, then?" said I. "Upon my soul, there's nothing in Euclid to beat it. Glass?"

"A little lump of common glass; a fragment of bull's-eye, perhaps."

"What's he hiding it for?"

"Because," said Captain North, in a soft voice, looking up and around, "he's mad!"

"Just so!" said I. "That I'll swear to now, and I've been suspecting it this fortnight past."

"He's under the spell of some sort of mania," continued the captain; "he believes he's commissioned to present a diamond to the Queen; possibly picked up a bit of stuff in the street that started the delusion, then bought a case for it, and worked out the rest as we know."

"But why does he want to pretend that the stone was stolen from him?"

"He's been mastered by his own love for the diamond," he answered. "That's how I reason it. Madness has made his affection for his imaginary gem a passion in him."

"And so he robbed himself of it, you think, that he might keep it?"

"That's about it," said he.

After this I kept no further lookout upon the Major, nor would I ever take an opportunity to enter his cabin to view for myself the piece of glass as the captain described it, though curiosity was often hot in me.

We arrived at Table Bay in twenty-two days from the date of my seeing the Major with the pistol in his hand. His manner had for a week before been marked by an irritability that was often beyond his control. He had talked snappishly and petulantly at table, contradicted aggressively, and on two occasions he gave Captain North the lie; but we had carefully avoided noticing his manner, and acted as though he were still the high-bred, polished gentleman who had sailed with us from Calcutta.

The first to come aboard were the Customs people. They were almost immediately followed by the harbor-master. Scarcely had the first of the Custom House officers stepped over the side when Major Hood, with a very red face, and a lofty, dignified carriage, marched up to him, and said in a loud voice—

"I have been robbed during the passage from Calcutta of a diamond worth fifteen thousand pounds, which I was bearing as a gift from the Maharajah of Ratnagiri to Her Majesty the Queen of England."

The customs man stared with a lobsterlike expression of face: no image could better hit the protruding eyes and brick-red countenance of the man.

"I request," continued the Major, raising his voice into a shout, "to be placed at once in communication with the police of this port. No person must be allowed to leave the vessel until he has been thoroughly searched by such expert hands as you and your *confrères* no no doubt are, sir. I am Major Byron Hood. I have been twice wounded. My services are well known, and, I believe, duly appreciated in the right quarters. Her Majesty the Queen is not to suffer any disappointment at the hands of one who has the honor of wearing her uniform, nor am I to be compelled, by the act of a thief, to betray the confidence the Maharajah has reposed in me."

He continued to harangue in this manner for some minutes, during which I observed a change in the expression of the Custom House officers' faces.

Meanwhile Captain North stood apart in earnest conversation with the harbor-master. They now approached; the harbor-master, looking steadily at the Major, exclaimed—

"Good news, sir! Your diamond is found!"

"Ha!" shouted the Major. "Who has it?"

"You'll find it in your pistol-case." said the harbor-master. The Major gazed round at us with his wild, bright eyes, his face a-work with the conflict of twenty mad passions and sensations. Then bursting into a loud, insane laugh, he caught the harbor-master by the arm, and in a low voice and sickening, transforming leer of cunning, said, "Come, let's go and look at it."

We went below. We were six, including two Custom House officers. We followed the poor madman, who grasped the harbor-master's arm, and on arriving at his cabin we stood at the door of it. He seemed heedless of our presence, but on his taking the pistol-case from the portmanteau, the two Customs men sprang forward.

"That must be searched by us," one cried, and in a minute they had it.

With the swiftness of experienced hands they found and pressed the spring of the pistol, the silver plate flew open, and out dropped a fragment of thick, common glass, just as

Captain North had described the thing. It fell upon the deck. The Major sprang, picked it up, and pocketed it.

"Her Majesty will not be disappointed, after all," said he, with a courtly bow to us, "and the commission the Maharajah's honored me with shall be fulfilled."

The poor gentleman was taken ashore that afternoon, and his luggage followed him. He was certified mad by the medical man at Capetown, and was to be retained there, as I understood, till the arrival of a steamer for England. It was an odd, bewildering incident from top to bottom. No doubt this particular delusion was occasioned by the poor fellow, whose mind was then fast decaying, reading about the transmission of the Koh-i-noor, and musing about it with a madman's proneness to dwell upon little things.

A NIGHTMARE
OF THE DOLDRUMS

The *Justitia* was a smart little barque of 395 tons. I had viewed her with something of admiration as she lay in mid-stream in the Hooghly—somewhere off the Coolie Bazaar, I think it was. There was steam then coming to Calcutta, though not as steam now is; very little of it was in any sense palatial, and some of the very best of it was to be as promptly distanced under given conditions of weather by certain of the clippers, clouded with studding sails and flying-kites to the starry buttons of their skysail mastheads, as the six-knot ocean tramp of today is to be outrun by the fourmasted leviathan thrashing through it to windward with her yards fore and aft.

I—representing in those days a large Birmingham firm of dealers in the fal-lal industries—had wished to make my way from Calcutta to Capetown. I saw the *Justitia* and took a fancy to her; I admired the long, low, piratic run of her hull as she lay with straining hawse-pipes on the rushing stream of the Hooghly; upon which, as you watched, there might go by in the space of an hour some half-score at least of dead natives made ghastly canoes of by huge birds, erect upon the corpses, burying their beaks as they sailed along.

I found out that the *Justitia* was one of the smartest of the Thames and East India traders of that time, memorable on one occasion for having reeled off a clean seventeen knots by the log under a main topgallant-sail, set over a single-reefed topsail. It was murmured, indeed, that the mate who hove that log was drunk when he counted the knots; yet the dead reckoning tallied with the next day's observations. I called upon the agents, was told that the *Justitia* was not a passenger ship, but that I could hire a cabin for the run to Capetown if I chose; a sum in rupees, trifling compared with the cost of transit by steam, was named. I went on board, found the captain walking up and down under the awning, and agreeably killed an hour in a chat with as amiable a seaman as ever it was my good fortune to meet.

We sailed in the middle of July. Nothing worth talking about happened during our run down the Bay of Bengal. The crew aforemast were all of them Englishmen; there were twelve, counting the cook and steward. The captain was a man named Cayzer; the only mate of the vessel was one William Perkins. The boatswain, a rough, short, hairy, immensely strong man, acted as second mate and kept a lookout when Perkins was below. But he was entirely ignorant of navigation, and owned to me that he read with difficulty words of one syllable, and could not write.

I was the only passenger. My name, I may as well say here, is Thomas Barron. Our run to the south Ceylon parallels was slow and disappointing. The monsoon was light and treacherous, sometimes dying out in a sort of laughing, mocking gust till the whole ocean was a sheet-calm surface, as though the dependable trade wind was never again to blow.

"Oh, yes," said Captain Cayzer to me, "we're used to the unexpected hereabouts. Monsoon or no monsoon, I'll tell you what: you're always safe in standing by for an Irishman's hurricane down here."

And what sort of a breeze is that?" I asked.

"An up-and-down calm," said he; "as hard to know where it begins as to guess where it'll end."

However, thanks to the frequent trade puffs and other winds, which tasted not like the monsoon, we crawled through those latitudes which Ceylon spans, and fetched within a few degrees of the equator. In this part of the waters we were to be thankful for even the most trifling donation of catspaw, or for the equally small and short-lived mercy of the gust of the electric cloud. I forget how many days we were out from Calcutta: the matter is of no moment. I left my cabin one morning some hour after the sun had risen, by which time the decks had been washed down, and were already dry, with a salt sparkle as of bright white sand on the face of the planks, so roasting was it. I went into the head to get a bath under the pump there. I feel in memory, as I write, the exquisite sensation of that luxury of brilliant brine, cold as snow, melting through me from head to foot to the nimble plying of the pump-brake by a seaman.

It was a true tropic morning. The sea, of a pale lilac, flowed in a long-drawn, gentle heave of swell into the south-west; the glare of the early morning brooded in a sort of steamy whiteness in the atmosphere; the sea went working to its distant reaches, and floated into a dim blending of liquid air and water, so that you couldn't tell where the sky ended; a weak, hot wind blew over the taffrail, but it was without weight. The courses swung to the swell without response to the breathings of the air; and on high the light cotton-white royals were scarcely curved by the delicate passage of the draught.

Yet the barque had steerage way. When I looked through the grating at her metalled fore-foot I saw the ripples plentiful as harp strings threading aft, and whilst I dried myself I watched the slow approach of a piece of timber hoary with barnacles, and venerable with long hairs of seaweed, amid and around which a thousand little fish were sporting, many-colored as though a rainbow had been shivered.

I returned to my cabin, dressed, and stepped on to the quarter-deck, where I found some men spreading the awning, and the captain in a white straw hat viewing an object out upon the water through a telescope, and talking to the boatswain, who stood alongside.

"What do you see?" I asked. "Something that resembles a raft," answered the captain. The thing he looked at was about a mile distant, some three points on the starboard bow. On pointing the telescope, I distinctly made out the fabric of a raft, fitted with a short mast, to which midway a bundle—it resembled a parcel—was attached. A portion of the raft was covered by a white sheet or cloth, whence dangled a short length of something chocolate-colored, indistinguishable even with the glass, lifting and sinking as the raft rose and fell upon the flowing heave of the sea.

"This ocean," said the captain, taking the glass from me, "is a big volume of tragic stories, and the artist who illustrates the book does it in that fashion," and he nodded in the direction of the raft.

"What do you make of it, boatswain?" I asked.

"It looks to me," he answered in his strong, harsh, deep

voice, "like a religious job—one of them rafts the Burmuh covies float away their dead on. I never see one afore, sir, but I've heard tell of such things."

We sneaked stealthily towards the raft. It was seven bells—half-past seven—and the sailors ate their breakfast on the forecastle, that they might view the strange contrivance. The mate, Mr. Perkins, came on deck to relieve the boatswain, and, after inspecting the raft though the telescope, gave it as his opinion that it was a Malay floating bier—"a Mussulman trick of ocean burial, anyhow," said he.

There should be a jar of water aboard the raft, and cakes and fruit for the corpse to regale on, if he ha'n't been dead long."

The steward announced breakfast; the captain told him to hold it back awhile. He was as curious as I to get a close view of the queer object with its white cloth and mast and parcel and chocolate-colored fragment half in and half out like a barge's leeboard, and he bade the man at the helm put the wheel over by a spoke or two; but the wind was nearly gone, the barque scarcely responded to the motion of her rudder, the threadlike lines at the cutwater had faded, and a roasting, oppressive calm was upon the water, whitening it out into a tingling sheen of quicksilver with a fiery shaft of blinding dazzle, solitary and splendid, working with the swell like some monstrous serpent of light right under the sun.

The raft was about six cables' lengths off us when the barque came to a dead stand, with a soft, universal hollowing in of her canvas from royal to course, as though, like something sentient, she delivered one final sigh before the swoon of the calm seized her. But now we were near enough to resolve the floating thing with the naked eye into details. It was a raft formed of bamboo canes. A mast about six feet tall was erected upon it; the dark thing over the edge proved a human leg, and, when the fabric lifted with the swell and raised the leg clear, we saw that the foot had been eaten away by fish, a number of which were swimming about the raft, sending little flashes of foam over the pale surface as they darted along with their back or dorsal fins exposed. They were all little fish; I saw no sharks. The body to which the leg belonged was covered by a white cloth. The captain called my attention to the parcel attached to the mast, and said that it possibly contained the food which the Malays leave beside their dead after burial.

"But let's go to breakfast now, Mr. Barron," said he, with a slow, reproachful, impatient look round the breathless scene of ocean. "If there's any amusement to be got out of that thing yonder there's a precious long, quiet day before us, I fear, for the entertainment."

We breakfasted, and in due course returned on deck. The slewing of the barque had caused the raft to shift its bearings, otherwise its distance remained as it was when we went below.

"Mr. Perkins," said the captain, "lower a boat and bring aboard that parcel from the raft's jury-mast, and likewise take a peep at the figure under the cloth, and report its sex and what it looks like."

I asked leave to go in the boat, and when she was lowered, with three men in her, I followed Mr. Perkins, and we rowed over to the raft. All about the frail bamboo contrivance the water was beautiful with the colors and movements of innumerable fish. As we approached we were greeted by an evil smell. The raft seemed to have been afloat for a considerable period; its submerged portion was green with marine adhesions or growths. The fellow in the bows of the boat, manœuvring with the boathook, cleverly snicked the parcel from the jury-mast and handed it along to the mate, who put it beside him without opening it, for that was to be the captain's privilege.

"Off with that cloth," said Mr. Perkins, "and then backwater a bit out of this atmosphere." The bowman jerked the cloth clear of the raft with his boathook; the white sheet floated like a snowflake upon the water for a few breaths, then slowly sank. The body exposed was stark naked and tawny. It was a male. I saw nothing revolting in the thing: it would have been otherwise perhaps had it been white. The hair was long and black, the nose aquiline, the mouth puckered into the aspect of a harelip; the gleam of a few white teeth painted a ghastly contemptuous grin upon the dead face. The only shocking part was the footless leg.

"Shall I hook him overboard, sir?" said the bowman.

"No, let him take his ease as he lies," answered the mate, and with that we returned to the barque.

We climbed over the side, the boat was hoisted to the davits, and Mr. Perkins took the parcel out of the stern-sheets and handed it to the captain. The cover was a kind of fine canvas, very neatly stitched with white thread. Captain Cayzer ripped through the stitching with his knife, and exposed a couple of books bound in some kind of skin or parchment. They were probably the Koran, but the characters none of us knew. The captain turned them about for a bit, and I stood by looking at them; he then replaced them in their canvas cover and put them down upon the skylight, and by-and-by, on his leaving the deck, he took them below to his cabin.

The moon rose about ten that night. She came up hot, distorted, with a sullen face belted with vapor, but was soon clear of the dewy thickness over the horizon and showering a pure greenish silver upon the sea. She made the night lovely and cool: her reflection sparkled in the dew along the rails, and her beam whitened out the canvas into the tender softness of wreaths of cloud motionless upon the summit of some dark heap of mountain. I looked for the raft and saw it plainly, and it is not in language to express how the sight of that frail cradle of death deepened the universal silence and expanded the prodigious distances defined by the stars, and accentuated the tremendous spirit of loneliness that slept like a presence in that wide region of sea and air.

There had not been a stir of wind all day: not the faintest breathing of breeze had tarnished the sea down to the hour of midnight when, feeling weary, I withdrew to my cabin. I slept well, spite of the heat and the cockroaches, and rose at seven. I found the steward in the cabin. His face wore a look of concern, and on seeing me he instantly exclaimed—"The captain seems very ill, sir. Might you know anything of physic? Neither Mr. Perkins nor me can make out what's the matter."

"I know nothing of physic," I answered, "but I'll look in on him." I stepped to his door, knocked, and entered. Captain Cayzer lay in a bunk under a middling-sized porthole; the cabin was full of the morning light. I started and stood at gaze, scarce crediting my sight, so shocked and astounded was I by the dreadful change which had happened in the night in the poor man's appearance. His face was blue, and I remarked a cadaverous sinking in of the eyeballs; the lips were livid, the hands likewise blue, but strangely wrinkled like a washer-woman's. On seeing me he asked in a husky whispering voice for a drink of water. I handed him a full pannikin, which he drained feverishly, and then began to moan and cry out, making some weak miserable efforts to rub first one arm, then the other, then his legs.

The steward stood in the doorway. I turned to him, sensible that my face was ashen and asked some questions. I then said, "Where is Mr. Perkins?"

He was on deck. I bade the steward attend to the captain, and passed through the hatch to the quarter-deck, where I found the mate.

"Do you know that the captain is very ill?" said I.

"Do I know it, sir? Why, yes. I've been sitting by him chafing his limbs and giving him water to drink, and attending to him in other ways. What is it, d'ye know, sir?"

"*Cholera!*" said I.

"Oh, my God, I hope not!" he exclaimed. How could it be cholera? How could cholera come aboard?"

"A friend of mine died of cholera at Rangoon when I was there," said I. "I recognize the looks, and will swear to the symptoms."

"But how could it have come aboard?" he exclaimed, in a voice low but agitated. My eyes, as he asked the question, were upon the raft. I started and cried, "Is that thing still there?"

"Ay," said the mate, "we haven't budged a foot all night."

The suspicion rushed upon me whilst I looked at the raft, and ran my eyes over the bright hot morning sky and the burnished surface of sea, sheeting into dimness in the misty junction of heaven and water.

"I shouldn't be surprised," said I, "to discover that we brought the cholera aboard with us yesterday from that dead man's raft yonder."

"How is cholera to be caught in that fashion?" exclaimed Mr. Perkins, pale and a bit wild in his way of staring at me.

"We may have brought the poison aboard in the parcel of books."

"Is cholera to be caught so?"

"Undoubtedly. The disease may be propagated by human intercourse. Why not then by books which have been handled by cholera-poisoned people, or by the atmosphere of a body dead of the plague?" I added, pointing at the raft.

"No man amongst us is safe, then, now?" cried the mate.

"I'm no doctor," said I; "but I know this, that contagious poisons such as scarlet fever and glanders, may retain their properties in a dormant state for years. I've heard tell of scores of instances of cholera being propagated through articles of dress. Depend upon it," said I, "that we brought the poison aboard with us yesterday from that accursed death-raft yonder."

"Aren't the books in the captain's cabin?" said the mate. "Are they?"

"He took them below yesterday, sir."

"The sooner they're overboard the better," I exclaimed, and returned to the cabin. I went to the captain, and found the steward rubbing him. The disease appeared to be doing its work with horrible rapidity; the eyes were deeply sunk and red; every feature had grown sharp and pinched as after a long wasting disease; the complexion was thick and muddy. Those who have watched beside cholera know that terrific changes may take place in a few minutes. I cast my eyes about for the parcel of books, and, spying it, took a stick from a corner of the berth, hooked up the parcel, and, passing it through the open porthole, shook it overboard.

The captain followed my movements with a languid rolling of his eyes but spoke not, though he groaned often, and frequently cried out. I could not in the least imagine what was proper to be done. His was the most important life on board the ship, and yet I could only look on and helplessly watch him expire.

He lived till the evening, and seldom spoke save to call upon God to release him. I had found an opportunity to tell him that he was ill of the cholera, and explained how it happened that the horrible distemper was on board, for I was absolutely sure we had brought it with us in that parcel of books; but his anguish was so keen, his death so close then, that I cannot be sure he understood me. He died shortly after seven o'clock, and I have since learned that that time is one of the critical hours in cholera.

When the captain was dead I went to the mate, and advised him to cast the body overboard at once. He called to some of the hands. They brought the body out just as the poor fellow had died, and, securing a weight to the feet, they lifted the corpse over the rail, and dropped it. No burial service was read. We were all too panic-stricken for reverence. We got rid of the body quickly, the men handling the thing as though they felt the death in it stealing into them through their fingers—hoping and praying that with it the cholera would go. It was almost dark when this hurried funeral was ended. I stood beside the mate, looking around the sea for a shadow of wind in any quarter. The boatswain, who had been one of the men that handled the body, came up to us.

"Ain't there nothing to be done with that corpus out there?" he exclaimed, pointing with a square hand to the raft. "The men are agreed that there'll come no wind whilst that there dead blackie keeps afloat. And ain't he enough to make a disease of the hatmosphere itself, from horizon to horizon?"

I waited for the mate to answer. He said gloomily, "I'm of the poor captain's mind. You'll need to make something fast to the body to sink it. Who's to handle it? I'll ask no man to do what I wouldn't do myself, and rat me if I'd do *that!*"

"We brought the poison aboard by visiting the raft, bo'sun," said I. "Best leave the thing alone. The corpse is too far off to corrupt the air, as you suppose; though the imagination's nigh as bad as the reality," said I, spitting.

"If there's any of them game to sink the thing, may they do it?" said the boatswain. "For if there's ne'er a breeze of wind to come while it's there—"

"Chaw!" said the mate. "But try 'em, if you will. They may take the boat when the moon's up, should there come no wind first."

An hour later the steward told me that two of the sailors were seized with cramps and convulsions. After this no more was said about taking the boat and sinking the body. The mate went into the forecastle. On his return, he begged me to go and look at the men.

"Better make sure that it's cholera with them too, sir," said he. "You know the signs;" and, folding his arms, he leaned against the bulwarks in a posture of profound dejection.

I went forward and descended the forescuttle, and found myself in a small cave. The heat was over-powering; there was no air to pass through the little hatch; the place was dimly lighted by an evil-smelling lamp hanging under a beam, but, poor as the illumination was, I could see by it, and when I looked at the two men and spoke to them, I saw how it was, and came away sick at heart, and half dead with the hot foul air of the forecastle, and in deepest distress of mind, moreover, through perceiving that the two men had formed a part of the crew of the boat when we visited the raft.

One died at six o'clock next morning, and the other at noon; but before this second man was dead three others had been attacked, and one of them was the mate. And still never a breath of air stirred the silver surface of the sea.

The mate was a strong man, and his fear of death made the conflict dreadful to behold. I was paralyzed at first by the suddenness of the thing and the tremendous character of our calamity, and, never doubting that I must speedily prove a victim as being one who had gone in the boat, I cast myself down upon a sofa in the cabin and there sat, waiting for the first signal of pain, sometimes praying, or striving to pray, and seeking hard to accustom my mind to the fate I regarded as inevitable. But a keen and biting sense of my cowardice came to my rescue. I sprang to my feet and went to the mate's berth, and nursed him till he died, which was shortly before midnight of the day of his seizure—so swift and sure was the poison we had brought from the raft. He was dropped over the side, and in a few hours later he was followed by three others. I cannot be sure of my figures: it was a time of delirium, and I recall some details of it with difficulty, but I am pretty sure that by the morning of the fourth day of our falling in with the accursed raft the ship's company had been reduced to the boatswain and five men, making, with myself, seven survivors of fifteen souls who had sailed from Calcutta.

It was some time about the middle of the fifth day—two

men were then lying stricken in the forecastle—the boatswain and a couple of seamen came aft to the quarter-deck where I was standing. The wheel was deserted: no man had grasped it since the captain's death; indeed, there was nothing to be done at the helm. The ocean floated in liquid glass; the smell of frying paint, bubbled into cinders by the roasting rays, rose like the stench of a second plague to the nostrils. The boatswain and his companions had been drinking; no doubt they had broached the rum casks below. They had never entered the cabin to my knowledge, nor do I believe they got their liquor from there. The boatswain carried a heavy weight of some sort, bound in canvas, with a long laniard attached to it. He flung the parcel into the quarter-boat, and roared out—

"If that don't drag the blistered cuss out of sight I'll show the fired carcass the road myself. Cholera or no cholera, here goes!"

"What are you going to do?" said I.

"Do?" he cried; "why sink that there plague out of it, so as to give us the chance of a breeze. Ain't this hell's delight? What's a-going to blow us clear whilst *he* keeps watch?" And he nodded with a fierce, drunken gesture towards the raft.

"You'll have to handle the body to sink it," said I. "You're well men, now; keep well, won't you? The two who are going may be the next taken."

The three of them roared out drunkenly together, so muddling their speech with oaths that I did not understand them. I walked aft, not liking their savage looks. Shouting and cursing plentifully, they lowered the boat, got into her by descending the falls, and shoved off for the raft. They drew alongside the bamboo contrivance, and I looked to see the boat capsize, so wildly did they sway her in their wrath and drink as they fastened the weight to the foot of the body. They then sank the corpse and, with the loom of their oars, hammered at the raft till the bamboos were scattered like a sheaf of walking-sticks cut adrift. They now returned to the barque, clambered aboard, and hoisted the boat.

The two sick men in the forecastle were at this time looked after by a seaman named Archer. I have said it was the fifth day of the calm; of the ship's company the boatswain and five men were living, but two were dying, and that, not counting me, left three as yet well and able to get about.

This man Archer, when the boatswain and his companions went forward, came out of the forecastle, and drank at the scuttle-butt in the waist. He walked unsteadily, with that effort after stateliness which is peculiar to tipsy sailors; his eyes wandered, and he found some difficulty in hitting the bunghole with the dipper. Yet he was a civil sort of man when sober; I had occasionally chatted with him during his tricks at the wheel; and, feeling the need of someone to talk to about our frightful situation, I walked up to him, and asked how the sick men did.

"Dying fast," he answered, steadying himself by leaning against the scuttle-butt, "and a-ravin' like screech-owls."

"What's to be done, Archer?"

"Oh, God alone He knows!" answered the man, and here he put his knuckles into his eyes, and began to cry and sob.

"Is it possible that this calm can last much longer?"

"It may last six weeks," he answered, whimpering. "Down here, when the wind's drawed away by the sun, it may take six weeks afore it comes on to blow. Six weeks of calm down here ain't thought nothen of," and here he burst out blubbering again.

"Where do you get your liquor from?" said I.

"Oh, don't talk of it, don't talk of it!" he replied, with a maudlin shake of the head.

"Drinking'll not help you," said I; "you'll all be the likelier to catch the malady for drinking. This is a sort of time, I should think, when a man most wants his senses. A breeze may come, and we ought to decide where to steer the barque to. The vessel's under all plain sail, too, and here we are, four men and a useless passenger, should it come on to blow suddenly—"

"We didn't sign on under you," he interrupted, with a tipsy scowl, "and as ye ain't no good either as sailor or doctor, you can keep your blooming sarmons to yourself till they're asked for."

I had now not only to fear the cholera but to dread the men. My mental distress was beyond all power of words to convey: I wonder it did not quickly drive me crazy and hurry me overboard. I lurked in the cabin to be out of sight of the fellows, and all the while my imagination was tormenting me with the first pangs of the cholera, and every minute I was believing I had the mortal malady. Sometimes I would creep up the companion steps and cautiously peer around, and always I beheld the same dead, faint blue surface of sea stretching like an ocean in a dream into the faint indefinable distances. But shocking as that calm was to me, I very well knew there was nothing wonderful or preternatural in it. Our forefoot five days before had struck the equatorial zone called the Doldrums, and at a period of the year when a fortnight or even a month of atmospheric lifelessness might be as confidently looked for as the rising and setting of the sun.

At nine o'clock that night I was sitting at the cabin table with biscuit and a little weak brandy and water before me, when I was hailed by someone at the open skylight above. It was black night, though the sky was glorious with stars: the moon did not rise till after eleven. I had lighted the cabin lamp, and the sheen of it was upon the face of Archer.

"The two men are dead and gone," said he, "and now the bo'sun and Bill are down. There's Jim dead drunk in his hammock. I can't stand the cries of sick men. What with liquor and pain, the air below suffocates me. Let me come aft, sir, and keep along with you. I'm sober now. Oh, Christ, have mercy upon me! It's my turn next, ain't it?

I passed a glass of brandy to him through the skylight, then joined him on deck, and told him that the two dead bodies must be thrown overboard, and the sick men looked to. For some time he refused to go forward with me, saying that he was already poisoned and deadly sick, and a dying man, and that I had no right to expect that one dying man should wait upon another. However, I was determined to turn the dead out of the ship in any case, for in freeing the vessel of the remains of the victims might lie my salvation. He consented to help me at last, and we went into the forecastle, and between us got the bodies out of their bunks, and dropped them, weighted, over the rail. The boatswain and the other men lay groaning and writhing and crying for water; cursing at intervals. A coil of black smoke went up from the lamp flame to the blackened beam under which the light was burning. The atmosphere was horrible. I bade Archer help me to carry a couple of mattresses on to the forecastle, and we got the sick men through the hatch, and they lay there in the coolness with plenty of cold water beside them and a heaven of stars above, instead of a lowpitched ceiling of grimy beam and plank dark with processions of cockroaches, and dim with the smoke of the stinking slush lamp.

All this occupied us till about half-past ten. When I went aft I was seized with nausea, and, sinking upon the skylight, dabbled my brow in the dew betwixt the lifted lids for the refreshment of the moisture. I believed that my time had come, and that this sickness was the cholera. Archer followed me, and seeing me in a posture of torment, as he supposed, concluded that I was a dead man. He flung himself upon the deck with a groan, and lay motionless, crying out at intervals." God, have mercy! God, have mercy!" and that was all.

In about half an hour's time the sensation of sickness passed. I went below for some brandy, swallowed half a glass, and returning with a dram for Archer, but the man had either swooned or fallen asleep, and I let him lie. I had my senses perfectly, but felt shockingly weak in body, and I could think of nothing consolatory to diminish my exquisite distress of mind. Indeed, the capacity of realization grew unendurably poignant. I imagined too well, I figured too clearly. I pictured myself as lying dead upon the deck of the barque, found a corpse by some passing vessel after many days and so I dreamt, often breaking away from my horrible imaginations with moans and starts, then pacing the deck to rid me of the nightmare hag of thought till I was in a fever, then cooling my head by laying my cheek upon the dew-covered skylight.

By-and-by the moon rose, and I sat watching it. In half an hour she was a bright light in the east, and the shaft of silver that slept under her stretched to the barque's side. It was just then that one of the two sick men on the forecastle sent up a yell. The dreadful note rang through the vessel, and dropped back to the deck in an echo from the canvas. A moment after I saw a figure get on to the forecastle-rail and spring overboard. I heard the splash of his body, and, bounding over to Archer, who lay on the deck, I pulled and hauled at him, roaring out that one of the sick men had jumped overboard, and then rushed forward and looked over into the water in the place where the man had leapt, but saw nothing, not even a ripple.

I turned and peered close at the man who lay on the forecastle, and discovered that the fellow who had jumped was the boatswain. I went again to the rail to look, and lifted a coil of rope from a pin, ready to fling the fakes to the man, should he rise. The moonlight was streaming along the ocean on this side of the ship, and now, when I leaned over the rail for the second time, I saw a figure close under the bows. I stared a minute or two, the color of the body blended with the gloom, yet the moonlight was upon him too, and then it was that after looking awhile, and observing the thing to lie motionless, I perceived that it was the body that had been upon the raft! No doubt the extreme horror raised in me by the sight of the poisonous thing beheld in that light and under such conditions crazed me. I have a recollection of laughing wildly, and of defying the dark floating shape in insane language. I remember that I shook my fist and spat at it, and that I turned to seek for something to hurl at the body, and it may have been that in the instant of turning, my senses left me, for after this I can recall no more.

The sequel to this tragic and extraordinary experience will be found in the following statement, made by the people of the ship *Forfarshire*, from Calcutta to Liverpool:—"August 29, 1857. When in latitude 2° 15′ N. and longitude 79° 40′ E. we sighted a barque under all plain sail, apparently abandoned. The breeze was very scanty, and though we immediately shifted our helm for her on judging that she was in distress, it took us all the morning to approach her within hailing distance. Everything looked right with her aloft, but the wheel was deserted, and there were no signs of anything living in her. We sent a boat in charge of the second officer, who returned and informed us that the barque was the *Justitia*, of London. We knew that she was from Calcutta, for we had seen her lying in the river. The second officer stated that there were three dead bodies aboard, one in a hammock in the forecastle, a second on a mattress on the forecastle, and a third against the coamings of the main-hatch; there was also a fourth man lying at the heel of the port cathead—he did not seem to be dead. On this Dr. Davison was requested to visit the barque, and he was put aboard by the second officer. He returned quickly with one of the men, whom he instantly ordered to be stripped and put into a warm bath, and his clothes thrown overboard. He said that the dead showed unmistakable signs of having died from cholera. We proceeded, not deeming it prudent to have anything further to do with the ill-fated craft. The person we had rescued remained insensible for two days; his recovery was then slow, but sure, thanks to the skilful treatment of Dr. Davison. He informed us that his name was Thomas Barron, and that he was a passenger on board the *Justitia* for Capetown. He was the travelling representative of a large Birmingham firm. The barque had on the preceding Friday week fallen in with a raft bearing a dead body. A boat was sent to bring away a parcel from the raft's mast, and it is supposed that the contents of the parcel communicated the cholera. There were fifteen souls when the vessel left Calcutta, and all perished except the passenger, Thomas Barron."

"TRY FOR HER IN FIFTY"

The following extraordinary story was told to me some years ago by the commander of a steamship in which I was making a voyage for my health. The captain who, as we shall see, had himself shared in the experience he related, began his tale thus:

"A good many years ago I was in Capetown, having been forced by illness to quit my post as second mate of a large ship bound to Bombay. A fortnight after the ship sailed, I recovered my health and was fit for work.

"In those days Capetown was without docks nor does this carry the memory very far back, either. Colonial progress is the foremost of the miracles of our century. You visit some Antipodean shore after a few years and note a growth of docks, piers, warehouses, an expansion of suburbs, a magical embracing of the hillsides by roof upon roof of charming villas, as at Natal, for example; and whilst you look, you shall think it rational to hold that more than a century has gone to the creation of this noble scene of civilization, and that the little struggling village you remember arriving at a few years before, with its dockless bay and its three or four small ships blistering under the eye of a roasting sun at their poor moorings alongside a rustic wooden wharf, was an imagination of your slumber.

"I was entirely dependent upon my profession. Sickness had heavily taxed my slender purse, and I was exceedingly anxious, when I was well enough for work, to obtain a situation. Ships brought up in the bay in those days, and discharged for the most part in lighters. The spacious breast of waters would offer again and again a grander show than is ever likely to be seen there in these or succeeding times. There was no Suez Canal; steam was by no means plentiful. All the trading to the East was by way of the Cape, and nearly everything bound round Agulhas looked into Table Bay for refreshment.

"I remember one of those mornings whilst I was hunting for a berth, that I counted a hundred and ten vessels at anchor in Table Bay. To be sure, I had witnessed as much as five hundred ships straining at their ground tackle at one time in the Downs. But that forest of spars had a wide area to distribute itself over in the waters streaming from the South Foreland down to the stretch that lies abreast of Sandwich. The hundred odd craft in Table Bay made a more imposing sight than the Downs picture, thanks, perhaps, to the solemn and magnificent scenery of mountain, whose lofty, silent terraces seemed, in the colossal sweep of them, to swell and thicken the ships into a stately, rocking crowd, and they lay in a tall mass of symmetric spires, the rigging of one knitting that of another past her, and the bright wind was painted with the colors of a dozen nations.

"I stood at the head of a little jetty or pier. Was there nothing to find me a berth worth six pounds a month in all that that gallant huddle of gleaming sides and coppered flanks? The water trembled like molten brass under the sun to the coral-white line of the opposite shore, where the land went away to strange hues of rusty red and sickly green, carrying the eye into the liquid blue distance in which hung a hundred miles off a range of magnificent mountains like pale gold in the far light, their sky-lines as clean cut in the full and even splendor of that magical climate as the top of Table Mountain, close at hand.

"I was watching a Malay fishing-boat sliding through the water with an occasional burst of spray off her weather bow, which arched a little rainbow for her to rush through, when I was accosted. I turned. It was the port-captain or harbormaster. I cannot remember the term by which his office was distinguished. He had sailed with my father some years earlier, and I had met him on two occasions in England. He had done me some kindness whilst I lay ill in lodgings in Capetown, and had assured me of his willingness to help me to find a ship when I should be well enough to go to sea. He was a Scotchman, with a hard, weather-colored face, and of a dry, arch expression of eye.

"'D'ye see anything to fit ye?' said he.

"'Ay,' said I, 'a plenty.'

"'Well, now,' said he, 'you're the very mon I was thinking of not half an hour ago. I was in Adderley Street, and met a captain who was here last year. His name's Huddersfield, He's in charge of a Colonial trader from a South American port, with a small consignment for this place, and is bound for Sydney, New South Wales, where his little ship's owned, chiefly, I believe, by himsel'.'

"'Is there room for me in her?'

"'Well, yes, I think you'll stand a chance. She lost her chief officer overboard when six days' sail from this port, and she's got to ship another man. Take my advice and go aboard this evening and see the captain. He's ashore till five or six o'clock.'

"'Which is the vessel?'

"He pointed to a large three-masted schooner that was lying within a hundred strokes of an oar almost abreast of us. She looked an exceedingly fine craft. A large Dutch Indiaman was rolling upon the swell of the sea within a few cables' length astern of her, and just ahead rode a Russian auxiliary frigate, very heavily sparred, with great gleaming windows in her stern, and a net-work of gilding on either quarter, so that the blue brine under her counter flashed as to the dart of a sunbeam whenever she lightly swayed; yet the schooner held her own in all points as a picture of beauty, and was not to be dwarfed. The gilded buttons of her trucks shone high in the azure of that afternoon; she was painted white, and a gleam of dark red, like some cold wet flash of sunset, broke from her metalled bends whenever she was moved by the inflowing heave of the water.

"I lingered by the shore for the remainder of the afternoon, watching the people coming and going from and to the shipping, until I fancied, indeed I was certain, that the man I wanted, dressed in white clothes and a wide-brimmed straw hat, had been put aboard the schooner by her own boat.

"When I got on board I found the little ship a very noble, flush-decked vessel, with a clear sweep of sand-bright, yacht-like plank running from the taffrail to the 'eyes'; the brass-work was full of the stars of the western sunshine. The glass of her skylights was dark and shining. Her ropes were Flemish coiled, as though, indeed, she had been a man-of-war. Everything was clean and neat. I guessed she was about three hundred tons burden. Her crew had knocked off for the day and were lounging about the windlass, two or three of them stripped to the waist washing themselves. They had a colonial air. This might have been owing to their dress of check shirt, open at the breast, no braces, here and there moleskins, and here and there a cabbage-tree hat.

"The second mate, a man whose name I afterwards ascertained was Curzon, was walking in the gangway smoking a pipe. I enquired if Captain Huddersfield was on board. He asked me what my business was, as though suspicious of a visit from a stranger after working hours. I was about to explain the reason that had brought me to the schooner, when Captain Huddersfield himself emerged through the little companion way, and stepped on deck, pausing a moment with the sharp of his hand to his brow to gaze in the direction of Capetown.

"He was a tall, gentlemanly-looking person, thickly bearded, the hair of a rich auburn; the skin of his face was much burnt by the sun; his eyes were of a liquid blue, and when he approached and directed them at me I seemed to find something glowing and tender in them, as though he were an enthusiast, a man of strange, perhaps high, but always honest imagining; a dreamer. He of all the men that ever I had met at sea the least corresponded in appearance with the received image of the nautical man, who, forsooth, whether in fiction or on the stage, must needs be a fraud from the landgoing point of view if he be not purple with grog blossoms, with eyes dim and staring with drink, with legs bent like the prongs of a pitch fork, and charged to the throat with a forecastle vocabulary, incommunicable even by initials!

"I must say of Captain Huddersfield that never afloat or ashore had I before beheld in any man a more placid, benevolent expression of countenance. His age seemed about forty.

"'That's the captain,' said the second mate.

"I lifted my cap and walked up to him. In a few words I told my business, adding that I held not only a chief mate's, but a master's certificate of competency. He eyed me critically but with kindness, and nodded with something of gravity on my mentioning the name of the port-captain. After we had exchanged a few sentences, he took me into the cabin, a bright, breezy little interior, aromatic with a quantity of plants which had evidently been recently brought aboard, and cheerful with mirrors and pictures, as though, in short, this gentleman was in the habit when he went to sea of carrying his parlor with him; and bidding me be seated, he asked a number of questions, all which I saw with much pleasure by the expression of his face I answered to his satisfaction.

The interview ended in his offering me the post of mate of the schooner on a lump wage for the run to Sydney, and early next morning I went on board with my chest, and took up my quarters in the cabin.

"I regarded this securing of a post as a fine stroke of luck, and was mighty thankful. Plentiful as was the shipping in Table Bay, I had suspected ever since I went ashore, a sick man, that my chance of getting a situation aft was small; that, in short, I should be obliged to get clear of the Cape by offering myself as a hand. A trip to Sydney was just to my liking, for amongst the ships there I should find no difficulty in procuring a berth owing to the gold craze which was emptying vessels of their crews, from mate to boy, before they were fairly berthed.

"Four days after I had signed the schooner's articles, we weighed and stood out of the Bay. We were just in time to escape the thrashing of a furious south-easter which came whipping and howling down Table Mountain, out of the magnificent milk-white softness of vapor that half veiled the grand height, sinking and lifting upon it. A wide surface of water was whitened by this strange local gale. The limits of the wind were sharply and extraordinarily defined by a line of foam, inside of which all was savage popple and boiling commotion, the ships in it straining wildly, their loose gear curving, their bunting roaring; whilst outside all was of a midsummer serenity, the water rolling like knolls of polished quicksilver, tarnished here and there by light breathings of wind which delicately stretched the sails of the Malay boats, and sent them glancing through it, till the cats-paw died out into a roasting trance of burnished brine.

"We were, as I have said, a three-masted schooner, square-rigged forward, with an immense hoist of lower-mast for a square foresail, and a length of flying jibboom that made us all wags from the golden gleam of the figure-head to the tack of the flying jib. I had never before been shipmate with fore and aft canvas. All my knowledge of the sea had been picked up under square yards. There was nothing I could not do with a full-rigged ship, nor need a square-rigger and an old hand be charged with egotism for saying so. But when it came to boom-mainsails and gaff-foresails, and ropes and rigging with unfamiliar names, I could only idly look on for a while. But I did not doubt I should be able to quickly learn everything necessary to be known, and, meantime, when we were well out at sea, with the high African land upon our port quarter, blue in the air, with distant mountains trembling towards their summits into silver, and the mighty Southern Ocean stretching over our bows away down to the white silence of the Antarctic parallels, I watched the behavior of the schooner with interest.

"The breeze was abeam, the whole hot distance of the rich blue ocean was in it, there was no land for hundreds of leagues to break or hinder it; the schooner leaned over and flashed her sheathing at the northern sun, and stretched along the deep with the look of a flying hare. The white water poured aft from her shearing stem, her riband of wake sparkled to midway the horizon in a soaring and sinking vein of silver full of frostlike lights and wreaths of foam bells. It was like yachting, and I reckoned upon a quick run to Sydney.

"From the hour of my coming aboard officially, Captain Huddersfield exhibited a very friendly, almost cordial disposition. He was a man of good education, a sailor first of all, but a gentleman also, not highly varnished perhaps, wanting in the airs and graces of the drawing-room, but abundantly possessed of those qualities which, when glazed and brightened by shore-going observance and habit, caused men to be esteemed for their breeding and bearing. He had a regard for me, I think, because, like himself, I was not wholly a copy of the dramatic and romantic notions of the sailor. I neither swore nor drank. I was ever of opinion that it did not follow, because a man got his living under the commercial flag of his country, he must needs cultivate all qualities of blackguardism as a condition of his calling. I could not for the life of me understand why an officer in the merchant service should not be able to behave himself on board ship and ashore with as lively a sense of his duty and obligations as a gentleman as if he wore the buttons of the State.

"Possibly my friend, the port-captain at Capetown, had prejudiced Huddersfield in my favor. Then again, though he lived in Sydney, he was an Englishman born; his native county was mine, and this little circumstance alone, all those watery leagues away from the old home, was enough to establish a bond between us. Nevertheless, I did not observe that he was very communicative about his own affairs. For the first few days until the furious weather set in we often conversed, but I never found that our chats left me with any knowledge of his past or of his business; as, for instance, how long he had lived in New South Wales, the occasion that had despatched him there, what his commercial interests were outside his schooner, whether he was married, and so forth.

"It breezed up ahead after we had been at sea a few days. The *Cambrian* looked well to windward, but she was still points off her course. Then again the great Agulhas Stream set us to leeward, and our progress was slow. On the 22nd day of the month, we then being four days out from Table Bay, the weather blackened on a sudden in an afternoon in the north, the lightning streamed like cataracts of violet flame on those sooty sierras of storm, the thunder rolled continuously, but it was not till the edge of the electric stuff, black as midnight, was over our mastheads, with sea and sky dim and frightful as though beheld in the deep shadow of a total eclipse of the sun, that the hurricane took us.

It came along in a note of thunder, sharp-edged with the continuous shrieking of wind; the sea boiled under it and raced with the diabolic outfly in a high white wall of water. It swept upon us with a flash in a whole sky-full of salt smoke, and the air was like a snowstorm with the throb and flight of the yeast; the trifle of canvas that had been left exposed vanished as a puff of steam would. The schooner lay over till her starboard shear poles were under, and then it was deep enough to drown a man in the lee scuppers.

It was doubtful for some time whether she would right, and I was clawing my way forward with some dim hope of getting at the carpenter's chest for an axe for the weather laniards, when the noble little craft suddenly rose buoyant, with the long savage yell of the gale in her rigging as she thrashed her lofty spars to windward.

After this she made fairly good weather of it, but for three days we lay under bare poles, sagging helplessly to leeward in the trough of that mighty ocean. The weather then moderated; within six hours of the breaking of the gale it was blowing a gentle wind out of the northeast; the sun shone brightly and the schooner flapped leisurely along her course under all plain sail and over a large but fast subsiding swell.

"During the time of violent weather Captain Huddersfield had seemed much depressed in spirits. I had attributed his dejection to the peril of those hours. We were a small ship for that tall southern surge. Moreover his risk in the vessel might be large for all I knew. I could not guess how gravely I misjudged one of the manliest intelligences that ever informed a sailor.

"We were seated alone at dinner on the first day of fine weather. He said, after regarding me steadfastly for some moments—

"'Do you attach any meaning to dreams?'

"'I do not,' I answered.

"'But when they recur?' said he.

"'No,' said I, 'not though they should recur for a month of Sundays.'

"'Do you know of any superstitions in connection with dreams?' he asked.

"'I remember,' said I, 'an old woman once told me that to dream of a smooth sea is a sign of a prosperous voyage, but of a rough sea a stormy and unprofitable one.'

"He shook his head with a little impatience, without smiling.

"'Then, again,' said I, taxing my memory to oblige him, for this sort of talk was sad stuff to my way of thinking; 'a sailor once told me that if you dream of a dolphin you're bound to lose your sweetheart. And the same man said that to dream of drowning was a promise of good luck. The hopefullest of all sea-dreams, I believe, is the vision of an anchor. 'Tis a fact,' said I, finding myself thoughtful for a moment, 'that I dreamt of an anchor the night before I received a letter from an uncle containing a cheque for two hundred pounds—the only money I ever received from a relative in all my life.'

"He was silent for a while, and then said, speaking in a very serious voice—'For three nights running the same odd vision has troubled me. I have thrice dreamt that I was becalmed in an icy atmosphere of Antarctic darkness. The stars rode brilliantly, but they made no light. Regularly through this black atmosphere there sounded, in a note of sighing, human with articulation, and yet resembling the noise made by the whale when it spouts its fountain, these mysterious words: *"Try for her in fifty!"*

"' "Try for her in fifty!" Over and over again it so ran: *"Try for her in fifty!"* Now, to have dreamt this *once* would be nothing; *twice* makes it remarkable; the *third* time of the same vision must affect even the most wooden of minds with a spirit as of conviction. I don't believe in dreams any more than you do, yet there ought to be some sort of meaning in the repetition of one, in such a haunting cry repeated on several occasions of slumber as, *"Try for her in fifty!"*

"'Well, sir, it's strange,' I exclaimed, 'and that's about the amount of it. I've somewhere heard of men rescued in a starving state from a desolate island through a dream. The captain's nephew was the dreamer, I think. The same vision troubled him three times, as yours did. He was a young Frenchman, and the dream made him importunate. The skipper shifted his helm to oblige the lad, and on sighting the island or rock found a little company of gaunt Selkirks upon it.'

"Thus we reasoned the matter a while; he conversed as though he was worried at heart; when I went on deck, however, I flattered myself I had left him with an easier mind.

"He did not afterwards in that day refer to the subject, nor next morning when he came out of his cabin soon after sunrise, did he tell me that he had again been troubled in his sleep by that mysterious haunting cry, sounding across the black cold ocean of his dreams like the noise made by a whale, when it spouts its fountain to the stars in some midnight hush.

"A few days after we had had that talk I have just repeated, almost immediately on making eight bells by our sextant, a man on the forecastle hailing the quarter-deck bawled out that there was a small black object on the lee bow. Captain Huddersfield levelled the telescope, and said the thing was a ship's quarter-boat with a man standing up in her. The weather was quiet at this time, the breeze a light one. The schooner was rippling leisurely forward with an occasional flap of her canvas that flashed a light as of the sun itself into the blue air all about the masts. The junction of sea and sky was in haze, with here and there a dim blue shadow of cloud poised coastlike upon the horizon.

"I took the glass from the captain and made out a boat with a mast but no sail. The figure of a man stood erect, and one arm hooked the mast. We shifted our helm, and presently had the boat alongside.

"Two men were in her. One lay motionless under the thwarts. The other, though erect on his feet, had barely strength to catch the rope's cod that was flung. The boat was of the ordinary pattern of ship's quarterboat. Whilst we leaned over the side looking down into her, the captain said—

"'What is the name written in the stern-sheets there?'

"My sight was good. I answered, 'Prairie Chief.'

"He started, and turned pale, with a look of astonishment and horror, but said nothing.

"Meanwhile, the two men were being got aboard. One was lifeless, and his looks seemed to tell of his having been frozen rather than starved to death. They were both dressed in the plain garb of the merchant sailor. The one that lived was assisted forward and disappeared in the forecastle in the company of two or three sympathizing seamen of our crew. Nothing so pleads to the humanity of the British sailor as the misery that is expressed by the open boat. In this case no appeal could have been more complete. I jumped into the little craft in obedience to the captain's orders and overhauled her, and found nothing to eat or drink. Her cargo was an empty beaker and some fragments of canvas which appeared to have been chewed. The very heart within me sickened at the story of anguish that was silently related by those dusky, doughlike lumps of canvas. We hoisted the boat aboard. The weather permitted us to do that, and it was too good and useful a boat to lose.

"In the afternoon we buried the body of the dead, nameless seaman; nameless, because it seemed that the other was incapable of relating his story; pain and famine had paralyzed the tongue in his mouth. The captain read the service; his manner was so subdued, his whole demeanor expressed him as so affected, that you would have supposed he was burying some dear friend or near relative. I had often attended a burial service at sea, but never one more impressive than this. All the desolation of the mighty deep seemed to have centred as in a very spirit, in the lifeless body that lay stitched in a hammock in the gangway.

"When the body was overboard the captain walked to the boat we had hoisted in, and stood with his first look of amazement and grief, musing upon, or rather staring at the name *Prairie Chief* painted in the stern-sheets. He then went to his cabin. When he again made his appearance some time afterwards he was extraordinarily reserved and gloomy. Throughout the watches he would ask if the man was better. I do not recollect that he addressed another word to me than that question.

"Next forenoon, some time about eight bells, the man was sufficiently recovered to come aft. I stood beside Captain Huddersfield, sextant in hand, whilst he talked to him. He said his name was James Dickens, and that he had been an able seaman aboard the barque *Prairie Chief*. The ship was from London bound to Sydney. South of the Cape they met with very heavy weather from the northward, which hove them to and drove them south; it was so thick the captain could not get an observation. The wind slackened and the captain made sail, defying the thickness; he was impatient and had already made a long passage, and was resolved, happen what might, to "ratch" north for a clear sky. In the middle of the day, when the smother upon the sea was so thick that the flying-jibboom end was out of sight from the wheel, a loud and fearful cry of 'Ice right ahead!' rang from the forecastle. The wheel was revolved, every spoke, with the fury of despair, by the helmsman; but the ship's time was come, and there was nothing in seamanship to manœuvre her clear of her fate. She telescoped into the ice and went to pieces.

"This, Dickens said, had happened about ten days before we fell in with the boat. The disaster was not so frightfully sudden but that there was time for some to escape. A number of people, said the man, got upon the ice. Amongst them were the captain, his wife, and a female passenger. Dickens particularly noticed these people, that is, the commander and the two women. He and three others drifted away in a boat. The barque went to pieces aloft when she struck; he was sure that none others saving himself and the three men escaped in the boats. It was the middle of the day when the ship ran into the berg, and the darkness happened so quickly after the disaster that he was unable to tell much of what followed. Two of his companions died whilst they were adrift and their bodies were dropped overboard.

"Whilst Dickens told his story I watched the captain. His features were knitted into an expression of consternation, yet he never once interrupted the man. When the sailor had made an end of his story, Huddersfield said, in a slow level voice—

"'Was your commander Captain Smalley?'

"'Yes, sir.'

"'Was one of the female passengers Mrs. Huddersfield?'

"'It was her name, sir.'

"The captain turned his eyes upon me and cried, with a sudden wild toss of his hands that somehow gave an extraordinary pathos to his words and looks, 'She is my wife!'

"Nothing was said for some moments. I was at a loss for speech. It was the same as hearing of the death of one beloved by the person you are with when the news is given to him; what can you say? Presently I said to the man—

"'Did you sight any ships whilst you were adrift?'

"'Nothing, sir.'

"'But won't the ice you ran into,' said I, 'be well within the limits of the ocean fairway?'

"He could not answer me this.

"'How far south did you drift?'

"He did not know.

"'If they are on the ice is it too late to rescue them, sir?' I inquired, addressing the captain, after another pause.

"He seemed too distracted by grief to heed my question.

"'I had hoped,' he said, speaking in short breathings and broken sentences, 'to find her safe at Sydney on my arrival there; she went home last year on a visit to her mother. It was arranged that Captain Smalley, an old friend, should bring her out. Ten days ago,' he muttered to himself, 'ten days ago.' He covered his eyes with his hand, then looking vacantly at his sextant, went to the rail and seemed to stare out to sea into the south.

"I was about to question Dickens afresh when the captain rounded upon us in a very flash of white face and wild, eager manner.

"'Try for her in fifty!' he cried, looking at me, but as though he saw someone beyond me. I viewed him with silent surprise. The very memory and therefore the meaning of the words he now pronounced had gone out of my head, and I did not understand him.

"'Try for her in fifty!' he repeated. 'I know what it means.'

"He went in a sort of a run to the wheel, and brought the schooner's head to a due southerly course, whilst he shouted in tones vibrating with the excitement that seemed like mania in the man then, with the workings of his face—I say he shouted for sail to be trimmed for the course he had brought the schooner to, and the seamen fled about the decks to my commands, alert and willing, but as astonished as I was. When sail had been trimmed the captain called to Mr. Curzon to keep her steady as she went, and requested me to follow him below.

"He stood beside the table and leaned upon it; his agitation was so extreme that I thought to see his mother in his eyes. His breathing continued distressingly labored for some time; indeed, the emotions and passions which tore him appeared to have arrested the faculty of speech. At last he exclaimed in a voice low with religious awe, yet threaded too with a note of triumph that instantly caught my ear—

"'Do you now guess the meaning of that dream which was three times dreamt by me?'

"Still I was at a loss and made no answer.

"'Try for her in fifty!' he exclaimed. 'That was the cry I

told you about. You remember the sentence, surely?'

"'Yes, clearly now, sir, that you recall it.'

"'Come, let's work out the latitude,' he said, 'and we'll find that iceberg's situation. My heart's on fire. Oh!' he cried, but softly, in a tone that thrilled through me, 'my wife is dear to me. I pray, I pray! we may not be too late."

"I still failed to grasp what was in his mind, and suspected that his reason had been a little weakened by the shock of the news he had received. When we had worked out our observations he exposed the chart he used to prick off the ship's course on, and mused upon it, and measured angles and distances.

"'It is at this season,' said he, 'that the ice breaks away out of the south and comes in fleets of bergs thickly crowding north. There's been heavy weather. We'll not allow for a larger drift than a league a day. Try for her in fifty. That's it. That will put the berg when the *Prairie Chief* struck it in about fifty-one.'

"I thought now I began to understand him. "'You mean fifty-one degrees of south latitude?'

"'Of course I do,' he answered.

"I measured the distance due south from the place where our ship then was, and made it a few hundred miles—I forget the figure.

"'It's a short run,' said he, looking at the chart. 'The boat did it in ten days, and that's not above three knots an hour.' I was silent. I shall strike the parallel of fifty degrees,' he continued, after a pause, 'then run away east. If I sight nothing I shall head back. I'll find her—under God,' he added, removing his cap, and glancing upwards with an expression of rapt devotion.

"This was an extraordinary undertaking, prompted as it was by an impulse bred of the imagination of a mind in slumber, yet by no means irrational, seeing that it was certain, if the seaman Dickens reported aright, there was a shipwrecked company upon an iceberg within a few days' sail.

"The crew were briefly told that Captain Huddersfield's wife had been aboard the *Prairie Chief* and that the schooner was going to seek the survivors of the wreck. It will be supposed, however, that no hint was dropped as to the mysterious voice which had spoken in the whisper of a giant in the captain's dream. Curzon, the second mate, said that apart from the heavy odds against our falling in with the particular iceberg we wanted, there was the certainty, should we strangely enough encounter the mass of ice, of our finding the people dead of cold and starvation. I answered there was no certainty about it, and quoted several instances of astonishing deliverances from floating bodies of ice as recorded in the old marine chronicles.

"Not until the fourth day did we strike the latitude of 50°, in which time we saw no ice. The ocean was of a marvellous rich blue, the heavens a deep and thrilling violet, with coasts of swelling white vapor of a rusty bronze in their brows lying upon the glasslike line of the horizon. We now headed due east; the sailors thought our quest was ended! Throughout the glittering frosty hours—the wind blew with a piercing breath down here—Captain Huddersfield kept a lookout. He was for ever crossing the deck to peer ahead, and again and again, slinging a binocular glass over his shoulder, he would go aloft on to the little fore-royal-yard, where he stayed till the bitter cold drove him down.

At midnight on this day we sighted a large ice-island; pale as alabaster under the moon, and shortened canvas to approach it. We hove-to till the grey of the dawn, when the rising sun gave us a magnificent picture of a floating mountain bristling with pinnacles, a principality of turrets and castellated eminences, majestic in solitude. The man Dickens said it was not the berg. We sailed round it, keeping a sharp lookout for the loose ice, and then observing no signs of life, save a number of birds, proceeded.

"This same day we fell in with five different bergs, of different sizes, all of which we approached, and carefully examined; but to no purpose. Then for some long hours we encountered no more ice; but all this while we sailed steadily on the parallel of 50° S., making a due east course.

"And now comes the amazing part of this tale. I went on deck at midnight to take charge of the schooner. On walking to the side as my custom was, and gazing steadily ahead—a corner of the moon at this time hung in the sky over the port-quarter—I beheld a dim faintness right ahead, a delicate gleam like some mysterious reflection of light in a looking-glass in a darkened room. A man came along from the forecastle, and sung out in a quiet voice that there was ice ahead. I bade him rout out Dickens; it was his watch below, but whenever ice was reported we had him up, and stationed him on the forecastle to keep a lookout, as the one and only man in the vessel who would know the berg we were in search of. I then ran to the companion hatch and called to the captain, who was lying upon a locker below, and he immediately arrived.

"The wind was scanty, and our speed through the water scarcely four knots, but hardly had day broken—the ice-island being then about a mile distant—when Dickens, who had remained on the forecastle throughout the dark hours, shrieked out—

"'The iceberg, sir!'

"It was a fine morning, the sea quiet, the wind a nipping air out of the southwest; the sun shone full upon the iceberg, and flashed it into a great moon-white floating heap, scored with ravines and gorges. The swell rushed in thunder into deep caverns. I saw many Gothic archways with birds flying in them; the mass was like a city of alabaster, the home of sea spirits, of ocean fowl of mighty pinion; the surf boiled in thunder on the windward points. I observed a shelf of the dead-white crystal sloping very gently like a beach into the wash of the water, and whilst I was gazing at it the captain, who was working away at the berg with a telescope, cried out fiercely; then growing inarticulate, he put the glass into my hand, gaping at the ice, and pointing to it.

"I leveled the glass, and immediately, distinguished a structure, contrived, as I presently saw, of the galley of a ship, and a quantity of wreckage. It stood in a great split in the ice, within musket-shot of the beach, and whilst I looked smoke rose from it.

"'There is life there!' I cried out.

"We hauled in, and then with the naked eye clearly perceived several figures making signs to us. When we were as close as prudence permitted, the long-boat was got over, and the captain and five men, one of them being Dickens, pulled away towards the berg. I stood off to improve my offing, and being full of the business of the schooner, had little opportunity to remark what passed on the ice-island.

"By-and-by the boat returned; she looked to be full of people. When she was alongside I saw two women in her. One was locked in the embrace of Captain Huddersfield; he had wrapped her in his coat, and held her to his heart. Both women were lifted over the side; three of the men were also handed up. The others managed to crawl on deck unaided. There were seven men and two women. They afterwards told us that fifteen in all had gained the ice.

"The wife of the captain of the *Prairie Chief*—he was amongst those who had perished—died before our arrival in Sidney. Mrs. Huddersfield, a stronger woman, quickly recovered, and was walking the deck in the sun, leaning on her husband's arm, within a week of her rescue.

THE *CHILIMAN* TRAGEDY

In the year 1863 I sailed as ship's doctor aboard the *Chiliman,* in the third voyage that fine Blackwall liner made to Melbourne. I had obtained the berth through the influence of a relative. My own practice was a snug little concern in a town some fifty miles from London; but a change was needed, a change for my health, such a change as nothing but the oceans of the world with their several climates and hundred winds could provide, and so I resolved to go a voyage round the world on the easy terms of feeling pulses and administering draughts, with nothing to pay and nothing to receive, a seat at the cabin table, and a berth fitted with shelves and charged with a very powerful smell of chemist's shop down aft in what is called the steerage.

I joined the ship at the East India Docks, and went below to inspect my quarters. I found them gloomy and small; but any rat-hole was reckoned good enough in those days for a ship's doctor, a person who, though of the first importance to the well-being of a ship, is, as a rule, treated by most owners and skippers with the same sort of consideration that in former times a parson to a nobleman received, until he had obliged my lord by marrying his cast lady.

First let me briefly sketch this interior of saloon and steerage, since it is the theatre on which was enacted the extraordinary tragedy I am about to relate. The *Chiliman* had a long poop: under this was the saloon, in those days termed the cuddy; cabins very richly bulk-headed went away down aft on either hand. Amid-ships was the table, overhead the skylights, and the deck was pierced by the shaft of the mizzenmast, superbly decorated with a pianoforte secured to the deck just abaft it. There were no ladies' saloons, smoking-rooms, bathrooms as in this age, though the ship was one of the handsomest of her class. If you sought retirement you went to your cabin; if you desired a pipe you stepped on deck; if you asked for a bath you were directed to the head pump.

The *Chiliman's* cuddy was entered from the quarter-deck

by doors close beside the two flights of steps which conducted to the poop. A large square of hatch yawned near the entrance inside, and you descended a staircase to the steerage where my berth was. The arrangment of this steerage resembled that of the cuddy, but the bulkheads and general furniture were in the last degree plain. I believe they charged about twenty-five pounds for a berth down here, and sixty or seventy guineas for a cabin up above.

Whilst I stood in my berth looking around me a little boxy-legged man, in a camlet jacket and a large strawberry mark on his cheek, peered in and asked if I was the doctor.

"Ay, Dr. Harris," said I.

"I'm the ship's steward, sir," said he. "That's where I sleep," and he pointed to a cabin opposite.

I was glad to make this man's acquaintance, and was very civil to him. I would advise all sea-going doctors on long-voyage sailing ships to speedily make friends with the head steward. I remarked upon the gloominess of my quarters, and said I was afraid when it came to my making up draughts I might blunder for the want of light. He answered that the sailors never expected much more than strong doses of glauber salts, and that in his experience passengers as a rule managed very well without physic until they got ashore again.

I asked him if we were a full ship. He answered pretty full. About half the steerage berths were taken, and the same number of cabins would be occupied in the saloon. The 'tween-decks were crowded, he told me.

After this chat I went on deck, where I made the acquaintance of the captain and the chief mate. The ship was still in the docks, and the captain had just come aboard, and was talking to the first officer when I walked up to them. The decks were full of life, and the scene charged with excitement and interest. Groups of 'tween-decks people stood about, and numbers of drunken sailors were bawling and cutting capers on the forecastle; some saloon passengers who had joined the ship in the docks walked the poop; Blue Peter was streaming at our fore-royalmasthead under the gray sky of the Isle of Dogs; in all directions rose the masts of ships, a complicated forest, bewildering with the lace-work and tracery of rigging. Cargo was swinging in and out; pawls of capstan and winch were ticking like gigantic clocks to the thrust of the handspike and the revolution of the handle; the air was full of the smell of distant climes; I seemed to taste coffee and nutmeg and a pungent tickling of black pepper, but the perfume of the greasy wool-bale was dominant, and suggested nothing of the sweetness of the Arabian gale.

The captain went below, the mate fell a-shouting, I walked to the brass rail that ran across the break of the poop, and gazed about me. The steerage passengers on the main-deck looked a shabbily-dressed lot of poor, distressed people—men, women, and children. I took notice that certain young fellows, apprentices or midshipmen, with brass buttons on their jackets and brass badges on their caps, warned them off the quarter-deck whenever they stepped abaft the mainmast. One of these young fellows came and stood beside me. He was a gentlemanly, fair-haired, handsome lad, now making, as he presently told me, his second voyage. I asked him why those poor people were ordered off the part of the deck that lay immediately beneath us. He said because it was the quarter-deck, to be used only by the second-class passengers.

"That dirty rabble," said he, looking with disgust at the third-class folks, "must keep to the waist and forecastle if they want air."

"And this fine deck of poop?" said I. "Nobody uses this," he answered, "but the saloon nobs, and the officers and the midshipmen of the ship."

Shortly before eleven the vessel hauled out of dock. There was much noise of yelling and swearing; at this time my sight and hearing were confounded, and I wondered that any mortal being should understand the exact thing to do in such a scene of clamorous distraction. People on the pier-heads shrieked farewells to those on board, and those on board sobbed and yelped in response. When we had floated over the cill, with the mud pilot on the forecastle almost apoplectic with unavailing wrath at some insult fired at him out of a hurricane lung on the wharf, a tug got hold of us, a couple of seamen lurched aft to the wheel, the hawser tautened, and away we went down the river in the fizzing wake of a pair of churning paddles.

The varied scenery of the Thames—I mean its maritime

details of craft of twenty different rigs and steamers of twenty different aspects thrusting up and down, some staggering athwart, others making a bee-line through the reaches—charmed and interested me, who was fresh from a long spell of inland, almost rural, life, and I lingered till I was driven below by the wet which came sweeping along in a succession of drenching squalls as we rounded out of Galleon's into Barking Reach. I spent the remainder of that day in putting my cabin to rights, examining the drugs (some of which, for antiquity, methought, might have gone round the world with Cook in his first voyage), and in providing for my own comfort as best I could, and at half-past six went into the cuddy to join the people at dinner, by which hour the ship had arrived at a mooring-buoy off Gravesend, and was lying motionless on her own shadow in the stream.

It was a sullen evening, already dark; and dirty blowing wet weather on deck. The muffled howling and hissing of the wind in the three towering spires of mast, and yard, and rigging communicated, I've no doubt, the particular brilliance and beauty I found in the appearance of the well-lighted cuddy, with its long table draped for dinner, sparkling with glass and plate, and a number ladies and gentlemen, along with the captain and chief officer, issuing from their respective berths to take their seats. Thirteen of us sat down, and when this was remarked by an elderly lady next the captain, a midshipman was sent for to neutralize the sinister influence of that number by making a fourteenth. The lad took his place with a countenance of happy astonishment. He heartily wished, I dare say, that thirteen people would sit down to dinner every day.

I understood that there were some eight or ten more passengers expected from Gravesend in the morning, I looked about me to see what sort of persons I was to be associated with on an ocean passage that might run into four months. No need in this brief record of a tragic event to enter into minute descriptions of the people: enough if I refer now to two persons who sat opposite me, both of whom were to prove leading actors in what I have to tell.

One of them was a man of about six-and-thirty years of age. He wore a heavy moustache slightly streaked with grey.

His eyes were dark, keen, and steadfast in their gaze—steadfast, indeed, to rudeness, for his manner of looking at you was scarcely less than a deliberate scrutinizing stare. His hair was thin on the top, bushy at the sides; his complexion dark as of one who has lived long under the sun. His voice was subdued, his whole bearing well bred.

His companion was a lady: a dark, very handsome woman of three or four and twenty. Her hair was black, without gloss, a soft, dark, rich black, and I never before saw a woman with so wonderful a thickness of hair as that girl had. Her large, fine, dark eyes had a tropic sparkle; there was foreign blood in the glances which flashed through the long lashes. Her complexion was a most delicate olive made tender by a soft lasting bloom, which rested like a lingering blush upon her cheeks. Her figure looked faultless, and doubtless was so. I put the man down as a happy fellow carrying a beautiful bride away with him to the Antipodes. You could not have doubted that they were newly married; his behavior was all fondness; hers that of the impassioned young wife who finds difficulty in concealing her adoration in public.

I have thus sketched them, but I own that I was not more particularly interested in the couple than in others of the people who sat on either hand. The chief mate of the ship, however, Mr. Small, who occupied a seat on my left, concluded that my interest was sufficiently keen to justify him in talking to me about them; and in a low voice he told me that they were Captain and Mrs. Norton-Savage: he didn't quite know what he was captain of, but he had gathered from some source he couldn't recollect that he had made a fortune in South America, in Lima or Callao, and had been married a few weeks only, and was going to live in Australia, as his wife's health was not good, and the doctors believed the Australian climate would suit her.

Early next morning the rest of the passengers came on board, the tug again took us in tow, and under a dark blue sky, mountainous with masses of white cloud, the *Chiliman* floated in tow of the tug into Channel waters, where a long flowing heave despatched a great number of us to our cabins.

We met with nothing but head winds and chopping seas

down Channel. The ship lurched and sprang consumedly, and the straining noises of bulkheads and strong fastenings were so swift and furious in that part of the vessel where I slept that I'd sometimes think the fabric was going to pieces at my end of her. I was very seasick, but happily my services were never required in that time.

I think we were five days in beating clear of the Channel; the weather then changed, the sky brightened into a clear azure, delicately shaded by clouds; a soft wind blew out of the west, and when I made my first appearance on deck I found the ship clothed in swelling canvas from truck to waterway; her sand-white decks were lively with people in motion and the swaying shadows of the rigging; a number of ladies and gentlemen walked the poop, and the captain, with a telescope at his eye, was looking at a small steamer that was passing us at about a mile with a color flying; Captain and Mrs. Norton-Savage stood beside him, also looking at the steamer; the foam spun along the ship's side in wool-white wreaths, and every bubble shone like a bit of rainbow, and the streak of the vessel's wake gleamed upon the flowing lines of the ocean astern as though she trailed a length of mother-o'-pearl.

All sights and sounds were beautiful and refreshing. I breathed deep, with exquisite enjoyment of the ocean air after my spell of confinement in my apothecary-shop of a cabin, and with growing admiration of the spectacle of the noble ship, slightly heeling from the breeze, and curtsying stately as she went, till you'd think she kept time to some solemn music rising up round about her from the deep, and audible to her only, such a hearkening look as she took from the yearning lift of her jibs and staysails.

Presently the captain observed me, called me to him, and we stood in conversation for some twenty minutes. I begged his leave to take a look round the ship, and he ordered a midshipman to accompany me. I peeped into the galley or ship's kitchen, then into the forecastle, a gloomy cave, dully lighted by a lamp whose vapor was poisonous with the slush that fed it, and complicated to the landlubber's eye by the glimmering outlines of hammocks, and the dark, coffinlike shapes of bunks and seamen's chests. I then descended into the 'tween-decks by way of the main-hatch, and took a view of the accommodation there, and found the cabins formed of planks roughly shaped into bulkheads with partitions which made mere pigeon-holes of the places. In truth the poor third class folk were always badly treated in those days at sea. They were ill-housed; they were half starved; they were elbowed, sworn at, and generally tyrannized over by all hands, from the captain to the cook's mate; and in heavy weather, when the hatches were battened down, they were almost suffocated. Yet they were better off than the sailors, who were not only equally half starved, half suffocated, and sworn at, but were forced to do the treadmill work of the ship also.

I regained the deck, glad to get out of this gloomy region of crying babies and quarrelling children, and grimy groups in corners shuffling greasy cards, and women with shawls over their heads mixing flour and water for a pudding, or conversing shrilly in provincial accents, some looking very white in deed, and all as though it was quite time they changed their country.

As I went along the quarter-deck on my way to the cuddy, I saw a young man standing in the recess formed by the projection of the foremost cuddy cabins and the overhanging ledge or break of the poop. I looked at him with some attention; he was a particularly handsome young fellow, chiefly remarkable for the contrast between the lifeless pallor of his face and the vitality of his large, bright, dark eyes. His hair was cropped close in military fashion; he wore a cloth cap with a naval peak. His dress was a large, loose monkey-jacket and blue cloth trousers cut in the flowing nautical style. On the beach of Southsea or the sands of Ramsgate he might have passed for a yachtsman; on the high seas and on the deck of a full-rigged ship with plenty of hairy sailors about to compare him with, nothing mortal could have looked less nautical.

I paused when in the cuddy to glance at him again through the window. He leaned in the corner of the recess with his arms clasped upon his breast and his fine and sparkling eves fixed upon the blue line of the horizon that was visible above the lee bulwark-rail. My gaze had lighted upon many faces whilst I looked over the ship, but on none had it lingered. It lingered now, and I wondered who the youth was. His age might have been twenty; handsome he was, as I have said, but his expression was hard, almost fierce, and certainly repellant. Whilst I watched him his lips twitched or writhed three or four times and exposed a grin of flashing white teeth that was anything but mirthful, I can assure you. His clothes were good, his appearance refined, and I concluded that he was one of the cuddy passengers who had come on board at Gravesend. He turned his face and saw me looking, and instantly made a step which carried him out of sight, past the cabin projection.

The steward came up out of the steerage at that moment, and wishing to know who was who in the ship I asked him to peep through the door and tell me who the melancholy pale-faced young gentleman in the nautical clothes was. He popped his head out and then said—

"He's a young gent named John Burgess, one of the steerage people. He occupies the foremost cabin to starboard beside the foot of them steps," said he, pointing to the hatch.

"Is he alone in the ship?" said I.

"All alone, sir."

"Where do those steerage people take their meals?"

"Why, in the steerage, at the table that stops short abreast of your cabin."

Nothing in any way memorable happened for a considerable time. The ship drove through the Atlantic impelled by strong beam and quartering winds which sometimes blew with the weight of half a gale and veiled her forecastle with glittering lifts of foam and heeled her till her lee-channels ripped through the seas in flashings fierce as the white water which leaps from the strokes of the thrasher's flails. The passengers had settled down to the routine of ship-board life. They played the piano, they sang, they hove the deck quoit, they formed themselves into whist parties. Both Captain Norton-Savage and his wife promised to become exceedingly popular with all the people who lived aft. The lady sang sweetly; she sang Spanish, English, and French songs. It was understood that she was a South American, of pure Spanish blood on one side. Captain Norton-Savage told a good story. He smoked excellent cigars and was liberal with them. He came to me one day and talked about his wife, told me there was consumption in her family, and asked what I thought of a sea voyage for her, and of the climate of Australia. I could find nothing to object to in the man except his stare. There was something defiant in his manner of looking at you; his speech was significant with it even when nothing more was meant than met the ear. I was misled at first, and sometimes troubled myself to look under his words for his mind; then I found out that it was his stare which was responsible for what his language seemed to carry, and so, with the rest of us, took him as he offered himself.

And still I never felt quite easy with him, though no man laughed louder at his humorous stories.

I was going one morning from my berth to the cuddy when, at the foot of the steps which conducted to the hatch, I met the young man called John Burgess. I had seen nothing of him for days. He came out of his cabin holding his cap. Plenty of light flowed through the hatch; he was very pale, and I thought seemed ill, and his eyes had a wild look. He was handsome, as I have said—at least, to my way of thinking; but there was an evil spirit in the delicate structure and lineaments of his face. I said "Good morning." He answered "Good morning" in a low voice, but with a manner of impatience, as though he wished me to pass on or get out of his road.

"Are you going to Australia for your health?" said I, for the sake of saying something.

"No," he answered.

"Are you English?"

"Pray who are you?" he exclaimed with a foreign accent. "I am Dr. Harris," I answered, smiling.

He looked uneasy on my pronouncing the word *doctor*, stepped back and grasped the handle of his cabin door, yet paused to say, "Are you a passenger, sir?"

"I am the ship's doctor," I answered.

Without another word he entered his cabin and shut the door upon himself. His behavior was so abrupt, discourteous, that I suspected his brain was at fault. Indeed, I made up my mind, in the interests of the passengers, and for the security of the ship, to keep my eye upon him—that is, by accosting him from time to time, and by watching him without seeming to watch whenever we should happen to be on deck together. And yet I was not altogether satisfied with my suspicion of his not being right-headed, either; I found my puzzlement going another way, but in a direction that I could by no means make clear to myself.

However, not to refine upon this matter: I think it was next day that, happening to come along from the forecastle where I had been visiting a sick sailor, I spied the young fellow standing before the mainmast in a sort of peeping posture; his eyes were directed aft; he was watching the people walking on the poop. I stopped to look at him, struck by his attitude. The great body of the mast effectually concealed him from all observers aft. He turned his head and saw me; his face was ghastly white, the expression wonderful for the tragic wrath of it.

On meeting my eyes he colored up, I never could have credited so swift a transformation of hue; his blush was deep and dark and his eyes shone like fire, He scowled angrily, stepped round the mast, and disappeared through the cuddy door.

After this I saw no more of him for a week. I questioned the steward, who told me the youth was keeping his cabin.

"What's his name again?" said I.

"John Burgess, sir."

"That's an English name, but he's not an Englishman," said I.

"We don't trouble ourselves about names on board ship, sir," he answered. "There be purser's names aft as well as forrard."

"Does he ever talk to you?"

"No, sir, he might be a funeral mute for talk."

"Does he come to the table for his meals?"

"No, sir; his grub's carried in to him."

"When did you see him last?"

"About an hour ago."

"Does he seem well?"

"Well as I am, sir."

I asked no more questions. There was a cheerfulness in the steward's way of answering which promised me he saw nothing peculiar in the lad. This was reassuring, for I knew he was often in and out of the young man's berth, and anything eccentric in his conduct would strike him. As for me, it was no part of my duty to intrude upon the passengers in their privacy.

We took the northeast trade wind, made noble progress down the North Atlantic, lost the commercial gale in eight or ten degrees north of the equator, and then lay "humbugging," as the forecastle saying is, on plains of greasy blue water, scarcely crisped by the cats-paw, and often, for hours at a time, without air enough to wag the fly of the vane at the masthead. One very hot night after a day of roasting calm I lingered on the poop for some while after my customary hour of retiring to rest for the refreshment of the dew-cooled atmosphere and the cold breath lifting off the black surface of ocean. The awning was spread over the poop; a few shadowy figures moved slowly under it; here and there a red star indicated a smoker sucking at a cigar; the water alongside was full of smoky fire rolling in dim green bursts of cloud from the bends of the ship as she leaned with the swell. But the stars were few and faint; down in the southwest was a little play of silent lightning; the noises of the night were rare and weak, scarce more than the flap of some pinion of cloth up in the gloom, or the jerk of a wheel chain, or the subdued moan of water washing under the counter.

I smoked out my pipe and still lingered; it was very hot and I did not love the fancy of my bunk on such a night. The passengers went below one by one after the cabin lamps were turned down. Six bells were struck, eleven o'clock. I took a few turns with the officer of the watch, then went on to the quarter-deck, where I found Captain Norton-Savage smoking and chatting with two or three of the passengers under the little clock against the cuddy front. The captain offered me a cigar, our companions presently withdrew, and we were left alone.

I observed a note of excitement in Captain Savage's speech, and guessed that the heat had coaxed him into draining more seltzer and brandy than was good for him. We were together till half-past eleven; his talk was mainly anecdotic and wholly concerned others. I asked him how his wife bore the heat. He answered very well, he thought. Did I not think the voyage was doing her good? I answered I had observed her at dinner that day and thought she looked very well in spite of her pallor. These were the last words I spoke before wishing him good night. He threw the end of his cigar overboard and went to his cabin, which was situated on the port side just over against the hatch down which I went to my quarter in the steerage.

All was silent in this part. The hush upon the deep worked in the ship like a spirit; at long intervals only arose the faint sounds of cargo lightly strained in the hold. Much time passed before I slept. Through the open porthole over my bunk I could hear the mellow chimes of the ship's bell as it was struck. It was as though the land lay close aboard with a church clock chiming. The hot atmosphere was rendered doubly disgusting by the smell of the drugs. Yea, more than drugs, methought, went to the combined flavor. I seemed to sniff bilgewater and the odor of the cockroach.

I was awakened by a hand upon my shoulder.

"Rouse up, for God's sake, doctor! There's a man stabbed in the cuddy!" I instantly got my wits, and threw my legs over the edge of the bunk.

"What's this about a man stabbed?" I exclaimed, pulling on my clothes. The person who had called me was the second mate, Mr. Storey. He told me that he was officer of the watch; a few minutes since one of the passengers who slept next the berth occupied by the Savages was awakened by a shriek. He ran into the cuddy, and at that moment Mrs. Savage put her head out and said that her husband lay dead with a knife buried in his heart. The passenger rushed on deck, and Mr. Storey came to fetch me before arousing the captain.

I found several people in the cuddy. The shriek of the wife had awakened others besides the passenger who had raised the alarm. Captain Smallport, the commander of the ship, hastily ran out of his cabin as I passed through the steerage hatch. Someone had turned the cabin lamp full on, and the light was abundant. The captain came to me, and I stepped at once to the Savages' berth and entered it. There was no light here, and the cuddy lamp threw no illumination into this cabin. I called for a box of matches and lighted the bracket-lamp, and then there was revealed this picture: In the upper bunk, clothed in a sleeping costume of pyjamas and light jacket, lay the figure of Captain Norton-Savage, with the cross-shaped hilt of a dagger standing up out of his breast over the heart and a dark stain of blood showing under it like its shadow. In the right-hand corner, beside the door, stood Mrs. Savage, in her night-dress; her face was of the whiteness of her bedgown, her black eyes looked double their usual size. I noticed blood upon her right hand and a stain of blood upon her nightdress over the right hip. All this was the impression of a swift glance. In a step I was at Captain Savage's side and found him dead.

"Here is murder, captain," said I, turning to the commander of the ship. He closed the door to shut out the prying passengers, and exclaimed—"Is he dead?"

"Yes."

Mrs. Savage shrieked. I observed her dressing-gown hanging beside the door and put it on her, again noticing the blood stains upon her hands and night-dress. She looked horribly frightened and trembled violently.

"What can you tell us about this?" said Captain Smallport.

In her foreign accent, strongly defined by the passion of terror or grief, she answered, but in such broken, tremulous, hysteric sentences as I should be unable to communicate in writing. That being suddenly awakened by a noise as of her cabin door opened or shut, she called to Captain Savage, but received no answer. She called again, then, not knowing whether he had yet come to bed, and the cabin being in darkness, she got out of her bunk and felt over the upper one for him. Her hand touched the hilt of the dagger, she shook him and called his name, touched the dagger again, then uttered the shriek that had alarmed the ship.

"Is it suicide?" said the captain, turning to me.

I looked at the body, at the posture of the hands, and answered emphatically, "No." I found terror rather than grief in Mrs. Savage's manner; whenever she directed her eyes at the corpse I noticed the straining of panic fear in them. The captain opened the cabin door, and called for the stewardess. She was in waiting outside, as you may believe. The cuddy, indeed, was full of people, and whilst the door was open I heard the grumbling hum of the voices of 'tween-deck passengers and seamen crowding at the cuddy front. The news had spread that one of the first-class passengers had been murdered, and every tongue was asking who had done it.

The stewardess took Mrs. Savage to a spare cabin. When the women were gone and the door again shut, Captain Smallport still remaining with me, I drew the dagger out of the breast of the body and took it to the light. It was more properly a dagger-shaped knife than a dagger, the point sharp as a needle, the edge razorlike. The handle was of fretted ivory; to it was affixed a thin slip of silver plate, on which was engraved "Charles Winthrop Sheringham to Leonora Dunbar."

"Is it the wife's doing, do you think?" said the captain, looking at the dagger.

"I would not say 'Yes' or 'No' to that question yet,' said I.

"She might have done it in her sleep."

"Look at his hands," said I. "He did not stab himself. Will you take charge of this dagger, captain?"

"All bloody like that!" cried he, recoiling.

I cleansed it, and then he took it.

We stood conversing awhile. I examined the body again; which done, the pair of us went out, first extinguishing the lamp, and then locking the door.

The passengers sat up for the remainder of the night, and the ship was as full of life as though the sun had risen. In every corner of the vessel was there a hum of talk in the subdued note into which the horror of murder depresses the voice. The captain called his chief officer and myself to his cabin; we inspected the dagger afresh, and talked the dreadful thing over. Who was the assassin? Both the captain and mate cried, "Who but the wife?" I said I could not be satisfied of that yet; who was Charles Winthrop Sheringham? who was Leonora Dunbar? It was some comfort anyhow to feel that, whoever the wretch might be, he or she was in the ship. There were no doors to rush through, no windows to leap from, no country to scour *here*. The assassin was a prisoner with us all in the ship; our business was to find out who of the whole crowd of us had murdered the man, and we had many weeks before us.

In the small hours the sailmaker and his mate stitched up the body ready for the toss over the side before noon. We waited until the sun had arisen, then, our resolution having been formed, the captain and I entered the berth which had been occupied by the Savages and examined such baggage as we found there. The keys were in a bag; our search lasted an hour. At the expiration of the hour we had found out, mainly through the agency of a large bundle of letters, but in part also through other direct proofs, that the name of the murdered man was Charles Winthrop Sheringham; that the name of the lady whom we had known as Mrs. Savage was Leonora Dunbar: that this Miss Dunbar had been an intimate friend of Mrs. Sheringham, and that the husband had eloped with her and taken a passage for Melbourne in the ship *Chiliman,* promising marriage in twenty solemn protestations on their arrival in Australia, the ceremony to be repeated should Mrs. Sheringham die.

This story we got together out of the letters and other conclusive evidence. The captain was now rootedly of opinion that Miss Dunbar had killed Sheringham.

"It's not only the dagger," said he, "with her name on it, which was therefore hers, and in her keeping when the murder was done; for, suppose someone else the assassin, are you to believe that he entered the Savages' berth and rummaged for this particular weapon instead of using a knife of his own? How would he know of the dagger or where to find it? It's not the dagger only; there's the stains on her hand and bedgown, and mightn't she have killed him in a fit of madness owing to remorse, and thoughts of a life-long banishment from England, and horror of the disgrace and shame he's brought her to?"

I listened in silence; but not yet could I make up my mind.

I met the stewardess coming to the captain with the key of the Savages' cabin; she wanted clothes for the lady. I asked how Mrs. Savage did, giving the unhappy woman the name she was known by on board.

"She won't speak, sir," answered the stewardess. "She's fallen into a stony silence. She sits with her hands clasped and her eyes cast down, and I can't get a word out of her."

"I'll look in upon her by-and-by," said I.

The body was buried at ten o'clock in the morning. The captain read the funeral service, and the quarter-deck was crowded with the passengers and crew. I don't think there was the least doubt throughout the whole body of the people that Mrs. Savage, as they supposed her, had murdered Sheringham. It was the murder that put into this funeral service the wild, tragic significance everybody seemed to find in it, to judge at least by the looks on the faces I glanced at.

When the ceremony was ended I called for the stewardess, and went with her to Miss Dunbar's cabin. On entering I requested the stewardess to leave me. The lady was seated, and did not lift her eyes, nor exhibit any signs of life whilst I stood looking. Her complexion had turned into a dull pale yellow, and her face, with its expression of hard, almost blank repose, might have passed for marble wantonly tinctured a dim primrose. She had exchanged her dressing-gown for a robe, and appeared attired as usual. I asked some questions, but got no answer. I then took a seat by her side, and called her by the name of Leonora Dunbar. She now looked at me steadily, but I did not remark any expression of strong surprise, of the alarm and amazement I had supposed the utterance of that name would excite.

I said softly, "The captain and I have discovered who you are, and your relation with Charles Winthrop Sheringham. Was it you who stabbed him? Tell me if you did it. Your sufferings will be the lighter when you have eased your conscience of the weight of the dreadful secret."

It is hard to interpret the expression of the eyes if the rest of the features do not help. I seemed to find a look of hate and contempt in hers. Her face continued marble hard. Not being able to coax a syllable out of her, though I spared nothing of professional patience in the attempt, I left the cabin, and, calling the stewardess, bade her see that the lady was kept without means to do herself a mischief.

That day and the next passed. Miss Dunbar continued dumb as a corpse. I visited her several times, and twice Captain Smallport accompanied me; but never a word would she utter. Nay, she would not even lift her eyes to look at us. I told the captain that it might be mere mulishness or a condition of mind that would end in madness. It was impossible to say. The stewardess said she ate and drank and went obediently to bed when ordered. She was as passive as a broken-spirited child, she said. For her part she didn't believe the lady had killed the poor man.

It was on the fourth day following the murder that the glass fell; it blackened in the northwest, and came on to blow a hard gale of wind. A mountainous sea was running in a few hours upon which the ship made furious weather, clothed in flying brine to her tops, under no other canvas than a small storm main-trysail. The hatches were battened down, the decks were full of water, which flashed in clouds of glittering smoke over the lee bulwark rail. The passengers for the most part kept their cabins. The cook could do no cooking; indeed the galley fire was washed out, and we appeased our appetites with biscuit and tinned meat.

The gale broke at nine o'clock on the following morning, leaving a wild, confused sea and a scowling sky all around the horizon, with ugly yellow breaks over our reeling mast-heads. I was in my gloomy quarters, whose atmosphere was little more than a green twilight, with the wash of the emerald brine swelling in thunder over the porthole, when the steward arrived to tell me that one of the passengers had met with a serious accident. I asked no questions, but instantly followed him along the steerage corridor into the cuddy, where I found a group of the saloon people standing beside the figure of the young fellow named John Burgess, who lay at his length upon the deck. I had not set eyes on him for days amid days.

I thought at first he was dead. His eyes were half closed; the glare of approaching dissolution was in the visible part of the pupils, and at first I felt no pulse. Two or three of the sailors who had brought him into the cuddy stood in the doorway. They told me that the young fellow had persisted in mounting the forecastle ladder to windward. He was hailed to come down, as the ship was pitching heavily and often dishing bodies of green water over her bows. He took no notice of the men's cries, and had gained the forecastle-deck when an unusually heavy lurch flung him; he fell from a height of eight or nine feet, which might have broken a limb for him only; unhappily he struck the windlass end, and lay seemingly lifeless.

I bade them lift and carry him to the cabin that I might examine him, and when they had placed him in his bunk I told them to send the steward to help me and went to work to partially unclothe the lad to judge of his injuries.

On opening his coat I discovered that he was a woman.

On the arrival of the steward I told him that the young fellow called John Burgess was a girl, and I requested him to send the stewardess, and whilst I waited for her I carefully examined the unconscious sufferer, and judged that she had received mortal internal injuries. All the while that I was thus employed some extraordinary thoughts ran in my head.

The stewardess came. I gave certain directions and went to the captain to report the matter. He was in no wise surprised to learn that a woman dressed as a man was aboard his ship; twice, he told me, had that sort of passenger sailed with him within the last four years.

"Captain," said I, "I'll tell you what's in my head! That woman below who styled herself John Burgess murdered Sheringham."

"Why do you think that?"

"Because I believe that she's his wife."

"Ha!" said Captain Smallport.

I gave several reasons for this notion; what I observed in the disguised woman's behavior when hidden behind the mainmast; then her being a foreigner, in all probability a South American, as Leonora Dunbar was, and so on.

He said, "What about the blood on Miss Dunbar's hand and night-dress?"

"She told us she had felt over the body."

"Yes, yes!" he cried, "doctor, you see things more clearly than I do." When I had conversed for some time with Captain Smallport, I walked to Miss Dunbar's cabin, knocked, and entered. I found her on this occasion standing with her back to the door, apparently gazing at the sea through the portholes; she did not turn her head. I stood beside her to see her face and said—

"I have made a discovery; Mrs. Sheringham is on board this ship."

On my pronouncing these words she screamed, and

looked at me with a face in which I clearly read that her silence had been sheer sullen mulish obstinacy, with nothing of insanity in it, pure stubborn determination to keep silence that we might think what we chose.

"Mrs. Sheringham in this ship?" she cried, with starting eyes and the wildest, whitest countenance you can imagine.

"Yes," I answered.

"Then it's she who murdered Sheringham. She is capable of it, she is a tigress!" she cried in a voice pitched to the note of a scream.

"That's what I have come to talk to you about, and I am glad you have found your voice."

"Where is she?" she asked, and a strong shudder ran through her.

"She is in her cabin below, dying; she may be dead even now as we converse."

She uttered something in Spanish passionately and clasped her hands.

"Now hear me," said I, "since you have your ears and have found your tongue. You are suspected of having murdered the man you eloped with."

"It is false!" she shrieked. "I loved him—oh, I loved him!"

She caught her breath and wept bitterly.

"In my own heart," said I, touched by her dreadful misery, "I believe you guiltless. I am sure you are so now that we have discovered that Mrs. Sheringham is on board. Will you answer a question?"

"Yes," she sobbed.

"You know that Sheringham was stabbed to the heart with a dagger?"

"Yes."

"It bears this inscription: '*Charles Winthrop Sheringham to Leonora Dunbar.*' Was that dagger in your possession in this ship?"

"No. Mr. Sheringham gave it to me. There was no such inscription as you name upon it. I left it behind when I came away. I swear before my God I speak the truth!"

Her voice was broken with sobs; she spoke with deepest agitation. Her manner convinced me it was as she represented.

I said, "Come with me and see the woman and tell me if she is Mrs. Sheringham." She shrank and cried out that she could not go. She was perfectly sane; all her stubbornness was gone from her; she was now a miserable, scared, broken-hearted woman. I told her that the person I took to be Mrs. Sheringham lay insensible and perhaps dead at this moment, and, by putting on an air of command, I succeeded at last in inducing, or rather obliging, her to accompany me. She veiled herself before quitting the cabin. The saloon was empty. We passed into the steerage, and she followed me into the cabin where the woman was.

The poor creature was still unconscious; the stewardess stood beside the bunk looking at its dying white occupant. I said to Miss Dunbar:

"Is it Mrs. Sheringham?"

She was cowering at the door, but when she perceived that the woman lay without motion with her eyes half closed, insensible and, perhaps, dead, as she might suppose, she drew near the bunk, peered breathlessly, and then, looking around to me, said—

"She is Mrs. Sheringham. Let me go!"

I opened the door and she fled with a strange noise of sobbing. I stayed for nearly three hours in Mrs. Sheringham's berth. There was nothing to be done for her. She passed away in her unconsciousness, and afterwards, when I looked more closely into the nature of her injuries, I wondered that she could have lived five minutes after the terrible fall that had beaten sensibility out of her over the windlass end.

I went to the captain to report her death, and in a long talk I gave him my views of the tragic business. I said there could be no question that Mrs. Sheringham had followed the guilty couple to sea with a determination so to murder her husband as to fix the crime of his death upon his paramour. How was this to be done? Her discovery at her home of the dagger her husband had given to Leonora Dunbar would perhaps give her the idea she needed. If Miss Dunbar spoke the truth, then, indeed, I could not account for the inscription on the dagger. But there could be no question whatever that Mrs. Sheringham had been her husband's murderess.

This was my theory: and it was afterwards verified up to

the hilt. On the arrival of the *Chiliman* at Melbourne Miss Dunbar was sent home to take her trial for the murder of Mr. Sheringham; but her innocence was established by—first, the circumstance of a woman having been found aboard dressed as a man; next, by the statement of witnesses that a woman whose appearance exactly corresponded with that of "John Burgess" had been the rounds of the shipping offices to inspect the list of passengers by vessels bound to Australia; thirdly, by letters written to Leonora Dunbar by Sheringham found among Mrs. Sheringham's effects, in one of which the man told the girl that he proposed to carry her to Australia. Finally, and this was the most conclusive item in the whole catalogue of evidence, an engraver swore that a woman answering to Mrs. Sheringham's description called upon him with the dagger (produced in court) and requested him without delay to inscribe upon the thin plate, "Charles Winthrop Sheringham to Leonora Dunbar."

And yet, but for the death of Mrs. Sheringham and my discovery of her sex, it was far more likely than not that the wife would have achieved her aim by killing her husband and getting her rival hanged for the murder.

THE SECRET OF
THE DEAD MATE

Black in the wake of the moon, in the heart of the trembling spread of white splendor, floated a boat. The night was breathless: beyond the verge of the eclipsing brightness of the moon the sky was full of stars. A man sat in the stern-sheets of the boat motionless with his chin on his breast and his arms in lifeless posture beside him. From time to time he groaned, and after he had been sitting as though dead for an hour he raised his head and lifted up his eyes to the moon, and cursed the thirst that was burning his throat, then shifted his figure close to the gunwale, over which he lay, with both hands in the water for the chill of it.

The moonshine was nigh as bright as day. The sea-line ran firm as a sweep of painted circle through the silver mist in the far recesses. An oar was stepped as a mast in the boat, and athwart it was lashed another oar from which hung a man's shirt and coat. She looked dry as a midsummer ditch in that piercing moonlight. At the feet of the man, distinctly visible, were two or three little pellets or lumps of rag, which he had been chewing throughout the day; but his jaws were now locked, the saliva had run dry, his sailor's teeth, blunted by junk and ship's bread, could bite no more moisture out of the fragment of stuff he had cut off his back. Oh! it is dreadful to suffer the agony of thirst, the froth, the baked and cracking up, the strangled throat, whilst beholding a vast breast of cold sea glazed into the beauty of ice by the moon, and whilst hearing the fountainlike murmur and refreshing ripple of water alongside!

The moon rolled slowly into the south-west, trailing her bright wake with her, and the boat and its solitary occupant floated into the shadow. Again the man lifted his head and looked around him. A soft breeze, but hot as the human breath, was blowing, and the shirt and coat dangling from the athwartship oar were lifting to the light pressure. The man saw that the boat was moving over the sea, but made no attempt to help her with the helm; once more he cast his eyes up at the moon and cursed the thirst that was choking him. But a boat, like a ship, has a life and a spirit of her own. The little fabric ran as though, with the sentience of a living organism, she knew there was something to hope for in the darkness ahead; her wake was a short, arrowlike line, and it streamed from her in emerald bubbles and circling wreaths of fire.

The sun rose, and the shadow of the earth rolled off the sea, which was feathering into the south-west to the steady pouring of the northeast wind. The boat ran straight, and now, the day being come, when the man looked up and ahead, he saw the shadow of land over the bows. Life sprang up in him with the sight, and a grin of hope twisted his face. With a husky groan he shifted himself for a grasp of the helm, and, laying his trembling hand upon the tiller, he held the boat—but not more steadily than she had been going—for the land.

He was a man of about forty-five years of age; half his clothes were aloft, and he was attired in fearnaught trousers of the boatman's pattern, and a waistcoat buttoned over his vest. Suffering had sifted a pallor into the sun-brown of his skin, and his face was ghastly with famine and thirst. His short yellow beard stood straight out. His yellow hair was mixed with grey, and lay clotted with the sweat of pain into long streaks over his brow and ears, covering his eyes as though he was too weak or heedless to clear his vision.

The speed of the boat quickly raised the land, and by noon under the roasting sun it lay within a mile. It was one of the Bahama Cays—a flat island, with a low hill in the midst of it, to the right of which was a green wood; the rest of the island was green with some sort of tropic growth as of guinea-grass. The breeze was now very light—the sun had eaten it up, as the Spaniards say. The man thought he saw the sparkle of a waterfall, and the sight made him mad, and as strong in that hour as in his heartiest time. He sprang from his seat, pulled down his queer fabric of oar and flapping shirt and coat, and flinging the two blades over, bent his back and drove the boat along. In a quarter of an hour her forefoot grounded on a coral-white beach that swept round a point clear of the foam of the breaker, and the man reeling out of her on to the shore, grasped her painter, and secured it to an oar, which he jammed into a thickness of some sort of bush that grew close to the wash of the water, and then, rocking and stumbling, he went up the beach.

It was an uninhabited island, and nothing was in sight upon the whole circle of the white shining sea saving the dim blue haze of land in the north and a like film or delicate discoloration of the atmosphere in the south-west. The man with rounded back and hanging arms and staggering gait searched for water. The heat was frightful; the sunshine blazed in the white sand, and seemed to strike upwards into the face in darting and tingling needles, white hot. He went towards the wood, wading painfully on his trembling legs through the guinea-grass and thick undergrowth, with toad-stools in it like red shields and astir with armored creatures, finger-long reptiles, of glorious hue, and spiders like bunches of jewels.

Suddenly he stopped; his ears had caught a distant noise of water; he turned his back upon the sun, and, thrusting onwards, came presently to a little stream, in which the grass stood thick, green, and sweet. He fell on his knees, and, putting his lips to the crystal surface, sucked up the water like a horse, till, being full nearly to bursting, he fell back with a moan of gratitude, his face hidden in his hands. He sat till the broiling sunshine forced him to rise. The slender stream narrowed in the direction of the wood, and he walked beside it; presently after pushing a little way into the green shade, he found the source in a rock rich with verdure and enamelled with many strange and beautiful flowers. The trees in this wood stood well apart, but their branches mingled in many places, and the shade they made was nearly continuous.

He threw himself down beside the source of the little stream to rest himself. The surf seethed with a noise of boiling through the silent, blazing atmosphere outside. The miserable castaway now directed his eyes round in search of food. He saw several kinds of berries, and things like apples, but durst not eat of them for fear of being poisoned. Being now rested and immeasurably refreshed, he cooled his head in the stream and walked to the beach, and picked up a number of crabs. He saw to his boat, hauling her almost high and dry. All that she contained besides the clothes which had served him for a sail, was a carpenter's hammer and a bag of spikes. He whipped off his waistcoat and put his coat on, and dropping the hammer into his pocket, returned to the wood with his collection of crabs; then with his knife he cut down a quantity of dry brush-wood and set fire to it with the old-fashioned tinder-box that seamen of this man's rating sometimes carried in those days to light their pipes. He roasted the crabs artfully, as one who has served an apprenticeship to hardship, and having eaten, he drank again, and then folded his arms to consider what he should do.

He knew that the island was one of the Bahama Cays, though which he could not imagine. But other islands were in sight. He guessed that New Providence was not out of reach of his boat, nor was the Florida coast remote, and then there was all the traffic of the Gulf of Mexico. He determined, whilst he reflected, to cook plenty of crabs and to seek for turtle, and so store himself with provisions. But how about watering his little craft? Fresh water, cold and sweet, there was in plenty, but he had nothing to put it in, and what could he contrive or invent to serve as a breaker? He thought to himself, if he could find cocoanuts he would let the milk drain, and fill the fruit with water, and so carry away enough to last him until he should be picked up or make a port.

He cast his eyes up aloft with a fancy of beholding in the trees something growing that would answer his purpose, and started, still looking and staring, as though fascinated or lightning-struck.

His eye had sought a tree whose long lower branches overshadowed the little stream, and amidst the foliage he thought he saw the figure of a man! The shape jockeyed a bough; its back was upon the tree; and now, straining his vision steadily under the sharp of his hand, the man saw that it was the skeleton of a human being, apparently lashed or secured to the bough, and completely clothed, from the sugar-loaf hat upon his skull down to the rusty yellow sea-boots which dangled amidst the leaves.

The sailor was alone, and the ghastly sight shocked him; the sense of his loneliness was intensified by it; he thought he had been cast away upon the principality of death himself. The diabolic grin in the tree froze the blood in his veins, and for awhile he could do no more than stare and mutter fragments of the Lord's Prayer.

He guessed from the costume that the figure had been lodged for a great number of years in that tree. He recollected that when he was a boy he had seen foreign seamen dressed as that skeleton up there was. It was now late in the afternoon, and with a shuddering glance aloft he began to consider how and where he should sleep. He walked out of the wood and gained the highest point of the little central hill, and looked about him for a sail. There was nothing in sight, saving the dim shadows of land red in the ether of sunset. The skeleton, as though it had been a devil, took possession of the castaway's soul. He could think of nothing else— not even of how he was to get away, how he was to store fresh water for his voyage. He did not mean to sleep in a tree: but the leaves provided a roof as sheltering as an awning, and he determined to lie down in the wood, and take his chance of snakes. Yet, before he could rest, he must have the skeleton out of it: the shadows would be frightful with the fancy of that figure above riding the bough and rattling its bones to every sigh of wind.

So with a resolved heart made desperate by superstition and fear, the sailor walked to the wood, and coming to the tree, climbed it by the aid of the strong tendrils of parasites which lay coiled round the trunk stout and stiff as ropes. He bestrode a thick bough close to the skeleton. It was a ghastly sight in that green glimmering dusk, darkening swiftly with the sinking of the sun. The flesh of the face was gone; the cloak hanging from the shoulders was lean, dusty, ragged as any twelfth-century banner drooping motionless in the gloom of a cathedral. The sailor saw that time and weather had rotted everything saving the bone of the thing. It was secured to the bough by what was, or had been, a scarf, as though the man had feared to fall in his sleep. The seaman stretched forth his hand, and to the first touch the scarf parted as though it had been formed of smoke; the figure reeled, dropped, and went to pieces at the foot of the tree.

The sailor had not expected this. He was almost afraid to

descend. When he reached the ground he fled towards his boat, and lay in her all night.

He went for a drink of water at daybreak, and passing the scattered remains of the skeleton—with some degree of heart, for daylight brought courage, and a few hours of sleep had given him confidence—he spied something glittering amongst the rags of the skeleton's apparel. He picked it up. It was a silver snuffbox. He opened it, and inside found a piece of paper folded to the shape of the box. It was covered with a scrawl in pencil, faint, yet decipherable. To the man it would have been all one, whether the writing had been Chinese or English; he could not read. But he was a wary and cunning old sailor; every instinct of perception and suspicion was set a-crawling by the sight of this queer faintly pencilled document, and by the look of the silver snuff-box which weighed very handsomely in his horny palm, yellow with tar. He pocketed the toy, and having refreshed himself with a drink of water, returned to the fragments of wearing apparel and old bones, no longer afraid, and with the handle of his hammer turned the stuff over, and in the course of a few minutes met with and pocketed the following articles: a stump of common lead pencil, three pieces of silver Spanish money, a clay pipe mounted in silver in the bone of an albatross's wing, a silver watch and hair guard, and a small gold cross.

He talked to himself with a composed countenance as he examined these trifles; then, having hunted after more relics to no purpose, he turned his back upon the bones and rags, and went about the business of the day.

During the morning he collected many crabs, but all the while he could not imagine how he was to carry away a store of water, till, chancing to look along the brilliant curve of beach, he spied a turtle of about three hundred pounds coming out of the sea, and then he made up his mind to turn a turtle over after dark, and cut its throat, and make a tub of the shell.

Happily for this castaway he was spared the distress of passing another night upon the island. Two or three hours before sundown, a steady breeze then blowing from the north, a large schooner suddenly rounded the western point of the island at the distance of a couple of miles, heading east, and steering so as to keep the island fair abeam. The man had collected plenty of brushwood to roast his crabs with; he swiftly kindled a fire, and made a smoke with damp leaves, and whilst this signal was feathering down the wind, he launched and jumped into his boat, and, with the nimble experienced hands of the seaman, crossed his oars and set his sail of shirt and coat, and slowly blew away right before the wind towards the schooner. She saw the smoke and then the boat, and hove to, and in three-quarters of an hour the man was aboard.

"Who are you?" said the master of the schooner, when the man stood upon the deck.

"Christian Hawke, carpenter of the *Morning Star*," he answered.

"What's become of your ship?" said the other.

"Don't know," answered Hawke.

"What's your yarn?"

"Why," answered Hawke, speaking in a hoarse level growling voice, "we was becalmed, and the captain told me to get into a boat and nail a piece of copper, which had worked loose, on the rudder. We was flying-light."

"Where from?" said the captain suspiciously.

"From New Orleans to Havannah, for orders."

"Well?" said the captain.

"Well," continued Hawke, "I was hammering away all right, and doing my bit, when a squall came along, and the ship, with a kick-up of her stern, let go the painter of her own accord and bolted into the thickness; 'twas like muck when that squall bursted, with me a-hollering; I lost sight of the vessel, and should have been a dead man if it hadn't been for that there island." After a pause: "What island is it, sir?" he asked.

"An island fifteen mile east of Rum Cay," answered the captain. Hawke had got it into his head that the paper in the snuff-box was the record of a treasure secret, but he was afraid to exhibit it and ask questions. He did not know in what language it was written, whether, in fact, it might not be in good English, and he thought if he showed the paper and it proved a confession of money-burial, or something of that sort, the man who read it, knowing where the island was, would forestall him.

On the arrival of the schooner at Kingston, Jamaica, Christian Hawke went ashore. He was without money or clothes, and at once sold the skeleton's watch and hair guard, for which he received thirty dollars, The purchaser of the watch looked at Hawke curiously across the counter after paying down the money, and said—

"Vere did you get this?"

"It's a family heirloom," answered Hawke, pointing to the watchguard with a singular grin.

"This here vatch," said Mr. Solomons, "is a hundred years old, and a vast curiosity in her vurks. Have you more of this sort of thing to sell? If so, I was the most liberal dealer of any man in Jamaica."

Hawke gave him a nod and walked out. He found a ship next morning and signed articles as carpenter and second mate. She was sailing for England in a week from that date, and was a plump, old-fashioned barque of four hundred tons. At the sailor's lodging-house he had put up at, he fell into conversation one evening, a day or two before he sailed, with a dark, black-eyed, handsome, intelligent foreign sea-man, who called himself simply Pedro. This fellow did not scruple to hint at experiences gained both as a contrabandist and piccaroon.

"D'ye speak many languages?" said Hawke, puffing at a long clay pipe, and casting his grave, slow-moving little eyes upon a tumbler of amber rum at his elbow.

"I can speak three or four languages," said the foreign seaman. Hawke surveyed him thoughtfully and then, putting down his pipe, thrust his hand in his pocket, and extracted the paper from the snuff-box without exposing the box.

"What language is this wrote in?" said he, handing the paper to his companion. The man looked at it, frowning with the severity of his gaze, so dim was the pencil scrawl, so queer the characters, as though the handwriting were the march of a spider's legs over the page. He then exclaimed suddenly, "Yes, I have it. It is my own language. It is Spanish."

"Ha!" exclaimed Hawke, "and what's it all about, mate?"

"How did you come by it?" said the man.

"Found it in an old French Testament," answered Hawke. The man glanced at him, and then fixed his eyes upon the paper and began to read. He read very slowly, with difficulty deciphering the Spanish, and with greater difficulty interpreting it. The two men were alone. The foreign seaman made out the writing to signify this:

"I who write am Lois do Argensola, that was second in command of the *Gil Polo*, commanded by Leonardo de Leon. In a terrible hurricane the ship that was bound from the Havannah to old Spain was lost. I escaped in a boat with Dona Mariana do Mesa and two seamen; both men went mad, and cast themselves overboard in the night. The Dona Mariana was my cousin. She was following her husband to Madrid. He had preceded her by two months. She had many valuable jewels, the gift of her husband, and some had been for many centuries in possession of her own family, who were nobles of Spain. Before the ship foundered the Dona urged me to save these jewels, which were in a box in her cabin. I found the box and threw it into the boat, and shortly afterwards the ship went down.

"After five days of anguish we arrived at a little island, and twenty-four hours afterwards the Dona Mariana expired. I had no spade to dig a grave, and placed her body in a cave on the left hand side of a little bay opposite the wood or grove where the fresh water stream begins. I have now been here six weeks, and have beheld no ship, and am without hope and feel as a dying man. Oh, stranger, who shall discover this my writing, to your honor as a man and to your charity as a Christian do I appeal. My own bones may rest in the place where I die—I care not, but I entreat that the remains of the Dona Mariana may be enclosed in a box, and carefully conveyed for interment to her relatives at Madrid, and that this may prove no profitless duty to him who undertakes it, behold! in the foot of the tree I am accustomed to climb at night, that I may sleep free from the sting of the scorpion you shall find a hole. There, within easy reach of your hand lies the box of jewels. This box and the remains of Dona Mariana I entreat of your Christian charity to convey to Alonzo Reyes, Villagarcia. Spain, and I pledge the honor of a Spaniard that one half the value of the jewels shall be given to you.—LUIS DE AR-GENSOLA. July, 1840."

"That's twenty years ago," said Hawke, sucking at his pipe.

"What'll you take for the secret?" said his companion.

"If I can find someone to help you to recover those jewels, what share will you give me!" Hawke pocketed the paper with a sour smile and went out of the room.

His ship sailed and all went well with her. On his arrival in England, as soon as he had taken up his wages and purchased a suit of clothes, he went down to Ramsgate where, in a little off street not far from the entrance to the pier, dwelt his brother Reuben. This man was by trade a boat-builder. He also owned some bathing-machines. The brothers had not met for some years, nor had they heard from or of each other since they were last together. Yet when Christian, after beating with a little brass knocker upon a little green door, turned the handle and entered straight into a dwelling-room, his brother Reuben, who sat at tea with his wife, two girls, and his wife's grandfather, exhibited no surprise. Their greeting was simply, "Hallo, Christian!"

"Well, Rube!"

Christian sat down and partook of tea with the family, and related his adventures to the great entertainment of the grandfather, who laughed till his cheeks were wet at all the pathetic parts—such as Hawke's description of his thirst and his feelings of loneliness when upon the ocean and when lying in the boat at the island. The women cleared away the tea-things and went out; the old grandfather fell asleep; then said Christian to his brother—

"Rube, I'm down here to have an airnest chat along with yer."

"So I guessed," said Reuben, who resembled his brother in face, manner, and tone of voice.

"Still got that cutter o' yourn?"

"D'yer mean the *Petrel?*"

"Yes,"

"She's a-lying in the west gully. She airnt me some good money last year as a pleasure-boat. I've been thinking of sending her out a-fishing."

"What's her tonnage?"

"Eighteen. Want to buy her, Christian?

"Not I. Suppose you and me goes down and takes a look at her." Reuben put on his coat and cap, and the brothers issued forth. Two square figures, the shoregoer rolling in his gait like the sea-farer, as though in fact, he was as fresh from the heave of the sea as the other. They walked along the pier till they came abreast of a stout little cutter lying at her moorings in the thick of a fleet of smacks hailing from Gravelines, Penzance, and other places. Christian viewed her in silence with the critical eye of an old sailor and a ship's carpenter to boot.

"How old's she, Rube?"

"Nine year."

"She'll do," said Christian. "Rube, I'm going to spin yer a yarn." They went leisurely along the pier, and as they walked Christian told his brother about the skeleton in the tree and the document in Spanish which he had found in the dead man's snuff-box. He produced the snuff-box and the paper, also the clay pipe mounted in the bone of an albatross's wing, and the small gold cross. Reuben listened with an eye bright and keen with interest and conviction. The mere sight of the silver box was as convincing to his mind as though he had been carried to the island, and stood looking at Argensola's bones and the hole in the tree in which the box of jewels lay hid.

That night the two brothers sat up late, deep in discourse. Christian put ten pounds upon the table.

"That's all I own in the world," said he. "It'll help to victual the boat."

"We shall want a navigator," said Reuben. "I'm rather ignorant myself of that art, and I don't suppose you've learnt yourself to read yet, ha' ye, Christian? There's young Bob Maxted knows all about shooting of the sun. Us two and him'll be hands enough. Shall we make shares?"

"No," said Christian; "you and me divides. T'other'll come along on wages."

"There's no doubt about the situation of the island, I suppose?" said Reuben. "No."

"Let's look at that there Spanish writing again."

Christian produced the snuff-box and Reuben opened the paper.

"Are you cocksure," said Reuben, fastening his eyes upon the dim scrawl, "that that there Pedro, as you call him, gave you the right meaning of this writing?"

"Yes; and there was my own ixpurrience to back his varsion."

"I'm rather for having it made into English again, Christian," said Reuben, thoughtfully. "Young Jones down at Consul Hammond's office speaks Spanish. What d'yer say?"

"No; I'm not a-going to trust any man but yourself with the secret. See here: if we come back rich—as'll follow—and you've bin meanwhile and shown that there paper to someone who understands it, what'll be thought? The gaff'll be blowed; the relatives of that there Mary Ann'll be getting wind of our haul, and'll come upon us for the jewels."

This and the like reasoning satisfied Reuben, who presently returned the paper to Christian, and, after drinking a final glass of grog, the two brothers went to bed.

Next day, and for some days afterwards, they were full of business. Young Maxted was willing to sail with them; they gave out vaguely that they were bound to the West Indies, partly on pleasure, partly on business. The true character of their errand was not revealed to Maxted, who had agreed for six pounds a month to navigate the little ship into the West Indian seas and back again. Reuben drew all his savings from the bank; twenty pounds and Christian's ten pounds formed their capital. They provisioned themselves with fore-castle fare, adding some bottled beer and a few gallons of rum, and on a fine morning at daybreak, when Ramsgate still slumbered, and the hush of the night yet brooded over the harbor, the three men hoisted their mainsail and jib, and blew softly down the gulley and round the head of the pier into the English Channel, which was by this time white with the risen sun, and beautiful in the south-west, where a hundred ships that had lain wind-bound in the Downs were flashing into canvas, and moving like a cloud before the light easterly breeze.

All went well down-Channel with the little craft. She was a stout and buoyant sea boat, with a dominant sheer of bow, coppered to the bends like a revenue cutter, and uncommonly stout of scantling for a vessel of her class. She was in good trim, and she plunged along stoutly, making fine weather of some ugly seas which ridged to her bow as she drove aslant through the Bay. By this time young Maxted had been made acquainted with the cutter's destination, and was steering a course for the little island. He plied his sextant nimbly, and clearly understood his business. The brothers represented to him that the object of their voyage was to recover some treasure which had been washed ashore out of a small Spanish plate ship and buried.

"We ain't sure," Christian Hawke told him. "that the island we're bound to is the island where the wreck took place. But the herrant's worth the cost and the time, and we mean to have a look round, anyhow."

Maxted was silent; perhaps with the proverbial heedlessness of the sailor he was satisfied to take things as they happened. The actual motive of the voyage could be of no interest to him. All that he had to do was to steer the little ship to an island and receive so many sovereigns in wages on their return.

They made a swift run for so small a keel; in fact, the island was in sight at the grey of dawn thirty-three days after the start from Ramsgate. Christian Hawke with a telescope at his eye quickly recognized the central hill, the soft, cloudlike mass of green shadow made by the wood or grove on the right, and the slope of the green land to the ivory dazzle of sand vanishing in the foam of the charging comber. He warmly commended Maxted's navigation, and both brothers stared with flushed faces and nostrils wide with expectation at the beautiful little cay that lay floating like a jewel full of gleams upon the calm blue brine right ahead.

They hove-to and rounded at about a mile from the land, and then let go their anchor in sixteen fathoms of water.

They next launched their little fat jolly-boat smack-fashion through the gangway, and Christian and Reuben entered her and pulled away for the land, leaving Maxted in charge of the cutter; but little vigilance was needed in such weather as that; the sea was flat, and bare, and as brilliant as the sky; under the sun the water trembled in a glory of diamonds to the delicate brushing of a hot, light breeze. Nothing broke the silence upon the deep save the low, organlike music of the surf beating on the western and northern boards of the island.

Whilst Christian pulled, Reuben steering the boat with an oar, he talked of his sufferings when in these parts, how his jaws had been fixed in a horrid gape by thirst, and of the terror that had besieged him when he looked up into the trees and beheld the skeleton. They made direct for the little creek into which Christian had driven his boat, and where he had slept on that first and only night he had passed on the island; and when her forefoot grounded they sprang out and hauled the boat high and dry, and then with hearts loud in their ears and restless eyes, directed their steps towards the little wood. Christian glanced wildly about him, imagining that in everything his sight went to, he beheld a token of the island having been recently visited.

"How long'll it be since you was here, Christian?" rumbled Reuben, in a note subdued by expectation and other passions.

"Five month," answered Christian, hoarsely.

They walked to the margin of the little wood, and arrived at the source of the stream that ran glittering and straying like pearls amidst the tall sweet green grass that grew in the bed of it. Reuben grasped Christian by the arm.

"What's that?" he cried.

It was a human skull, and close beside it were the complete bones of a human skeleton, together with a little heap of rags. It looked as though the stuff had been raked together for removal and forgotten.

"That wasn't how they was left," exclaimed Christian, coming to a halt and looking at the bones and rags. "There's been a hand arter me here in that job."

"A boat's crew may ha' landed and shovelled the stuff together out of a sort o' respect for the remains of something that might have been a sailor," exclaimed Reuben. "Where's the tree with the hole in it?"

Christian walked to the place where he had been seated when his eye went to the skeleton aloft. "That'll be the tree," said he.

It was a large tree, the trunk of the bigness of an English chestnut, but dwarfed in altitude; its beauty was in the spread and curve of its branches. In the hinder part of the trunk—speaking with regard to its bearings from the source of the stream—about five feet above the ground was a large hole, partly concealed by the festooning drapery of the leaves of a rich and vigorous parasite, which soared in coils to the summit of the tree. Christian put his hand in.

"Stand by for snakes!" shouted Reuben.

The other drew out a little common brass tobacco-box. "What's here?" cried he.

"Try for the jewel box!" exclaimed Reuben. Christian entered his hand again and felt round.

"There's nothen more here," said he.

"Has it fallen to the bottom?"

"There ain't no hole for it to fall through," cried Christian, still feeling. "It's tight as a locker." He looked at the common little brass tobacco-box, then opened it, and found inside a slip of paper, folded to the shape of the box, as though in imitation of the snuff-box document in Christian's possession. The handwriting was a bold scrawl in ink. With a trembling hand and ashen face the poor fellow presented the paper to his brother, who, putting on his glasses, read aloud as follows—

"I would have been glad to take a small share to help you to find the jewels, but you would not put a little money in my way, though by interpreting Luis de Argensola's dying request in writing I was the instrument of your discovering that there lay a treasure to your hand. I therefore arranged with another to seek for the jewels: the situation being exactly known to me, because of your ignorance of the Spanish language, and perhaps of the art of reading, for at the end of the document, in three lines which it did not suit my purpose to interpret to you, Don Luis states how the island bears—that, in short, it is between ten and fifteen miles east of Rum Cay.

My friend, I have found the jewels, and thank you for a fortune. They consist of pearl and diamond necklaces, brooches, bracelets, earrings, smelling-bottles, rings, and diamond ornaments for the hair. I should say they will not fetch less than £10,000.—Your amigo of Kingston, PEDRO.

"I have left the skeletons to your pious care to coffin and carry to the representatives at Villagarcia. You will find the remains of the Lady Mariana de Mesa in a cave on the west side of the island."

The two men burst into a storm of oaths, and the little wood rang with forecastle and 'longshore imprecations. When they had exhausted their passions they knelt and drank from the spring of water, then walked to the boat, launched her, and returned to the cutter.

They arrived in England safely in due course, but some time later Reuben was obliged to compound with his creditors. Christian Hawke died in 1868 on board ship, still a carpenter.

THE TRANSPORT *PALESTINE*

In the spring of 1853 the hired transport *Palestine,* which had been fitting out at Deptford for the reception of a number of convicts, was reported to the Admiralty as ready for sea.

The burden of the *Palestine* was 680 tons, and the number of felons she had been equipped to accommodate in her 'tween-decks was 120. My name is John Barker, and I was second mate of that ship. The commander was Captain Wickham, and her chief officer Joseph Barlow. The *Palestine* was an old-fashioned craft, scarcely fit for the work she had been hired for. Official selection, however, was probably influenced by the owners' low tender. Good stout ships got £4 7s. 6d. a ton; I believe the *Palestine* was hired for £3 15s.

A guard from Chatham came aboard whilst we were at Deptford, consisting of a sergeant and ten privates, under the command of Captain Gordon and Lieutenant Venables. Shortly afterwards Dr. Saunders, R. N., who was going out as surgeon in charge of the convicts, took up his quarters in the cuddy. On the day following the arrival of the doctor and the guard, we received instructions to proceed to Woolwich and moor alongside that well-known prison-hulk H. M. S. *Warrior.* It was a gloomy, melancholy day; the air was full of dark vapor, and the broad, grey stream of the river ran with a gleam of grease betwixt the grimy shores. A chill wind blew softly, and vessels of all sorts, to the weak impulse of their wings of brown or pallid canvas, dulled by the thickness, sneaked soundlessly by on keels which seemed to ooze through a breast of soup.

I had often looked at the old *Warrior* in my coming and going, but never had I thought her so grimy and desolate as on this day. A pennant blew languidly from a pole-mast amidships; she was heaped up forward into absolute hideousness by box-shaped structures. Some traces of her old grandeur were visible in a faded bravery of gilt and carving about her quarters and huge square of stern, where the windows of the officials' cabins glimmered with something of brightness over the sluggish tremble of wake which the stream ran to a scope of a dozen fathoms astern of her rudder. All was silent aboard her. I looked along the rows of heavily grated ports which long ago had grinned with artillery, and observed no signs of life. Indeed, at the time when we moored alongside, most of the criminals were ashore at their forced labor, and those who remained in the ship were caverned deep out of sight hard at work at benches, lasts, and the like in the gloomy bowels of the old giantess.

The *Palestine* sat like a long-boat beside that towering fabric of prison hulk. We were no beauty, as I have said, and the little vessel's decks were now rendered distressingly unsightly by strong barricades, one forward of the foremast, leaving a space betwixt it and the front of the topgallant forecastle, and the other a little abaft the mainmast, so as to admit of some area of quarter-deck between it and the cabin front. Each barricade was furnished with a gate; the main-hatch was fortified by oak stanchions thick studded with iron nails, the foot of them secured to the lower deck. This timber arrangement resembled a cage with a narrow door, through which one man only could pass at a time. The main-hatch was further protected by a cover resembling a huge, roofless sentry-box. To this were attached planks of heavy scantling, forming a passage which went about ten feet forward; there was a door at the end of this passage, always guarded by a sentry with loaded musket and fixed bayonet.

The convicts came aboard at nine o'clock in the morning following the day of our arrival alongside the hulk. We were to receive our whole draught of 120 at once from the *Warrior,* and then proceed. I stood in the waist and watched the prisoners come over the side. It was an old-world picture, and the like of it will never again be seen. The day was as sullen as that which had gone before; the tall spars and black lines of rigging of our ship glistened with dripping moisture. A guard of six soldiers were drawn up along the front of the poop commanding the quarter-deck; each bayonet soared above the motionless shoulder like a thin blue flame. Captain Gordon and Lieutenant Venables stood near the men; at the break of the poop, grasping the brass rail, Dr. Saunders, scrutinizing the convicts with a severe, almost scowling face as they arrived.

The unhappy wretches were heavily fettered, and the long chains attached to the leg-irons clanked with a strange effect upon the hearing as the heavy tread of the many feet awoke a low thunder in the hollow deck. They were marched directly to their quarters in the 'tweendecks. I observed their faces as they passed through the hatch, and was struck by a general expression of light-heartedness, as though they were over-joyed at getting away from the horrors of the prison hulk and the spirit-breaking labor ashore, with a bright chance of for-tune in the sunny lands beyond the seas to which the ship was bound.

And certainly the convict in those days was out and away more tenderly dealt with than were the greater mass of the poor, honest emigrants. They were well clothed and better fed than the sailors in the forecastle; those who were ignorant were taught to read and write; they were prayed for and elo-quently admonished, and their health was rendered a matter of sincere concern to both the skipper and the doctor in charge. I recollect that the felons in our ship were dressed in coarse grey jackets and trousers, red stripes in the cloth, Scotch caps, and grey stockings and the ship's number of the criminal was painted on a square yellow ground on the arm and back.

On the afternoon of the day of embarkation a tug took us in tow, and we went away down the river on a straight course for Dungeness, where the steamer cast us adrift. Until we were clear of soundings I saw little of the convicts. We met with very heavy weather, and most of the prisoners lay as sea-sick as young ladies in their gloomy quarters. I had occasion once in this time to enter the barracks, as the soldiers' bulk-headed compartments were called, where I got a sight of the convicts in their 'tween-decks. The soldiers slept under the booby-hatch in cabins rudely knocked up for their accom-modation. Their quarters were divided from the prison by an immensely strong barricade bristling with triangular-headed nails, and loopholed for muskets, so that, in the event of a disturbance, the soldiers could fire upon the convicts within without passing the barricade. There was a strong door on the starboard side of this barricade, at which a sentinel with a loaded weapon was posted day and night.

I forget the occasion of my going below. It was blowing strong, and a high sea was running, the ship was laboring heavily, and the straining and groaning of the bulkheads and temporary fastenings were so distracting that I could easily believe the convicts supposed the ship was going to pieces. I put my eye to a loophole in the barricade and saw the picture. Sleeping-shelves for the reception of six men in a row ran the length of the 'tween-decks on either hand in two tiers. There was a suffusion of pale light round about the main-hatch, but it was like a sulky, thunderous twilight elsewhere, in the midst of which the shapes of the prisoners moved or lay motionless as though they were phantoms beheld in a dream, tragically colored by storm, by the cannonlike roar of hurling seas, and the wild springs and dives of a ship in angry waters. That scene of 'tween-decks is the most memorable of my life's impressions but I have no words to communicate it. It was not so much the details of the picture itself—the pale light under the hatch, the spiritlike figures of the felons, the lines of glimmering bunks, the bulging bulkheads of the hospital in the gloomy corner right forward; it was the deep human meaning that I found in it—the fancy of the sins, and the conscience, and the memories, the burning hopes, the biting griefs which made up the human life contained in that shadowy timber sea-tossed jail; this it was that gave to the scene its marvellous impressive significance.

Many of the prisoners were under life sentences; some were being exiled for fourteen, and some for terms of seven years. Never a man of them all would probably see England again. Indeed, it used to be said that not one in every hundred transported convicts returned to his native country.

When we got out of the Channel we met with quiet weather. The prisoners, heavily ironed, were brought up to help to do the ship's work and take exercise. They were but to assist the seamen in washing the decks down. They were also set to various jobs calculated to prove useful to themselves. It was a strange sight to a sailor's eye to see the convicts in their barricaded enclosure scrubbing with brushes at the planks, their chains clanking as they toiled, the burly boatswain of the ship bawling at the top of his pipes as he swished the water along, warders (themselves picked convicts) roaring commands to their fellow-prisoners; you saw the red coat of a sentry, the gleam of his bayonet on the forecastle; such another sentry clasped his musket at the main-hatch, and a third stood at the gate of the quarter-deck barricade. Overhead swelled the white sails, lifting to the milky softness of topgallant-sail and royal; the blue sea flashed in silver glory under the newly risen sun; smoke blew briskly away from the chimneys of the convicts and the ship's cabooses; you saw the cook leaning out of his galley door watching the scrubbing convicts: aft, on the sand-white stretch of poop, the captain and the surgeon in charge of the prisoners would be walking, whilst the mate of the watch, with one arm circling a backstay, might be standing at the poop-rail talking to Captain Gordon or the subaltern, answering questions about the ship, the names of sails, her rate of progress, or with long out-stretched arm pointing into the dark blue far recess to some growing star of canvas, or to some blackening fibrelike line of steamer's smoke.

It was not until we had closed the Madeira parallels, where the weather was hot and the azure slope of billow winked with the leaps of flying-fish, that the doctor gave orders for the convicts' irons to be removed. The whole of the prisoners were massed on deck and harangued by him before they were freed. Dr. Saunders had a stern face; he was a dark-skinned, smooth-shaven man, with heavy eyebrows and a lowering look, and I thought him a bully until I had sat a few times at the table when he was present, and exchanged a few sentences with him on deck, and then I guessed he was belied by his expression of feature and was a good man at root, kind, and even warm-hearted, though sternly masked for professional and penitentiary purposes. He addressed the mass of upturned faces on the quarter-deck, sermonized them indeed, assured them that it grieved him as much to hear the clank of their chains as the wearing of the irons oppressed and degraded them. He begged them to live on good terms with one another, to guard against evil language, to love God and keep His Word, and so to resolve as to assure themselves in the time coming, in a new land, in the day of their enlargement, of an honorable and prosperous future.

Some listened doggedly, some as though they would like to laugh out, some with a little play of emotion in their faces. They then went below, and their irons were taken off.

Until we reached the latitude of (call it) 5° N. all went as things should with us. The convicts were orderly and seemed well under the control of the doctor. Every day schools were held above or between decks; addresses on all sorts of topics were delivered to the prisoners by the doctor; Divine service was celebrated three times on Sundays; you'd sometimes hear the fellows down the hatchways singing psalms of their own accord. The doctor once at table with a well-pleased countenance told the captain that one of the worst of the many ruffians who were being lagged was now become the most penitent of all the prisoners.

"He talked to me about his past," Dr. Saunders said, "with the tears in his eyes, and in a voice broken by grief. I have great hopes of the poor fellow. Time was, and not long ago, when I looked upon him as a Norfolk Islander: I should never be surprised to hear that he was favored when out in the colony and was doing exceedingly well."

"Is it the square powerfully-built man, pitted with smallpox, with little black eyes, and a coal-black crop of hair?" asked Captain Gordon.

The doctor inclined his head.

"His name's Simon Rolt," said Lieutenant Venables. "I was in town at the time of his trial, and, having plenty of leisure, went one day down to the Old Bailey. He was convicted—"

Dr. Saunders lifted his hand with an expressive look. Indeed, it was never his wish that the prisoners should be named, and he was deaf to all inquiries concerning the crimes for which they were being transported.

Well, we had been driven by prosperous winds to the parallel of 5° N. Here the breeze failed. It was the zone of equatorial calms, where the dim, hot, blue water fades out into a near silver faintness of sky, and where the lofty white canvas of the stagnated ship melts into the azure brine under her, like quicksilver cloudily draining through the keel. For the past week the heat had been fierce; but always had there been a breeze to fill the windsails and render the roasting atmosphere of the 'tweendecks endurable. But now, when the wind was gone, the temperature was scarcely to be supported, even by the most seasoned of our lobscousers. The pitch lay like butter in the seams of the planks; the wheel, flaming its brass-clad circle to the small high sun, turned red-hot in the grip of the helmsman; the tar came off the rigging in strings upon the fingers like treacle, and the hush of the heat lay upon the plain of ocean as the silence of the white desert dwells upon its leagues of dazzling sand.

I had charge of the ship during the second dog-watch, that is, from six to eight. Some little time after sundown, and when the sky over our mastheads was full of large, dim, trembling stars, whilst the sea floated from alongside in a breast of ink into the obscurity of the horizon, Dr. Saunders approached Captain Gordon, who was talking to the commander of the ship close to where I stood, and exclaimed—

"The heat is too much for the people below. A hundred and twenty souls in those low-pitched contracted 'tween-decks: the sufferings of slaves in the Middle Passage can't be worse."

"What's to be done, sir?" said Captain Wickham. "The wind don't come to the mariner's whistle in these times."

"We must have detachments of them on deck," said Dr. Saunders. "We must let a third of them at a time breathe the open air and relieve the demands upon the atmosphere below. It may be done," he added, with perhaps the least hint of doubtfulness in his manner.

Captain Wickham did not speak.

"It ought to be done," said Lieutenant Venables, crossing the deck out of the shadow to port with a lighted cigar in his mouth. "It's hell, Gordon, in the barracks."

"You'll want the guard to fall in, doctor?" said Captain Gordon.

"Oh yes, if you please."

The necessary orders were given; five or six soldiers mounted the poop ladder, and ranged themselves along the break, the muskets loaded and the bayonets fixed as usual. The doctor left the deck, and in some ten minutes' time a file of shadowy figures wound, serpentlike, past the main-hatch sentry into the barricaded inclosure. They broke into little companies, and all were as still as the dead; but I could *feel* in their postures, in their manner of grouping themselves, the exquisite relief and delight they found in drinking in the moist night air.

This detachment remained an hour on deck. When they went below, and the next lot came up, the time was half-past eight. I had been relieved at eight bells by the chief officer; but the heat in the cabin was so great that after I had stayed a few minutes in my berth I filled a pipe and went on to the quarter-deck, where I stood smoking in the recess under the poop. The quarter-deck barricade was about six feet tall, and the figures of the convicts behind it were not to be seen where I stood. Nothing was visible but the stars over either bulwark-rail, and the festooned cloths of the main course on high, and the dim square of the becalmed topsail above it floating up and fading in the darkness of the night.

All on a sudden an odd, low whistle sounded forward or aft—I can't tell where; an instant later the figure of a convict sprang on to the top of the starboard bulwarks, where, poising himself whilst you might have counted ten, he shrieked aloud, "O God, have mercy upon me! O Christ, have mercy upon me!" and went overboard.

Silence lasting a moment or two followed the splash; the hush of amazement and horror was broken by loud cries from the convicts, sharp orders delivered over my head in the voice of Captain Gordon, followed by the tramp of the soldiers striding quick to the break of the poop clearly to command the people within the barricades with their muskets. I heard Mr. Barlow, the mate, roar to the man at the wheel, "Do you see anything of him there?" And Captain Wickham shouted once or twice, "Man overboard! Aft, some hands, and clear away the starboard quarter-boat." Meanwhile I had observed the form of Dr. Saunders rush down the poop ladder and run headlong past the sentry into the barricaded enclosure, where now at this time his stern, clear voice rang out strong as he ordered the convicts to fall in and return to their quarters.

I sprang to the side to look for the man that was gone, but saw nothing. The sea was like black slush: there was scarce an undulation in it to flap the softest echo out of the lightest canvas. I saw no fire in the water. Something was wrong with the quarter-boat. They were a long time bungling with the falls, and I heard the voice of an enraged seaman harshly yell, "Who the blooming blazes has bin and stepped 'em in this fashion!"

"Jump for the port boat, men! jump for the port boat!" shouted Mr. Barlow. "The man'll have sounded the bottom whilst you're messing about with those tackles."

I ran on to the poop to lend a hand. The captain, quickly making me out, told me to get into the boat and take charge. We were lowered, and rowed away round the vessel under her counter to look for the man to starboard, from which side he had jumped. The oars as they dipped made no fire in the water. We headed for the spot whence the convict had sprung, and then worked our way along the bends and afterwards went a few strokes astern, and then rowed round to port, conceiving that the poor devil might have risen on t'other side the ship.

"Do you see anything of him?" shouted Captain Wickham. "Nothing, sir."

"Hook on! He's gone—there's no more to be done," called down the captain. We had spent half an hour in the hunt and the man was undoubtedly drowned. Who was the convict that had destroyed himself? After I had regained the ship, and whilst I was ordering one of the boat's crew to go aft and coil away the end of the starboard main-brace, which I had noticed hanging over the side, the doctor arrived on the poop, walking slowly. The guard was by this time dismissed: all was silent and motionless on the main-deck betwixt the barricades; the only figures down there were the main-deck and quarter-deck sentries; but there was much stir forward upon the forecastle, where the sailors were stepping from side to side, peering over the rail with some fancy, no doubt, of catching sight of the floating body of the drowned convict.

The doctor, Captain Wickham, Captain Gordon, and the subaltern came together in a group within easy earshot of where I stood.

"It's the man Simon Rolt," said the doctor. "I shall be blamed for allowing the convicts to come on deck after the regulation hours."

"Rolt! D'ye mean your religious enthusiast, doctor?" said Captain Gordon.

"Lucky he was the *only* one!" exclaimed the commander of the ship. "Suicide should be contagious in this heat amongst fellows primed with such memories as sweeten the sleep of your people."

"I would rather have lost five hundred pounds than that it should have happened," said Dr. Saunders.

"Do the prisoners take it quietly?" inquired Captain Gordon.

"As I could wish," answered the doctor. "They seemed awed and frightened." The conversation ran thus for awhile. The party then went below to drink some grog, and after finishing my pipe on the quarter-deck I turned in.

I was aroused at midnight to take charge of the ship. I walked the deck until four, and nothing whatever happened saving that at about five bells there suddenly blew a fresh little breeze out of the north-west gloom: it brightened the stars, and the night felt the cooler for the mere sound of foam alongside. This breeze was blowing when I left the deck, and we were then moving through the water at five knots.

At six o'clock I was awakened by the chief officer putting his hand upon my shoulder. The look in his face startled me, and instantly gave me my wits.

"Mr. Barker," said he, "the captain lies dead in his bunk. He's been strangled—garrotted somehow. Come along with me. Who in the devil's name done it?"

I sprang out of my bunk and clothed myself quickly. The morning had fully broken: it was another brilliant day and the wind gone, and my cabin porthole glowed in a disc of splendor against the sea under the sun. I followed the mate to the captain's cabin. The poor man lay with his face dark with strangulation: his features were convulsed and distorted, his eyes were starting from their sockets, and froth and blood were on his lips. Dr. Saunders stood beside the body: it seems that the mate had roused him before coming to me.

"Is he dead, sir?" inquired Mr. Barlow.

"Ay; he has been throttled in his sleep. This must be the work of one of your crew," said Dr. Saunders, speaking low and deliberately, and sending a professional glance under a frown full of thought and wonder at the corpse.

"Why one of the crew," cried Mr. Barlow, "in a shipload of convicts? With ten soldiers and a sergeant besides?"

"Convicts!" exclaimed the doctor. "You'll not wish me to believe, sir, that the guard is in collusion with the prisoners? And you'll have to prove *that* to persuade me this is the work of a convict."

Mr. Barlow retorted; whilst they argued the dreadful matter I looked about me, but witnessed nothing to speak to a struggle. Through the large open stern window the silver-blue sea was sheeting to the horizon, and the cabin was full of the light glowing upon the water. I was very well acquainted with the furniture of the captain's cabin, which was right aft on the starboard side; everything was in its place. The doctor exposed the throat of the body, and showed us certain livid marks, which he said signified that the captain had been killed through compression of the windpipe by a pair of giant-strong hands. Powerful indeed the murderer must have been to destroy so vigorous a frame as Captain Wickham's in silence, suffocating him as he lay, with never a sound to penetrate to the adjacent cabins where Gordon slept and Dr. Saunders and Lieutenant Venables.

I roused those officers; they viewed the body, and then the lot of us went into the cuddy, where we held a council. Dr. Saunders again asserted that the murder must have been done by one of the sailors—at all events by someone belonging to the ship. The mate would not hear of this. Yes, if there was nobody but the ship's company in the vessel, then indeed the murderer would have to be sought for in the forecastle.

Captain Gordon said that he knew his men; he'd stake his life upon their dutifulness and loyalty.

"If the murderer is one of my people," said Dr. Saunders, "he passed the sentry to enter the cuddy. How was *that* managed unless the sentry permitted him to pass?"

"The sentry might have been dozing," said I.

"No, sir," cried Lieutenant Venables, bringing his fist in a passion on the table; "you are a sailor, Mr. Barker; you don't know soldiers."

"Could the convict have returned to his quarters unobserved even supposing him to have slipped past a nodding sentry?"

"A preposterous conjecture!" exclaimed the doctor. "How would he know where the captain slept? The murderer is no convict, Gordon."

It was settled that the mate and I should overhaul the ship's company for evidence, whilst the doctor and the military officers made inquiries for themselves amongst the prisoners and soldiers. I followed the mate on deck. He called to the boatswain to pipe all hands. The whole of the crew assembled on the quarter-deck, and Mr. Barlow told them that Captain Wickham had been murdered. He added that the ship must be searched from end to end, and he called upon the crew to do their utmost to help me and the boatswain to ransack the forecastle for evidence.

"I have no fear of the result, my lads," he exclaimed. "If the doctor and military officers can clear the guard and prisoners so much the better; it is my duty as your acting commander to see *you* cleared also, anyhow, and smartly, too, if you'll help."

The men sung out to me to come forward at once; many were their exclamations charged with the heavy oaths of the forecastle; and as they rolled forwards I heard them swearing that if the convicts hadn't done it then the murderer was one of the *guffies* (soldiers).

Well, the boatswain and I thoroughly searched the forecastle, but it was a fool's quest after all; we hardly knew what to look for. The sailors heartily helped us, threw open their chests, pulled their hammocks to pieces, forced us to overhaul their persons, but what for? It was not as though literally blood had been shed. There was no knife with damning signs upon the handle and blade to seek for. The only weapon used had been the hands. Our search, then, forward was wholly profitless.

I was an hour in the forecastle, and when I went aft the doctor and officers were still hard at work questioning and hunting after evidence below. They came to Mr. Barlow presently, and told him that they were fully satisfied the murder had not been the work of a convict. As to any of the soldiers being concerned—Captain Gordon indignantly refused to discuss the subject, nay, to listen to a syllable from us mates on that head.

"Is there nobody missing forward amongst the crew?" the doctor asked.

"Nobody," answered Mr. Barlow. "And how does it stand with *your* people?"

"Every man jack can be accounted for, of course."

"Search the ship!" exclaimed Captain Gordon.

"For what?" rejoined the mate. "There's no man missing; we're seven weeks out; what do you expect, gentlemen, to find hidden below at this time of day?"

"I'm for searching the ship, nevertheless," said Captain Gordon. "Good God! when such a murder as this has been done, would you stop short just when discovery may be within reach of another stride?"

The mate, with some color in his cheek, answered, "The ship shall be searched." I headed one little gang and the boatswain another, and we thoroughly overhauled the hold from the fore to the after peak. The ship's lading consisted of agricultural implements and light Government commodities for the colony. Her after-hold was filled with provisions, barrels of flour, casks of rum, great cases of tinned meat, and other such things. A large portion of the steerage, too, under the cuddy was filled with Government stuff, mattresses, blankets, and so forth, not to mention three hundred sets of irons.

Our search occupied some time: there was much ground to cover. Perhaps we did not seek very strenuously. For my part, I never for a moment imagined that there would or could be anyone not belonging to the ship in hiding below. Suppose a stowaway: it would scarcely serve his purpose to make his first appearance on deck as a murderer, and the murderer of the captain of the ship of all men! And yet, though I felt quite certain that the criminal was not amongst our crew, I was equally sure he was not amongst the prisoners. One had but to reason a little to understand that it was not the work of a convict. Every night the 'tween-decks prison gate that gave upon the barracks was strongly secured. No convict could have made his way through it, and beside it was posted the sentry. Equally well secured and guarded was the main-hatch entrance. The murderer, then, was not a convict. Was he a soldier?

We buried the body of the captain that morning, and Mr. Barlow took command of the ship. When night came a sentry was posted at the cuddy door (this was in addition to the usual guard), and the sergeant received instructions to make the rounds of the cuddy from time to time to see that all was well. In this work he would be assisted by the mate of the watch and by the ship's boatswain, who would now serve as second mate.

The night passed quietly. From time to time Captain Gordon or Lieutenant Venables illustrated his restlessness by coming on deck and flitting about, calling to the cuddy-door sentry and asking me questions. This was during my watch, during the silent passages of which I deeply pondered the matter of the murder, but could make nothing of it. Had it been done by someone walking in his sleep? Someone of us who, utterly unconscious of his deed, had viewed the corpse of the strangled captain with horror and astonishment?

I turned in at four, leaving the ship in the hands of the boatswain, and when I came on deck at eight I found a fresh breeze blowing off the beam, a wide scene of dark blue sea running in lines of froth, and the bluff bows of the *Palestine* bursting in thunder through the surge and driving the foam before her beyond the flying-jibboom end. The brightness of the day, the beauty of the scene, the swift dance of the old hooker, put some heart into all of us who lived aft. Yet we could talk of nothing but the murder. I suggested somnambulism; the doctor listened to me with a dark smile, then walked away. Mr. Barlow said that sooner or later we should find out that one of the soldiers had done it. In the course of the day Captain Gordon and Dr. Saunders went below, where they stayed long, questioning closely. I was on deck at dinner-time, and heard Mr. Barlow warmly defending himself against the accusation of the two military men, who, as I gathered, had declared that he exhibited an indifference and seemed to fail in his duty by neglecting to push his investigations to further lengths in the forecastle. This talk made me feel very hot; but Mr. Barlow was well able to take care of himself, and wound up a highly-flavored protest against Captain Gordon's observations by asserting that his own suspicions strongly pointed to the soldiers.

Well, the precautions of the previous night were renewed on this; the cuddy door was guarded, and from time to time one or another made the rounds of the cabins. I had the morning watch, that is, from four till eight. The hour was about half-past six. The watch was busy in washing down the forecastle and foredeck, and a number of convicts were scrubbing at the planks in the prison enclosure. I stood at the brass rail watching a picture that was full of life and color. A light breeze followed us; the sea was a delicate blue, and rolled in flowing folds, and the sails sank like breathing beasts to the curtsying of the ship upon the swell. It was fiery hot, and the sunshine came tingling off its own reflections in the sea like clouds of flaming needles.

I turned, and found the ship's steward at my elbow. His face was as white as veal. I never could have imagined the countenance capable of such an expression of horror as his carried. His mouth was dry, and he mumbled, without articulation, and put out his hand, as though feeling for something in the air.

"Oh, sir!"

"What is it?"

"Dr. Saunders—"

"What of him? What of him?"

"Murdered, sir! His throat cut. God have mercy, it's a sight that's going to last me for ever!"

For some moments I stood motionless, idly and mechanically exclaiming, "Dr. Saunders murdered! Dr. Saunders murdered!" Then, calling to one of the best seamen in my watch, I bade him look after the ship whilst I ran below, and the steward followed me down the companion ladder. I went straight to the doctor's berth. It was next Captain Gordon's, on the starboard side. The steward, in his fright and flight, had left the door open, and I had no need to enter the berth to witness the dreadful spectacle.

"Murder!" suddenly screamed the steward at my elbow, in some hysteric paroxysm of horror. "Who's doing it? who's doing it?"

His loud cries awakened the sleepers round about; in a moment Captain Gordon, Lieutenant Venables, and Mr. Barlow rushed out of their cabins. The group of us entered the cabin of the slaughtered man and looked at the corpse, and then stood staring at one another. The head was half severed; under the bunk the cabin floor was black with blood; but, as in the case of the murder of the captain, so now—everything was in its place.

We went into the cuddy, closing the door upon the murdered man. It was scarcely to be realized that *he* had fallen a victim. One somehow felt the terror in it more strongly than in the assassination of the commander of the ship, although, to be sure, as captain, his had been out and away the more valuable life.

"Venables," cried Captain Gordon, "tell the sergeant to fall in the guard at once. Mr. Barlow—do not think I wish to dictate—will not you be acting wisely in summoning the whole of the ship's company aft, acquainting them with this second crime, and making them understand that whilst the villain who has done these things remains undiscovered, no man's life is safe aboard this vessel?"

Mr. Barlow simply bowed, but in a manner that let Captain Gordon know his wishes would be complied with; I followed him on deck, he was deathly white and dreadfully agitated and horror-stricken. I spoke to him; he stared wildly at me and merely cried, "Who is it that's doing it? Who is it that's doing it?"

But already the news of this second murder had gone forward; no need for the boatswain to sound his whistle; all hands were on deck, and they came tumbling aft with scared looks to the first cry I raised. The guard had assembled on the poop, but when the mate and I came on deck the last of the convicts who had been helping to wash down was passing through the boarded gangway into the hatch, with the subaltern waiting to see him disappear. The three sentries, forward and amidships, stood motionless, the bright lines of their bayonets close against their cheeks.

By this time the mate had collected his mind; he addressed the crew with passion and in strong language, told them what had happened, swore that no man's life was safe, and exhorted them as Englishmen to work like fiends to discover the assassin if he was one of them.

"Whoever the murderer is, he don't sling his hammock *in*

our fo'k's'le," shouted a sailor. Another bawled, "We'll do everything that's right, sir, but don't let the guffies reckon that there's any bloody cut-throats amongst *us.*"

"Look out for your man in the 'tween-decks," shouted a third.

A whole volley of this sort of thing was fired off by the crew. Captain Gordon spoke to them quietly, and then turned to his own men; his manner was gentlemanly and dignified. The full spirit of the British officer was expressed in him as he stood speaking, with one hand grasping the brass rail.

This time the murder was one of real bloodshed; there should be a clue, therefore, to hunt after, were it but a fragment of stained apparel, or an unowned knife with marks of human butchery upon it. The sailors roared to me to follow them forward and watch them overhaul their forecastle. But nothing came of it. As before, every chest, every bunk, every hammock was ransacked, and now the seamen handled one another's clothes. But it was all to no purpose, and I came out of the forecastle hot as fire and sick at heart, and went aft with my report to Mr. Barlow.

They had not been idle at the cuddy end of the ship. It was owing to the suggestion of Lieutenant Venables that two convicts, who had been thief-takers in their day, hounds of justice, afterwards cast, the one for housebreaking, the other for "smashing": it was owing to the subaltern that these two men were brought out of the prisoners' quarters and put to the task (guarded by a couple of soldiers) of discovering the murderer. One was a thick-set, beetle-browed man, the other slim, with a cast eye and a fixed leering smile. They spent the whole day in this hunt. They searched every cabin aft, questioned the soldiers who had been on sentry duty at the cuddy door during the night, explored every box, locker, whatever was to be met with in that way. They tumbled my clothes about in my cabin and obliged me to undress myself; but then they served Gordon, Venables, and Barlow so. They swore the murders were *not* the work of a convict; indeed, it was perfectly certain no prisoner could by any possibility break out of the 'tween-decks during the night when the gates were secured and the sentries posted.

The two convict-searchers then went to the forecastle, but the Jacks there, on learning the object of the fellows' visit, said that no blooming oakum-pickers would be allowed to pass through the forescuttle; they had overhauled one another and all that their sea-parlor contained, and the second officer who had looked on had gone away satisfied; and a powerful sailor acting as the crew's spokesman swore with a huge oath that if the two prisoners attempted to enter the forecastle the men would lash them back to back and heave them overboard.

Captain Gordon asked that the hold should be again thoroughly searched. I put in at this, and said the boatswain and I and others had overhauled the ship's inside from fore to after peak.

"No good in walking round and round a job," exclaimed Mr. Barlow. "What's been done *is* done, gentlemen. There's no murderer under hatches. How's he to come up unseen? The cuddy-door sentry guards the steerage-hatch; the main-hatch and forecastle are watched by your men."

There was nothing more to be done. The body of the doctor was dropped over the side, and it was now for Captain Gordon and the subaltern to see after the prisoners. A feeling of consternation took possession of us all. Every man looked at his fellows with more or less of distrust. Who was to be the next victim, and who was the fiend that was doing these murders? Where did he lurk? Which of all the people you saw moving about the ship as soldiers, sailors, prisoners was he? And what was his object?

The arms chest was brought into the cuddy, and the four of us who now occupied the after part of the vessel slept with loaded weapons at our side, and every half hour during the night, at the sound of the bell, the cry, "All's well!" went from sentinel to sentinel, and regularly at every hour an armed soldier, and one of the seamen under the eye of the mate of the watch—whether the boatswain or myself—went the rounds of the cuddy, pausing, listening, looking into the cabins to see that all was right.

This was precaution enough, you might think, with the addition of a cuddy-door sentry urged into exquisite vigilance by stern instructions and by fear for his own throat.

Well, after the doctor was found murdered, ten days passed, and nothing in any way to alarm us happened. In this time we sneaked across the equator, and our taut bowlines snatched some life for the ship out of a dead-on-end southerly breeze, with a short, staggering roll of foaming blue water and a heavy westerly swell. It fell out, by the revolution of the watches, that I took charge of the deck on this tenth day from eight o'clock till midnight. The military officers turned in at eleven. Mr. Barlow stayed to yarn with me, and our talk was mainly about the two murders, and I noticed that the mate still seemed to believe that it was the work of a soldier. He went below whilst someone was striking five bells—half past eleven. I watched him pass under the skylight; he stood a moment or two looking up at the lamp as though he thought the dim flame should be further dimmed, then drank a glass of water and passed out of sight.

The boatswain relieved me at eight bells. I gave him the course and certain instructions, and specially exhorted him to see that the round of the cuddy was punctually made. I went to my cabin by way of the quarter-deck; a sentry stood posted, as usual, at the cuddy door, and I could dimly discern the figure of a second soldier at the main-hatch. My cabin was immediately abreast of the one that had been occupied by Dr. Saunders. Before lying down I looked to the brace of pistols we all of us aft now slept with, and then, as heretofore, peeped under the bunk, and took a careful squint round about. . . .

I was startled into instant broad wakefulness by a heavy groan, the report of a musket, and a sharp savage cry as of a man cursing whilst he stabs and slays another. The report of the musket in the resonant interior of the little cuddy sounded like the explosion of a magazine. I rushed out in trousers and shirt, grasping one of the pistols; but I was not the first. Captain Gordon and Lieutenant Venables were before me; Mr. Barlow sprang through his cabin door as I ran through mine; the boatswain was also tumbling down the companion steps, and I heard the noise of the feet of the watch racing aft along the deck, and exclamations of the soldiers coming through the booby-hatch.

The figure of a man lay upon the cuddy floor between the

table and the steerage hatchway, and beside him stood a sentry in the act of wrenching his bayonet out of the prostrate body. I turned up the lamp; the cuddy was fast filling. There was a universal growling and crying of questions.

"See to the prisoners, Venables!" I heard Captain Gordon say, and the subaltern shoved through the crowd to the door, calling for the guard.

"Turn him over. Who is it?" exclaimed Mr. Barlow.

I drew close to the motionless man on deck. Meanwhile the soldier who had killed him was standing at attention with his eyes fixed on Captain Gordon, and the bayonet in his musket dripping red in the lamplight. A couple of seamen turned the body—it had fallen sideways to the thrust of the steel, with its face upon deck.

"Stand out of the light," cried Mr. Barlow.

"Great heavens!" exclaimed Captain Gordon; "it's the prisoner Simon Rolt!"

Simon Rolt! There before us on the deck, dead, with the thrust of a bayonet through his heart, with a long, gleaming sheath-knife firmly grasped in his right hand, lay the corpse of the man who had fallen overboard—whom we all supposed lay drowned at the bottom of the sea weeks ago— whom we had all as utterly forgotten as though his memory had been no more than one of the bubbles which had floated to the surface with his plunge! We could not credit the evidence of our sight. Then, indeed, the suspicion of some enormous scheme of treachery as concerned the convicts seemed to visit all in that cabin assembled, as though we had been one man.

"He'll have had a confederate," shouted a voice.

"He was for murdering the officers, and then the convicts 'ud have rose and killed all hands," bawled another with lungs of storm.

"Silence!" cried Captain Gordon, and he questioned the sentry, who, standing bolt upright, in a cool, collected way, told this story. Having crossed the deck, leaving the cabin door on his left, he happened to glance through the window into the interior, and saw what he supposed was a shadow cast by the dimly-burning lamp upon the head of the steerage steps. He shrank and put himself out of sight of it, though commanding it still, and presently he saw it stir and crawl into the shape of a human head and shoulders. The sneaking subtle bulk rose clear of the steps, and noiselessly as the shadow of a cloud it was creeping aft into the gloom under the table when the sentry swiftly stepped into the door and challenged it. Up sprang the man: in a few beats of the heart his long knife would have been through the soldier; but the redcoat was too quick for him: the bayonet pierced the devil's breast, and at the same moment the musket, which the soldier had cocked, exploded. The convict fell dead with a single groan, but the soldier in his rage stabbed him thrice to make sure of him, cursing him loudly as he drove the steel home.

Some seamen picked up the body and put it away in one of the cabins. The cuddy was then cleared and a wet swab brought along to cleanse the deck; but until dawn the sailors stood about in the waist and gangways talking. A quiet wind held the canvas motionless, and the ship stole softly through the shadow of the darkest hours of the night. Mr. Barlow told me that when daybreak came I must go into the hold and find out where the villain had hidden himself. The military men and the mate and I lingered in the cuddy in conversation.

"Was it Rolt himself who jumped overboard, or was the figure some dummy?" said Captain Gordon, who immediately added, "Oh, it must have been the convict. How could he have got aft?"

"I saw him jump. Many must have seen him," said I.

"How did he get on board?" exclaimed Lieutenant Venables.

"I'll tell you what's in my head, gentlemen," said I. "I've been turning the matter over; you'll find I'm right, I believe. There was the end of the main-brace hanging over the quarter. I took notice of it as we pulled under the ship's stern. That brace was taken off its pin and lowered by a confederate hand. I heard a low whistle sound through the ship before the man sprang."

"So did I," said Captain Gordon. "You'll remember, Venables, I asked you if you heard it?"

"We'll find out who was at the wheel that night when the

man jumped overboard," exclaimed the mate.

"Pray go on with your notions, Mr. Barker," said Captain Gordon. "I fancy you've hit the truth."

"Why," I continued, "Suppose the thing preconcerted, and Rolt with a confederate amongst the crew; the whistle signalled all ready for the jump; a few silent strokes would bring the convict to the end of the main-brace, and the rest signified merely a hand-over-hand climb, with the mizzen-chains as a black hiding-place till the ship was silent. I take it that the man got round into the captain's cabin window; he found it open, entered, and strangled the commander, who probably started up on the villain entering."

"That'll be it certainly, gentlemen," said Mr. Barlow, looking from one to another of the officers. "The convict," he continued, "found the cuddy empty, and made his way into the steerage. But he would need a plan of the ship in his head to hide himself. Who's the scoundrel amongst the crew that helped him?"

At daybreak the boatswain and I went below into the steerage. We found the after-peak hatch-cover off, whence it was clear that the man had hidden in that part of the ship. We again thoroughly examined the hold, but we could not imagine how and where the man had secreted his square powerful form so as to completely baffle our first search. We found a large cask about a quarter full of ship's bread. The head was off and lying near. The boatswain thought that the convict might have concealed himself in that cask, heading himself up in it; and to prove that this could be done he got in, holding the head, which he put on when he was inside. If this cask had been the convict's hiding place it is certain in our first search none of us had meddled with it, or beyond doubt we should have discovered him.

And now to end this strange yarn. Mr. Barlow found out that a seaman named Mogg was at the wheel on the night Rolt jumped overboard. The mate and I—indeed, all of us aft—were persuaded that whoever stood at the wheel at that time was the convict's confederate, because the main-brace must have been dropped into the sea and belayed by some-one, who, standing near, could fling the rope overboard swiftly over the side without being observed. Certainly the brace had not been long overboard when the whistle sounded; Mr. Barlow or myself would have noticed it, wondered at such an unusual piece of lubberliness, and ordered the thing to be hauled in and coiled down.

However, that Mogg was Rolt's confederate was made almost certain a little later on when some of the crew came to Mr. Barlow and me to say they had heard Mogg speak of Rolt as his cousin. He was put into irons, but was dumb for a month, then, swearing that the memory of the murders lay as heavy on his soul as though he had committed them, he confessed that he had agreed with Rolt to help him to escape and hide in the after part of the ship, of which he gave him a plan. They had twenty different schemes. One had been this of the convicts jumping overboard when Mogg was at the wheel and the main-brace over the side. The opportunity they awaited came with several marvellous conditions for successful execution of the stratagem when the doctor on a breathless night brought the prisoners up in batches to breathe. Mogg said he had passed Rolt on his way to the wheel, and settled everything in a few whispers, and the signal was to be a long, low whistle. It was then he had given him the knife out of his sheath. The intention of the convict, as we gathered from Mogg, was to kill all the officers but myself; I was to be left to navigate the ship. He and Mogg reckoned that when the crew and the soldiers found themselves without commanders they would become demoralized, and allow the convicts to seize the ship. The seaman denied that he had tampered with the falls of the starboard quarter-boat.

We handed Mogg over to the police on our arrival, and they sent him in a ship sailing immediately to take his trial in England.